THE *ELDRIDGE* INCIDENT

K.W. GARLICK

Visit our website at **www.StillwaterPress.com** for more information.

First Stillwater River Publications Edition

ISBN-10: 1-950339-32-7
ISBN-13: 978-1-950339-32-7

Library of Congress Control Number: 2019911688

1 2 3 4 5 6 7 8 9 10

Written by K.W. Garlick
Published by Stillwater River Publications, Pawtucket, RI, USA.

Publisher's Cataloging-In-Publication Data
(Prepared by The Donohue Group, Inc.)

Names: Garlick, K. W. (Kenneth W.), 1949- author.
Title: The Eldridge incident / K.W. Garlick.
Description: First Stillwater River Publications edition. | Pawtucket, RI, USA : Stillwater River Publications, [2019] | Series: [Madame Alice tales]
Identifiers: ISBN 9781950339327 | ISBN 1950339327
Subjects: LCSH: Eldridge (Ship)--Fiction. | Destroyers (Warships)--United States--History--20th century--Fiction. | Clairvoyants--United States--History--20th century--Fiction. | Missing persons--United States--History--20th century--Fiction. | LCGFT: Historical fiction. | Paranormal fiction. | Ghost stories.
Classification: LCC PS3607.A7498 E55 2019 | DDC 813/.6--dc23

This is a work of fiction. While, as in all fiction, the literary perceptions, and insights are based on experience, all names, characters, places, and incidents either are products of the author's imagination or are used fictitiously.

The views and opinions expressed in this book are solely those of the author and do not necessarily reflect the views and opinions of the publisher.

DEDICATION

This novel is dedicated to the men and women of the armed forces. Their sacrifices are numerous and go beyond the obvious. There are the missed holidays, birthdays, and special events; the time away from their families is costly and can never be recaptured. Too many of us take these little life events for granted; American military families do not.

ACKNOWLEDGMENTS

I want to thank Sam Goodwin for his assistance and hospitality. He and I spent several hours exploring the USS *Casin Young*, a Fletcher class destroyer, tied off at the Charlestown Naval Shipyard in Massachusetts. His many years of service in the US Navy provided valuable insight into what life might have been like on a WW II destroyer; again, many thanks to Sam. You are a class act!!!

Thanks to Johan Bjuman for his incredible art work on my book cover and Travis Garlick for his coordinating and formatting that artwork.

BOOK I

BREWSTER MORRISON

The phone rang. *Probably my sister*, Candace Morrison thought to herself; *she often calls around this time*. "Hello."

"Is Lieutenant Commander Morrison available?" a very martial voice inquired; after all the years she recognized the precise, mechanical intonation.

She explained her husband was not home but would be shortly. A Captain Broadbent said it was important that her husband return his call as soon as he arrived home. He gave the number, thanked, her politely and hung up. A serious sounding voice and the urgency in which to return the call unnerved her. She returned to the comfort of preparing dinner for her husband. There was war ranging throughout the globe, these types of phone calls must happen all the time. That thought did not comfort her.

Her husband, Brewster Morrison or Brew as she called him, after graduating from Annapolis, 'Valedictorian, Class of '39 was assigned to the navy's research and development division in Bethesda, MD. Within 18 months he became the directing officer. He was responsible for the discovery and advancement in the area of radar technology and remote-control transmission and was making remarkable progress. Navy brass was impressed. He had been blessed with numerous young, intelligent, and hardworking people. They needed no

1

motivation; their country was at war and patriotism was in ample supply.

After kissing and hugging Brew when he finally arrived, she told him of Captain Broadbent's important call and how unnerving it was to her. Candace leaned into his chest and hugged him again, her swollen abdomen complicating the attempt; she was almost eight months pregnant and the last three weeks had been rather difficult.

Now they sat at the tiny kitchen table and picked at their late meal. A sobering telephone conversation with Captain Broadbent had stolen their appetite and had suddenly turned their world upside down. Brewster Morrison's talents were required elsewhere; his results at the navy's research center had shined a bright light on him. A more pressing matter demanded his leadership qualities. He was ordered to leave for Philadelphia the next day. A car would pick Brewster up at 0530, he would be driven to the small airport in Annapolis where a plane would be waiting for his own sequestered flight to the naval shipyard in Philadelphia. He should be prepared for an extended stay.

Lt. Commander Morrison explained the precarious condition of his young wife's pregnancy, his tone heavy with concern. The focused captain recognized the legitimate fears of the situation. He did not need a highly regarded officer distracted from a project that would demand his full commitment. His orders were quite clear: facilitate Lieutenant Commander Morrison's transfer quickly, logistics and cost were irrelevant.

"We will make arrangements for your wife to join you in a few days," Captain Broadbent offered. "In the meantime, just be ready at 0530 tomorrow morning. Forget about what you've been doing these last two and a half years. The navy has a new path for you. You will be exposed to a diverse new reality. See you tomorrow." And he hung up, the dial tone suddenly stimulating his concerns. That's how it works in the military, orders and instructions get passed down and concerns are dealt with later.

A sleepy chauffeured car ride—Brew slept poorly that night—and a cold, jarring plane ride to Philadelphia had him sitting in Captain Broadbent's office at 1100 hours that morning. An early December snowfall the night before spoke of the approaching holiday season and the anticipation it brings. Lt. Commander Morrison sensed there would be very limited time for good cheer in his family's Christmas plans.

Captain Broadbent's conference room was filled with navy brass: an admiral, two other captains, two attending lieutenants, and an ensign. Three other gentlemen, two of them wearing ill-fitting and wrinkled suits and the other rather plainly dressed, sat next to each other at the end of a long conference table. Their long hair and unshaven faces made them stand out like crows among the peacocks.

Introductions were made and the two ruffled dignitaries were revealed as German scientists who, with the aid of various European underground networks, had been smuggled out from the German research facility at Peenemunde. The other was their American counterpart. They stood, nodded their heads, and returned to their seats.

Admiral Carlson took charge of the meeting, directing the assembly to join the professors at the table. He began to outline the project that Lt. Commander Morrison would be responsible for.

"Mr. Morrison, the navy, with the aid of these brilliant men, Professor Muller and Professor Bjurman," and he nodded towards the foreigners, "and an impressive supporting cast are in the process of making some rather remarkable advancement it the area of, ah…ah," he stuttered, "well for now we're calling it…Deceptive and Evasive Technology or DET. I'm not sure I understand it, even marginally. But it is the goal of the Defense Department to adapt this technology to a US navy vessel. It is expected that this cutting-edge technology will make a ship completely invisible."

Admiral Carlson awkwardly paused and let the American professor translate his opening comment into German for the two researchers.

When the translation was finished, he began again. "Commander Morrison you have come highly regarded and recommended—" He stopped and turned to the American researcher, "Let the professors know they're going to have to wait a bit for the translation part to come

3

their way, I'll be damned if I'm going to stop every thirty seconds and wait for this bullshit to happen, besides I think our German friends have been here long enough to get the gist of what we're chatting about. Isn't that right gentlemen?" He nodded his head and extended his arm and open palm to the professors. From their chairs they subtly bowed their heads, but appeared clueless as to what had just been directed at them. They turned to their interpreter, nodded and replied "*Ja! Ja!*" when the admiral's pointed comments were translated.

"As I was saying, Morrison, you got a reputation that's way in front of you, so I want you to take this project by the horns and move it along. From what I have been told we are on the verge of something truly brilliant, something that will give us the superior hand militarily and globally, something that might end the goddamn war."

He stopped and walked to the office window and stared out at the snow-covered scene before him, paused a few seconds, and then spoke to the dingy view. "Too many young boys dying or coming home with their limbs separated from their souls," and then he turned back to the room, "and you Lieutenant Commander Morrison will make sure this project happens. Gentlemen, let's finish this meeting and then I will meet privately with Mr. Morrison."

Admiral Carlson was everything Brewster had heard he was: blunt, plain talking, hard ass and focused. Had to be if you headed up navy intelligence. He outlined the staff they had put in place to support him. Brewster would have plenty of that; brass did not want to repeat the tragic events of their last project director.

"Professor Kincaid here," and the admiral pointed to the plainly dressed civilian, "will oversee the research end of things and will report directly to you and Lieutenant Commander Grant, who will head up the construction efforts to prepare the USS *Eldridge* for active duty." Admiral Carlson turned to his left and the officer next to him tipped his hand in acknowledgement.

Project overviews, schedules, and expectations were reviewed. They discussed futuristic project related theorems. Brewster tried to let it all sink in. There would be a learning curve, a rather demanding one he surmised.

Admiral Carlson saw no purpose in further overwhelming his new project officer. Time for a little one on one. Asking those that were now part of Brewster's team to wait in the adjoining lobby, he dismissed the remaining officers. Papers were repacked into leather briefcases. Handshakes and a "welcome aboard" were offered to the new project director. Two men with the burden of a difficult mission had the room to themselves.

"Lt. Commander Morrison, let me give you some more background on the madness you're about to sink in up to your ass."

He shared more highly classified data on how the Defense Department and then the US Navy with the aid of defecting German scientists, the two he just met, had developed a process that would render a navy destroyer undetectable to enemy radar and visually invisible to nearby hostile ships.

"It was a concept I could hardly believe myself, such a futuristic approach, but then some early encouraging results showed the viability of the project. Mr. Morrison, get used to the term 'Quantum Physics.' You are about to enter a whole new world. Let me tell you how you ended up here."

The admiral told how Project Rainbow was moving steadily ahead, marked by initial impressive results, but then the mission abruptly stalled. The project director committed suicide; apparently the stress of the job, and then discovering his wife in bed with his best friend on an unexpected early visit home, had pushed him over the edge. His replacement just wasn't getting it done. They had been too hasty, not thorough enough in their selection process.

"Brewster, I'm putting a lot on your food tray, this Project Rainbow is priority one in all of the military, not just the navy. It will take you a while to get up to speed with the complexity of 'Rainbow,' but you can handle it. Your accomplishments at the R&D center in Bethesda were just too impressive to ignore. Most of the retrofitting is done; you'll need to finish that up. Training the crew and beta testing your device will be your biggest challenge. The ship leaves Philadelphia on June 9th, hell or high water. I have been directed to provide whatever resources you need for this project," he paused and reflected on what he was about to share with his junior officer, "but remember, the more you demand from my department, the quicker I will expect results. You and your new bunch of dick skinners better get results."

Brewster Morrison listened to the briefing in total amazement. Nothing he had accomplished or studied before could have prepared him for what had just been handed off to him. The navy had in their possession a vessel, the USS *Eldridge*, which was in the process of being retrofitted with a bevy of bizarre hardware and machinery that would render it invisible to any and all enemy vessels.

Now his commanding officer spoke of a whole new area of science. Something the admiral called quantum physics, and it was about to become his new world. He was excited and apprehensive at the same time.

"Admiral Carlson, this is a lot to take in." Brew slowly straightened from his chair. "I suppose the sooner I jump into the swamp the better off I will be."

"That's the spirit, Commander," and the admiral rose from his own chair and forcefully patted him on the back. "We'll be talking a lot in the coming months, so we can stop with the title prefix, call me Bob and I'll call you Brewster. We'll both be tired miserable pricks when this is finished, but let's get this goddamn war over. Too many of our fine boys are being sacrificed to a cause that is never just. People ask me why I joined the navy, 'isn't it just part of the war machine?' they say, and it is. War is an inevitable part of our human existence, especially for our country. I just strive as hard as I can to bring it to a successful conclusion as quickly as possible and I demand that of anyone under my command." He pulled a cigarette from a pack in his blazer's inner pocket, placed it lazily in his lips, flipped his zippo lighter, and pulled the flame in with a deep breath. "Good luck, Brewster. Talk in a bit." He turned and left the room

Brewster Morrison stood alone in the conference room. He was about to manage a very complex operation with five times the staff he had in Annapolis. A now dysfunctional group had lost their focus; his immediate concern would be to get them quickly back on task.

Admiral Carlson promised him whatever resources he would require and that directive had come from President Roosevelt himself. But the edict was clear: take charge and get results.

He knew his phone call home to Candace this evening would be a tale of unbelievable details.

An ensign waiting in the lobby pushed his head through the conference room door. "Lt. Commander, we need to get over to our field office. You're expected for another briefing."

Commander Morrison joined his new staff in the lobby. They boarded a waiting navy bus and were driven to the far end of the ship-yard to a large, secluded, and heavily guarded hanger.

Naval authorities found housing for their new Project Rainbow director and quickly facilitated the relocation of his pregnant wife.

On December 7th 1943, Morrison assembled his team and attacked the project. Long days and a focused supporting cast produced speedy results. The project was soon back on track. Admiral Carlson and his staff were pleased and impressed.

Lt. Commander Morrison even found time to be at his wife's side for the delivery of their son Clarke Michael Morrison on the 23rd.

The retrofitting was completed and the training and testing that could be done while in wet dock was as far as it could go. Sea trials were the next step and began on April 1st, 1944. They would try to mimic battle conditions.

With the goal of enhancing the Eldridge's fire power, the navy had retro-fitted the standard 5 inch mounts with 8 inch 200mm batteries. The added re-enforcing steel plating would make her a little top heavy and might compromise her speed and handling but her broadside would be lethal.

Off the coast of southern New Jersey, they would engage their secret weapon and did their target training on a barge towed far behind the assisting USS *Blackwell.*

After two months of rigorous testing and development, the USS *Eldridge* left the port of Philadelphia on June 9, 1944. She was bound for the Pacific theater. Her check-ins were on schedule and thorough. Information relayed back to naval command showed a very unique warship performing well beyond expectations. It was difficult to reign in the optimism.

USS *ELDRIDGE*

They had been a proud ship when they departed Philadelphia harbor on their top-secret mission. A whole new crew, recruited from all over the country, spoke to the uniqueness of their mission. To no one's surprise, during the retrofitting of their new ship and the training efforts, a complete clampdown on the crew's movement and exposure was implemented, placed in seclusion they were watched continuously. They had been a mishmash of personalities and their training had been bizarre and demanding, but they had jelled and were now confident in their skills and each other. They were housed in separate barracks, isolated from other personnel, with buses moving them from lodging to work details. Even the name of their ship was purposely withheld from them, not revealed until their journey began and the canvas that covered their ship's name removed. There was a lot of anticipation and they knew important information would be shared once they were underway. They would soon be told they were key players in their country's most classified project. The USS *Eldridge* DD-628 mission was top secret, its potential remarkable, but the risks extremely high.

They were two days out from home port when Capt. Milton Van Noy convened his officers and senior petty officers in his confined wardroom. He would lay out their mission and destination.

"Gentlemen, we are heading for the Pacific theater, more specifically the Philippine and East China Seas. As you know, we have installed some very strange equipment aboard the *Eldridge*. A large area forward of the engine room has been retrofitted with a foreign apparatus as well as numerous large seawater pumps. Numerous open water valves have been installed along both sides of our outer hull. For the last three months we have been undergoing intensive sea trials and you no doubt have all heard strange noises and felt the shaking the ship has experienced. Some parts of the ship's hull and bulkheads have become too hot to touch. All of us have experienced the very trying side effects, none of you ever shrank from your mission or duty and I am proud of you.

"I would like to introduce you to the three civilians that have been with us from the very inception of this mission," he continued. "No doubt you have seen their comings and goings on the ship." He asked the three noncombatants to stand. "Gentlemen, this is Professor Klaus Bjurman and Professor Hans Mueller, they defected from Germany about eighteen months ago and have been critical in developing this new weapon; and this is Professor Michael Kincaid, their American counterpart. I will not go into the specifics of their invention, because quite frankly I'm not sure I completely understand them. The navy has designated it Project Rainbow and from this point on we will refer to that area of the ship as the Rainbow Room. But gentlemen," and he paused, "this device when activated will render the USS *Eldridge* invisible to all ships, foreign or domestic."

Jaws dropped and there was stunned silence in the wardroom. Slowly, rank and file sought out each other's expressions and reactions, a bizarre reality had been thrust upon them, instinct told them to dismiss such a concept. It was as if they had suddenly been transported to a world that was completely foreign to them; measured belief and dogged acceptance would be all that they could muster at this point.

"I know this is difficult to comprehend," Captain Van Noy carried on. "I will let Professor Kincaid better define this and what lies ahead for us, hopefully it will bring about the rapid end to this horrible war." He turned and extended his arm in the direction of the three deans.

Mr. Kincaid spoke briefly to his German workmates in their native tongue and they nodded their comprehension. He turned to the officers before him and made his best attempt in layman's terms to explain the science behind their device and how it operated. Most of it was beyond their understanding. Blank stares were all they could offer.

"Perhaps this is a little overwhelming for most of you; it was my initial reaction too."

The American professor did make it clear that Project Rainbow was the sole creation of the two very gifted German scientists.

"Gentlemen, we have become a guinea pig for the United States Navy and our country. This is a work in progress and we will be testing and developing this new weapon as we navigate the oceans. Should we encounter any enemy vessels along the way, we have a clear directive to engage and destroy that vessel with the use of our special weapon.

USS *ELDRIDGE*

They began their long journey to the Pacific, testing their device as they traveled. Deep in the bowels of their ship, a special detail at the direction of the learned Germans would begin their strange routine. A crash course in German for the Americans and a crude understanding of English made the process smooth and relatively flawless, anything more demanding would be coordinated through the American professor.

Seaside valves would be opened and huge pumps activated. The sudden demand for power would load down the ship's steam turbines and the ship would shudder and vibrate. The mysterious device within its own thick bulkheads would be engaged. The *Eldridge* would begin to pulsate over its entire length, a piercing heat would radiate out from the containment room. Crew members, sometimes at the far reaches of the ship, would experience a sensation of a pressurizing heat and humidity, like they had suddenly been wrapped in an invisible hot blanket, others would complain of nausea, sometimes severe. Some crew members would experience brief hallucinations during the activation. Daylight became blurred or indistinct, light and images immediate to them seemed to rush in on them and then through them, causing the intense heat they experienced. There was dizziness and nausea throughout the ship. Visually, objects in the

11

distance appeared stable and their identifying colors distinct. But when sailors looked closely about their surroundings, visions swirled inward and past them, a collapsing kaleidoscope of light, funneling around them, moving swiftly to the center depth of their vessel. They were now unseen and yet, but for the bizarre side effects that had briefly challenged them, they sensed nothing different about their presence on a vast ocean. The whole process took perhaps a minute before the dizziness stopped, nausea passed, and 20-20 vision was restored to the crew.

The first visible evidence of their vanishing capabilities began when seagulls or albatrosses flew blindly into the super structure or hull of their warship and then fell stunned to the sea below. It became a comical event that the crew of the *Eldridge* looked forward to during the testing of their secretive ruse.

They were sailing undisturbed in calm waters when they made their first contact.

"Sonar," Seaman Hanes's voice rang loud and crisp on the pilot house speaker; there was an edge. "Captain we just got pinged, we've got an enemy sub in the area, gotta be a kraut."

Captain Van Noy picked up the phone line that led directly to the sonar room and Seaman Hanes's station. He knew that edge to Hanes's voice spoke volumes and sensed the urgency in his sonar man's voice.

"Go ahead Hansey, what else can you tell me?" Van Noy knew what this trusted tech was about to tell him might lead to the first test of their classified weapon in real combat conditions. Petty Officer Hanes was battle tested, he and the captain had seen a lot of central Pacific action on their previous destroyer and he had insisted on Hansey's expertise on the *Eldridge*. The navy had facilitated his transfer. He trusted Hanes completely.

"My guess is our heinie is 4800 yards at 165 degrees. I'm hearing a little commotion; he's probably going to general quarters right now."

"Forty-eight hundred yards," Van Noy repeated. "That's still on the fringe, he won't be sending any fish just quite yet. He'll want to get closer," he hesitated, "if he can. Do you think Schultzy knows we're on to him?"

"Captain, I pinged him twice for bearing and distance and then for conformation. If his sonar man is worth his shit, he knows we got a sniff of him."

"Thanks Bill." The captain used his first name when he was grateful for potentially critical information and to re-enforce a job well done.

He hung up his phone with sudden conviction. "Commander Preston, let's go to general quarters. Notify the people in the Rainbow Room we will need to engage their mechanism as soon as they are ready and light a fire under their ass. We've got a German sub trying to put us on the bottom. Helmsman, bring us to 165, all ahead two thirds, let's give Gerry the smallest profile we can."

U-235

Verner Vukic suddenly pressed the headphones against his sweaty temples. The German sonar technician quickly leaned out from his cramped station and yelled down the short passageway to the con room.

"Kapitan, ich habe einen treffere bei 320 grads, about 2600 yards, it's an American destroyer, Fletcher class, I know the sound of those twin-screw diesels all too well.

It was late afternoon and they had been steaming at snorkel depth as was their practice during the day. Snorkeling allowed them to travel under diesel power with their extended funnel just above the surface. It also allowed them to bring air in for the engines and some limited fresh air for the crew. It was still a hot and steamy con room and the crew, including their kapitan, was missing most of their proper dress.

But now battle stations had been sounded and they were scrambling.

Kapitan Herman Schuster shouted his orders, "Secure all diesel engines, engage battery drive, emergency dive, bring us to 80 meters, all ahead full, schnell! Schnell!!"

Orders were loudly and carefully repeated, uniforms were re-adjusted, and hats returned to their sweaty crowns. Tension and an edgy awareness had suddenly replaced a mundane, dreary environment. War can have that kind of effect. Kill or be killed.

Kapitan Schuster leaned back towards the sonar room. "Verner, as soon as you can verify the Yank's speed and distance, I'll bring her to periscope depth. Whenever you're ready Seaman. Does the American know we're on to him?"

"Oh, he's onto us, he pinged us twice; if I had to guess he became aware of us probably a minute after I picked him up. There's a lot of scrambling going on right now, probably ringing battle stations. And Kapitan!! They're not making any effort to hide their location. A lot of cavitation in the props, like their engines are loading down for some reason. Suddenly a lot of strain, real noisy, nothing I've heard before."

His curiosity piqued, Kapitan Schuster leaned closer to his sonar man's station. "What's your guess Seaman?"

"It's a Fletcher class alright, but something else is going on. What, I just don't know, Kapitan." And he didn't.

He had been probing the Atlantic waters for the last three years. He knew the sounds the commercial T-50 freighters made, the American destroyers, both the Roosevelt and the new Fletcher class, British destroyers, the escorts and their corsairs which dotted the north Atlantic, even the French escorts the Brits were now using. He knew them all, but this was different. A loud mechanical noise and then the sudden sound of gushing water, lots of it too. And then a pulsating humming noise, probably at sixty cycles, emanated from the bowels of the American destroyer.

"It's a sound I've never heard before, Kapitan. Makes me a little nervous. He's turned a smaller profile to us, probably straight on to us, that's funny, his engines are screaming right now but he's probably doing 15 knots at best. Bearing is still 165 five degrees."

"Alright Helmsman, bring us to periscope depth," Kapitan Schuster ordered.

Compressed air was released into the ballast tanks and they were soon at periscope depth.

"Open," the kapitan ordered, and the periscope was quickly at shoulder height and he scanned the horizon at the bearing and distance his sonar man had given him.

"Are you sure of the coordinates you just gave me Verner, I see nothing in that direction."

"He should be right there, Kapitan," the bewildered sonar tech responded. "I have him at 800 meters, same bearing, 165."

Kapitan Herman Von Schuster swiveled his periscope in all directions, his panic and frustration obvious. "Verner, I can see nothing in any direction." He abruptly stood away from his station, his concentration intense. He was at the sonar station in several quick steps. Gunther knew the routine; he quickly removed his ear piece and placed it on his commander's head. Kapitan Schuster adjusted the headset and listened intently. His orders were instant and loud.

"Down scope, emergency dive, bring us to 200 meters, rig for silent running."

There were rushed but deliberate actions. Men scrambled to their battle stations, valves and levers were hastily operated. Forward ballast tanks flooded with sea water, dive plane levers suddenly pushed forward as far they could go. No one uttered a word.

Kapitan Von Schuster whispered to his sonar man, "Something is crazy wrong here, get back on that headset. Tell me where this American destroyer is. It's about to get quite ugly."

"He should have been right there at 165, should have filled up your viewing portal," his tech responded with confidence. "Did it get foggy really quick?"

"It's as clear as a summer's day," his kapitan whispered, and then the first depth charge exploded. The sub shook violently, light bulbs popped and bulkheads groaned with the stress. Then another explosion, this time a little further away, two potable water lines popped and sailors scrambled to stop the gushing with isolation valves.

Von Schuster grabbed the intercom and softly addressed the engine room. "Give me all this lady has got. Be ready for emergency blow." And then he turned to his crew in the con room. "I want to bring us up on the stern of this phantom US destroyer. Ready stern tubes five and six." Two more explosions wracked the sub, further

16

away, but men were still jostled about the control room and it was suddenly dark. Flashlights were turned on; one by one new bulbs were installed and the depressing and crippling darkness was peeled back. Those present in the con room stood frozen, holding onto stanchions or piping. Their faces covered in sweat, they looked to their kapitan for direction and deliverance.

"Verner," the kapitan yelled into his radio set. "Where is this bastard?"

"Kapitan he's gone hard over to starboard, my guess, he's coming back for another run on us. He'll be on our ass at 325 degrees, 600 meters. I can give you a firing solution sir!" he screamed.

"Seaman Vukic, I got to put a set of eyes on him to make any firing solutions worth it, you know that."

"Surface, emergency blow," the kapitan shouted. "Gun crew, be ready to move; I want our deck mount active as soon as possible. Torpedo room, be ready. Verner, I need constant updates of where our Yank is."

High pressure air was suddenly flooding the forward ballast. The bow rose quickly and men once again held onto hand supports and leaned forward as their vessel pushed to the surface. Sea water rushed by and the sound was like a million rodents running along their outer hull, and then suddenly the sense of floating like a balloon in a summer breeze. The sub briefly hung in the air, suspended by their quick, forceful rise to the surface, their feet briefly free of their burden and their stomachs now home to butterflies. The boat crashed back to the ocean and men were scrambling. Forward and aft hatchways were opened. Crew members were rushing to their stations. Kapitan Schuster was just as quickly on the bridge with his supporting officers. Binoculars searched the waters around them in all directions.

"Verner!" Kapitan Schuster screamed.

"He's at 265. Coming straight on. 300 hundred meters."

Men in the conning tower turned to the direction given and raised their binoculars. Nothing was there, only the blue green of an empty ocean stretching out to a disappearing horizon.

"Kapitan," came the voice of his torpedo officer, "tubes five and six are ready."

Those in the bridge turned to their leader. The kapitan was at a loss, his stomach turned with indecision, and then the deck gun exploded. Those in the conning tower instinctively ducked below its protective steel walls. In a brief moment they rose to see the boat's surface 88mm mount was gone and their shipmates with it. Men and steel suddenly absent, only flame and gore remaining.

"Kapitan, 265 degrees 200 meters, he's right there," sonar man Verner Vukic screamed in Kapitan Schuster's headset. Herman once again turned to the bearing given. Nothing. And then explosions ripped the forward hull of U-235. He was about to give the orders for an emergency dive and then his spirit was suddenly and violently separated from his form. An American destroyer's eight-inch salvo tore into the sub's conning tower. His last thought floated there above his sub, now a twisted inferno full of men dear to him. They would soon be joining their kapitan in the next universe. U-235 was gone, a casualty of war.

USS *ELDRIDGE*

"Captain, our kraut just went below us at 150 feet. Gutsy move! Thought he would have turned tail." William "Hansey" Hanes, sonar tech, relayed his findings to Van Noy through his headset to the bridge loudspeaker.

"Yeah it was a heady move, our charges were set too deep for his course; he managed to get past them before they blew. Can't imagine we did any real damage, rattled their brains a little," Van Noy shared with his subordinates.

Those in the bridge waited for their next orders. The *Eldridge* had gone to general quarters a few short minutes ago and the ship was battle ready.

"Captain, we have a lot of heat coming from the Rainbow Room," Ensign Cabral, one of the three phone talkers in the pilot house, announced, his ship's phone held to his chest. "Really affecting the crew in the engine room, complaining of dizziness and nausea. One man passed out."

"Ensign Cabral, we're trying to focus on a German submarine that has got some real bad intent right now. Your job is to keep those men under your command focused. Don't need to hear trivial shit like this right now; we can deal with this after the fact, clear?"

19

The ship had begun to experience these symptoms when the *Eldridge* engaged its secretive device, and the indicators were becoming more pronounced. Legitimate concerns were being raised, but Van Noy would not tolerate dissension from anyone. He had his orders and he would follow them. His forceful leadership on this mission had become his new identity. Van Noy had convinced himself his years of hard work and dedicated service to the US Navy had promoted him to this position of leadership. Hard toil and commitment would be demanded of every sailor onboard his lethal destroyer.

They had been ordered to the Philippine Sea to seek out the Japanese, now the only real naval threat to the free world, as Van Noy saw it, but if they sunk a few German warships along their way to that wide swath of ocean, all the better. It was the captain's belief that the German navy had been dealt with and was no longer a threat.

The Japanese navy, however, still was. They had inflicted severe damage to the seventh fleet at Pearl Harbor and Van Noy had personally experienced the horror of that event. The Japanese navy continued their assault on Allied shipping all over the Pacific. Captain Van Noy's memories of that day were horrific and would haunt him for the rest of his life.

Captain Van Noy had been assigned to the Pacific fleet at Pearl Harbor in April of 1941. He and his wife Vivian loved their new home in paradise. Vivian had given birth to a beautiful little girl in October of the same year. Their two-year-old son Max would not have the challenges of being an only child. Other than long intervals of separation that the navy regularly demands, they could not have been a happier family.

The new Fletcher class destroyers were just starting to come on line. Captain Van Noy had been lucky enough to be given the command of one of these cutting-edge vessels, the USS *Michigan*.

Naval fleets in countries all over the world were being upgraded and expanded. America's answer to that aggressive build-up was the Fletcher class destroyer.

At 378 feet and a beam of only 38.5 feet, she displaced 2100 tons of water. 60,000 hp twin-screw turbo engines could propel the *Michigan* through ocean waters at 40 knots or about 45 miles an hour. She was an engineering marvel with impressive firepower. Forward and aft dual-purpose 5 inch, 127 mm guns with MK 12 fire-control radar were included.

At midship they carried ten 21 inch MK 15 torpedo tubes. Five 40 mm Bofors AA mounts and seven single 20 mm Oerlikon weapons were stationed about the ship. Two 50 caliber and four 30 caliber machine guns also defended their vessel. Shallow water inlets were not obstacles to the Fletcher class; she drew 17.5 feet of water. They were put to sea with a crew of 296, including 33 officers. At 15 knots they had the range of 5500 nautical miles.

The USS *Michigan* DD-676 was the new rising star within the seventh fleet. December 4th 1941, the *Michigan* had just returned from a four month assignment in the Philippine Seas and once again they had set the bar high with their performance. Van Noy and his ship were the talk of Pearl Harbor

His wife met him at the wharf when they tied off, and he held his little girl for the first time. He felt a sense of pride and accomplishment. A career he felt he was destined for and a loving, supportive family to sustain him had made each day special.

One Sunday morning they were on their way home from an overnight stay with the Keenan's, another navy family they were close with. In two hours, they would attend their daughter's christening at the Good Shepard Church in Honolulu. Milton Van Noy drove his navy gray, '39 Plymouth along the winding shore line drive, his captain's flag flying from its front bumper staff. Palm trees glistened in the early morning sun; a soft breeze seemed to make their feathered fronds wave a friendly greeting. Needing to be ready for their 9:30 service, they had gotten an early start for home. The windows were rolled down and soft tropical air filled their car. Vivian held their napping baby girl in her arms and young Max was slumped into his father's side, also comfortable in a deep slumber. He looked at his striking family and took it all in. This was a simple, beautiful moment in time he would cherish the rest of his life.

The peaceful ride was interrupted by a huge explosion, a navy ship in the harbor burst upward into the morning air, flame and debris filled the sky. Suddenly there were planes everywhere, bearing down on the resting American fleet. Van Noy immediately recognized the Japanese identifiers on their wings. Japan had displayed some aggressive posturing in the last few months and an attack that had been speculated for the last several weeks was finally upon them.

More explosions erupted all over the harbor; towering flames with heavy dark smoke gave evidence of their destructive force. Japanese planes buzzed all about like angry hornets defending their hive. Van Noy pulled their Plymouth off the shoreline road, stopped, and looked out across the bay. He tried to understand the horror before them. Muffled screams of terror and pain now floated across the inlet.

"Oh, my lord," was all Vivian could offer. Her eyes wide and her mouth open in terror-stricken disbelief.

Planes were beginning to attack anything that moved. "I need to get to my ship, let's get you home first." With that, he forcefully found first gear and was fishtailing down the road as the rear wheels searched for traction. An enemy fighter buzzed them, so close he could see the leather helmeted pilot, his piercing eyes filled with intent.

He drove quickly through the madness; his instinct to protect and survive now consumed him. The road before him erupted in violent puffs of dirt. The bullets quickly working their way to his car. The hood and front windshield of their auto erupted into dozens of tiny explosions. Instinctively his right arm reached across to shield his family. His wife screamed in terror, and then her body fluttered like a limp doll as the bullets tore into her chest and throat. A piercing, burning sensation slashed into his right shoulder and they were suddenly careening into a roadside ditch. They bounced along the trench before they found the trunk of a large palm tree and he fell into a numbing darkness.

His cataleptic trance lasted only short moments. The smell of gasoline and toxic burning rubber snapped him out of his unconsciousness and moved him past the pain tearing at his upper torso. The twisted wreck that was once his car was on its driver's side door. Vivian lay pressed against him. Her lifeless body, scarlet red with the blood of her and their murdered baby. She still clutched Courtney in her limp arms. Young Max's skull had been split apart from the bullets that were manufactured for that very evil purpose. His little boy's brain matter and blood were splattered all over his navy whites.

Pure horror and grief took possession of his body. He no longer cared about living. He wanted to die there with his family. He knew the dripping gas that seemed everywhere would soon find a smoldering flame and the ensuing inferno would be their funeral pyre. He was now in hell and its flames were just seconds away.

The thought of his family burning for hours in this steel coffin suddenly seemed horrific. He could not tolerate that finale for them. They were dead but they deserved better. He scrambled from his would-be metal and glass crypt and began the process of removing their bodies from their car. Zombie-like in his movements, he laid their bodies along the side of the road, away from the wreckage.

All around him a newly horrific war had started down its path of death and destruction. Battleships, cruisers, and destroyers all helpless to defend themselves from the onslaught in the sky above exploded at their berths. Enormous flames shot skyward, taking hundreds of souls with them.

Enemy dive bombers were now attacking the airfields at Schofield Barracks, hospitals were strafed and bombed. Once their primary targets had been dealt with, Japanese fighters began an indiscriminate campaign of attacking anything and everything. America had been dreadfully unprepared for this attack and was paying a heavy price.

Captain Van Noy, like a loyal sentry, stood by his brutalized young family and was numb to the carnage all about him. The crippling pain in his shoulder and the blood that oozed from his wound the only things that reminded him he was alive and that this was not a twisted horrific nightmare. Suddenly another enemy plane began to strafe his burning vehicle.

Its engine ever louder roared its evil intent, drowning out all other sounds of battle around him. He stood there frozen and traumatized, his arms limp by his side, holding a bloodied hat in his right hand. The Japanese Zero began to fire its weapons and the bullets once again raced along the ground towards him. Van Noy no longer cared if he lived or died. The projectiles once again tore into his family's now lifeless forms, and they spasmed with the impact. No enemy shells found the captain; he stood there alone in his pain and loss. But now a focused expression crept across his face. He stared intently out across Pearl Harbor with its image of devastation, and he knew he would make them pay. They should have killed him with his family, but they had not. Now there would be war and vengeance would be his.

Captain Van Noy convalesced in a stateside hospital and in four months was returned to active duty, and once again given command of a Fletcher class destroyer. Issues of his fitness for command were overlooked. The country was at war; high-ranking, experienced combat officers were in short supply.

He pushed his crew and ship hard. There were numerous engagements and his ship became one of the most decorated vessels in the Pacific campaign.

"Captain he is blowing his ballast tanks, he's coming up real fast," his sonar man warned all on the bridge. The sudden information quickly had Van Noy back in the moment, his bitter reflections of that December day suddenly vanishing.

"Seaman Hanes, I need a bearing and distance," he demanded.

"Bearing three-one-zero degrees, directly aft of us, about 400 yards Captain," was the confident reply.

"Gun crews, be ready to fire on my command. I want to blow him out of the water the second he is on the surface.

Hans Mueller, the German scientist who had been the co-creator of their secret weapon installed now in the bowels of the *Eldridge*, was present on the bridge, his anticipation to actually see his weapon used to its fullest wartime intent at its peak. A broad smile took control of his face and he rubbed his hands in excitement. Hans should have been in the Rainbow Room with his accomplice Klaus. It was critical that their new device work flawlessly, but their testing had been rewarding, with only some minor deviations. Klaus could handle any ripple that the system might create; after all, it was his invention too.

Hans would not miss this opportunity to see their system perform in its first hostile application. All his years of research and his hatred of Hitler's evil plan to rule the world had brought him to this point. He would not miss it.

The bow of the submarine burst through the surface, like a huge dark gray whale gulping at millions of tiny krill. The stern of the sub pulled back forcefully and it crashed back into the mid-Atlantic waters. Forward and rear hatchways flew open and crewmen scrambled to their gun positions. Officers could be seen in the conning tower with their binoculars searching the vast ocean. Its identifier U-235 clearly visible.

"Fire," the order came loud and clear. At this distance they were fish in a barrel.

Eldridge's rear 8 inch turrets opened fire. Aft 40 mm gun crews zeroed in on the hapless sub and raked it from bow to stern. There were immediate explosions along the hull and then the bridge suddenly erupted. The bow was quickly beginning to sink below the waves then a huge explosion ripped the boat apart. The sub disappeared below the whitecaps in about 30 seconds. The whole process consuming less than 5 minutes.

"That big one must have been the forward torpedo room," Lieutenant Estrella offered. "Shall we search for survivors, Captain?"

"This mission cannot afford those kinds of gestures, Lieutenant. Besides I do not believe there are any." He stared briefly at where U-235 had slipped below the waves. "Bring us to 165 degrees, all ahead one third. Secure from battle stations."

Captain Van Noy turned to Professor Mueller. "You seem quite pleased with the outcome of your system in its first hostile action," he paused, "and you should feel every sense of validation. It performed brilliantly, our enemy had no idea we were close enough to reach out and touch him."

"I am ecstatic, Captain." He turned to Van Noy, straightened his tie, squared his shoulders. "Sehr Glucklich," he reinforced in his native German.

"Care to join me in my cabin for a glass of brandy?" the captain offered. The professor nodded his head "Jah," and they left the bridge together.

Leaving word with his attending yeoman that he and the professor were not be disturbed, the captain closed his cabin door behind them. He poured them a small tumbler of brandy and, proposing a toast, he handed the glass to his cabin guest.

"To our first enemy fatality, hopefully the start of many successful engagements with our powerful new weapon."

"Jah," Hans offered, and they clinked their snifters. The professor was beaming with pride over his invention's successful debut. The cloaking of their ship had been flawless; the U-boat, totally unaware of their presence, had been destroyed in brief moments. It was a lopsided victory.

"However, Professor, I think we need to talk about something that looks like it may become a problem. I will let you decide that." He turned to the professor and looked him squarely in the eyes. "Is your invention becoming unstable? Our last beta test outside Philly harbor, we lost Seaman Galuska, and there were multiple episodes of nausea and vomiting. The crew complained of excessive heat in parts of the ship. Some were treated for second degree burns, and just now with the U-boat, another crew member gone, a rather grotesque death, very unnerving to my ship."

"Captain Van Noy, I too am aware of these strange, alarming incidents." And he told the captain how he and his fellow countryman had researched the abnormalities. He and Klaus determined that they may not have adequately designed enough cooling for their cutting-edge innovation, but felt that if they maximized the output of their cooling pumps the system would operate more stably.

"Have you shared this information with Professor Kincaid, your American counterpart?" he asked cautiously.

"No, we have not, Klaus and I are still looking at our numbers," he answered, wondering the reason for such an inquiry. "We will share our findings with the professor immediately, if you so wish."

"No, I prefer you did not." A glint of steel entered his voice. "Professor Mueller, you and I will need to form a new relationship. One I believe you will understand and welcome once I reveal its intent."

Van Noy had been given a file on both his German researchers. He learned of Hans' tragic past, a past almost parallel to his own, where wife and family had been ripped from his life, taking all meaning and identity with them. The captain had witnessed Hans' daily toil, knowing he walked about almost like a ghost, as he did; they were faint representations of who they used to be.

Van Noy told how their mission should never be compromised, regardless how unstable their cloaking device became. He felt the two of them now shared a common tragic bond. He knew of Hans' tragic loss of his family in Germany and the heartbreaking events that led up to it. He too shared the horrific death of his family in Hawaii to the empire of Japan, another sadistic war machine on the other side of the world.

"You and I have lost our families to very sadistic regimes. These soulless bastards have brought unimaginable cruelty to our world for purely selfish and evil intent. We have suffered a loss that few could ever possibly understand. These barbaric shitholes must pay for their inhumanity. Our passion for revenge must keep us focused. We must strike back at Germany and Japan and we have the weapon to do that. There is no alternative. I completely understand your pain and I don't believe I have judged you incorrectly. Is that true?"

Hans was stunned by what Van Noy had just shared with him. It was a lot to take in, but he sensed that he had found a brother in arms, someone who understood his pain and desire for revenge on any level.

"Captain, you have dumbfounded me with this new strategy; although it does intrigue me with its potential, it is a little overwhelming. To think all this time, I have been on board an American vessel with a captain so similarly consumed with hate and retribution as I am. In a twisted way it's rather comforting."

"Professor, we will have more conversations about what we have to do, the challenges we must face together." The captain's voice was full of commitment. "But I need to know that you are as resolved as I am to use this new weapon of yours to kill as many of the bastards as possible. Are you professor?"

"Is this something that only you and I will be party to?" Hans inquired.

"If you think your associate Klaus can be trusted, he could be included in this undertaking. But that would be the extent of it. The more people involved in our covert efforts, the greater the risk."

Hans had begun to doubt Professor Klaus Bjurman's commitment to their project. They were old friends and had been through a lot together, but lately Klaus had voiced concerns about the viability of their device. It irritated Hans. There had been some heated discussions. A few hiccups should be expected and he was disappointed that Klaus did not have the same passion for revenge as he did, probably because he had a family safe and secure in the United States. But now he had been blessed with Captain Van Noy, a person just as driven as he was for recompense.

Hans did not hesitate in his reply. "No, I do not think adding Klaus to our plans would be a good idea. He lacks the commitment. This will be our pact only."

"Good! We will talk more, but remember you must always be supportive of our mission and minimize whatever events transpire on this ship, especially those pertaining to your device. We will not compromise our mission for any reason."

Enough had been said, they had formed their pact and their path forward had been simplified. They would conspire together. Hans excused himself and returned to his cabin.

HANS

Hans would keep his pact with the American captain. Although he did not see it as a pact, only a blessing, an answer to his prayers. Punishing the German war machine after what they had done to him and his family had become his single purpose. But now, he had just turned on his good friend Klaus, had violated their trust, transformed his long-time reliable friend into the enemy. The thought conflicted him; he had become Judas, but the kiss, the betrayal would come later.

Hans sat on his bunk and stared across their confined stateroom at his old friend. Feelings of guilt and deceit came flooding in as he thought back on all the years they had invested in their friendship.

"Klaus, what a strange journey this has been, and now we're at this bizarre moment in time." Hans's words were friendly and engaging, hoping a little reflection might soothe their escalating tensions. "Our days at the university, did you ever imagine we would be on board such a futuristic ship bound for the south Pacific, and with a very deadly responsibility attached to it? All those years ago, I could never have imagined such an outcome for us."

Klaus removed his reading glasses and placed them and his engineering book on the small table next to his chair. "Yes, it has been a very odd trip, a very sad one for you my friend. You have no idea how much it pains me."

They had studied together at the Technical University of Berlin. Bjurman and Mueller were classmates and they both attended seminars when the prominent scientists Albert Einstein and Nikola Tesla had been invited to lecture. Einstein was beginning to discuss a whole new area of science called quantum physics, as well as unified field theory, which tried to reconcile the fields of electromagnetism and gravity into a single field. The whole notion of interstellar black holes, gravity, and how it might even bend light, possibly even warping the fabric of time itself, was fascinating and consumed them. Tesla had proposed several pioneering theories in his revolutionary thesis, 'Dynamic Theory of Gravity.'

Klaus and Hans soon became the gifted protégés of the university's proud engineering program. They were recommended to Adolph Hitler's aggressive war machine and after graduating, Klaus was sent to Peenemunde Army Research Center for development of the V-1 rocket. Hans was assigned to the Kummersdorf Facility where they began research on the V-2 missile. No other career path was offered them. Both men cared little for their work on the development of these guided missiles that promised only indiscriminate death and destruction. On their own, they began to secretly research theorems that Einstein and Tesla had postulated. They began to share their ideas through the mail. Hans was researching something potentially brilliant. Klaus sensed his good friend was on to something quite remarkable.

In small, tentative experiments, Hans discovered that some light within its own spectrum could be delicately influenced by intense gravity or extremely dense objects. The whole concept captivated Klaus and he encouraged Hans's research, but also warned him of the prying eyes of the SS.

However, their research became distracted; rumors of mistreatment and even imprisonment of Jews throughout Germany began to find its way to their individual facilities. Letters from their extended families told of Jewish businesses being harassed and even closed down by the government. More and more Jewish families would suddenly disappear in the early hours and their homes and other assets confiscated by the state. Families of Jewish heritage soon began to flee Germany.

Returning home at the end of a long day of research became unsettling for these family men as each day brought more news of ever-increasing exploitation of their Jewish brethren. Cousins, aunts and uncles were suddenly disappearing. It all became real and very alarming. It had hit home.

The two professors decided they would discontinue sending letters; too much was a stake, they had families now. Weeks later, incoming and outgoing mail at both research facilities was severely restricted and what little posting made it through the screening process was opened and obviously read. Klaus and Hans soon lost contact with each other, another forfeit because of their Jewish heritage. Hans continued his secret research on his own, always fearful of the SS and their ring of spies.

"Klaus, did I ever tell you of the time I was severely beaten for not wearing my Jewish star prominently enough for my neighbors' standards? Imagine it, people I considered my friends."

Hans rarely spoke of his early days, probably because many of the memories were so painful. However, Klaus knew it was a healing process that Hans needed to go through. He would listen, and listen long, Hans would spare no detail. Each past action, thought, and discussion were permanently embedded in his consciousness and then allowed to fester in the tragedy that had become his life.

"I'm very sorry that such a thing was done to you," he offered. "Tell me about it, perhaps it might help."

Hans stared at Klaus, as if looking right through him, and began his tale.

Hans told him of his initial days at the research facility at Kummersdorf. Life had been good for a short time and he had tolerated his work. It was not the research he wanted to immerse himself in, but the pay was good and he provided for his family. Then Hitler's regime began to turn on its Jewish associates and life soon became difficult for him and his young family. He had married his high school love Emma, and they had added a daughter.

The Nazi regime, with its new policy of persecution of Jews all over Germany, was escalating. Special government documents were required to be carried by Jews at all times. Jewish businesses were being targeted with vandalism and boycotts. A new government edict demanded that Jews wear Star of David identifiers on their clothing and that they be clearly visible.

The last few weeks, he had begun to walk home from his engineering job at the end of his work day. It was a long walk, but the bus was crowded and often he was forced to give up his seat. Three times he had been asked to leave the lorry when it became overloaded. Finally, it got to the point where he often was not allowed to board the bus.

The walk home became a welcome escape from the harassment and pressure that his work had become. Away from his neighborhood, he was invisible, just another working man heading home mixed in with all the other toilers. He pulled his Cossack hat low on his forehead and wore his overcoat over his suit jacket. With its yellow star hidden underneath, it did not invite persecution. As he got nearer to his own locality, he would remove his outer coat so all those that knew the Jew Hans Mueller also recognized that he was conforming to the new government policy. He hated his neighbors and despised their racist rule.

The day of his beating, it had been an especially cold and snowy day and he had kept his overcoat on. The raw elements of the day had allowed him to momentarily forget about the racist moniker, now hidden underneath his overcoat. A neighbor wrought with a jealousy and anger he had been taught to direct towards his Jewish brother recognized him. He and several of his intoxicated comrades had just stumbled from a beer hall and chose to point out to Hans his lapse of proper dress and remind him of the consequences. They dragged him down an alley and beat him. It could have been a fatal beating if not for the local Orpo officers that had stumbled onto the scene. They dispersed the bullying thugs, not before congratulating them on a job well done and adding to Hans's discomfort and humiliation by thumping the backs of his thighs and calves with their nightsticks. The remaining walk to his home was painful. Limping home, his Jewish star now stained and disgraced with his own blood. His wife shrieked in disbelief when she greeted her husband in their entryway.

"It was then I knew we must leave Germany," Hans told his friend, and he continued his tale.

"We need to get out of Germany," he told his wife several nights later at the dinner table, bruises and cuts slowly starting to heal. He was hunched over from the pain and humiliation that had been inflicted. His superiors at work showed little compassion and told him he would be closely watched.

His Emma was so frightened; both at a loss as to where to turn. She reminded him of the escalating madness. "Irving Sandman's business was closed down and they were moved from their home with only about a two-hour notice. They were physically beaten, all of them, and no one did a thing to stop it."

"It has become very dangerous for all Jews. It is only my research at Kummersdorf that has prevented us from becoming part of the missing." He was overcome with despair. "And I wonder how long that will insulate us.

"I know of a vessel that will be leaving Bremen, it is bound for America. Workers at my plant have talked about it. It may be our last chance to escape."

"They will never let you leave, you are too good of a scientist, a good little Jew," she said sarcastically, and then started to cry.

The next day Hans began thinking of fleeing his native Germany, emigrating from the homeland would be very difficult. The racist regime was now limiting the number of Jews it would allow to leave Germany, especially those involved in Nazi research and development. Hitler would not compromise his war effort even it meant employing Jewish scientists. It was also becoming very expensive;

many Jews spent their life savings and left all of their possessions to the government authorities.

He knew he would have to concoct an act of stealth and deception. They would never allow Hans to freely leave. Airports, shipyards, train stations, and border crossings were being watched carefully. Hans discovered through contacts at work that a steamer, a United States vessel called the *St. Louis,* would be leaving Bremen in six weeks. They were taking on Jewish passengers wishing to leave Germany and speculation was that it might be the last ship leaving the fatherland with Jewish travelers on board. Hans knew his family must be on that ship.

Night after night on his walk home from work, Hans tortured himself with thoughts of escape for him and his family. Every judgment steered him into a wall, he knew no one that could orchestrate the passports and the passage on the *St. Louis.* Any inquiries among his co-workers would surely bring about their demise. Work and the feeling of dread for his family were suffocating. He slept very little at night and stress had taken his appetite.

Hans strode through the early evening hours, his heavy overcoat with its Jewish star now prominently displayed pulled tight against the harsh winds. A thick woolen scarf was wrapped snuggly around his neck and raw, dried cheeks. A man, a stranger, soon fell in stride next to him. He was a tall, thin man and he too was dressed for the raw elements. The stranger wore the same religious identifier as Hans did. He was much older than Hans, his long, thick, gray beard helped in that conclusion.

"Hello Hans," he whispered. "Please keep walking, I will explain everything, but suddenly stopping here and confronting me will only bring attention to you. We must appear to be two old Jews commiserating in our misery."

Hans slowed his pace gradually and glanced at his new companion, taking in everything around him. "How do you know my name?" he asked quietly

"You'd be amazed how much I know about you, Mr. Hans Mueller. I work at the Kummersdorf Facility as do you. I know you are a valued engineer there and people outside our country, people in the global scientific community, are aware of that and want to facilitate your escape. But it won't be easy; we don't have a lot of time. The ship that has everyone talking leaves in just a few weeks."

He was stunned by this stranger's knowledge of him. They kept their walk slow and relaxed like two men discussing the recent frigid temperatures. On the inside Hans was anything but relaxed, his heart pounded in his chest and his mouth was suddenly dry.

His suspicions and dreaded fear of the Gestapo froze him with terror. "Who are you, I do not wish to escape from Germany and I know nothing about any ship."

"My name is Fredrick Deinmer and relax, I am here to help you, your wife, and little girl. You must learn to trust me, but unfortunately we don't have a lot of time. Go home to your wife and talk about what I have just told you. I will meet you again tomorrow on your way home. Think about what you want to ask me." He patted Hans on the shoulder like an old friend, strode off towards the town square, and disappeared among the throngs of people.

That night Hans told his wife of the stranger who had entered his life. Emma was terrified of the possibilities. "He could be with the police. Perhaps they want you to lead them to others with the same desire to escape. You must be careful. I would not trust him."

"There are so many reasons not to trust him, but something inside me tells me he is indeed a friend. I'll listen to him tomorrow when we walk, if he comes."

The next day Fredrick was there at the town square where they had parted company, and he fell in next to Hans and they began their delicate conversation. Hans, wanting to trust, was frozen on the inside with skepticism and suspicion. Fredrick tried to project confidence and conviction. Each day the same rendezvous and the same discussion with Fredrick's pressing objective of Hans's escape at the center of it. They would part company with Fredrick reminding him that time was running out.

Hans would return home with more understanding of this stranger who now suddenly had the potential of becoming their liberator. The questions conceived the night before with his wife were satisfied the following day. Hans learned that Fredrick, much to his amazement, was not Jewish; he simply attached the six-pointed symbol to his overcoat knowing it would allow him some small liberty when approaching Hans. When Hans asked who Fredrick was working for or his contacts within Germany, Hans was told that trust was a two-way street. Such information could be very dangerous if it fell into the wrong hands. If compromised, their mission would expose many good people and their families to the ruthless tactics of the Gestapo. When the time was right Fredrick would share everything.

"Why do you help me, a Jew?" he asked, stunned. "No one helps the Jews in this terrible country. Germany has lost its soul."

"I wish I could help all Jews," Fredrick whispered with quiet desperation. "There are a lot of people that think the same way as I do. That is why we will get you out of this godless nation. You have to trust me."

That night he told his wife that it was time to trust Fredrick. Emma was consumed with fear but knew they had reached a critical point.

"What has happened to our world?" she moaned, her eyes welling and her voice soft with despair. "We will have to leave our families behind; perhaps we will never see them again."

"We are at a crossroads my dear; if we don't leave soon, I am convinced we will never see our families or each other again. Hitler means to annihilate our people."

Tomorrow Hans would commit fully to Fredrick's plan. It was their only chance for escape.

That night they slept with their little girl between them. They caressed their infant daughter and each other, their eyes searching each other's depth wondering if this would be their last night together as a family. Despite the circumstances forced upon them they had loved each other deeply and lived with the conviction that their god would not forsake them.

The next day on their walk home he told Fredrick. "Our lives are in your hands. Take whatever you need from us."

HANS

ST. LOUIS

The ship was the SS *St. Louis*, a 365-foot steamer, and word had traveled fast that she was taking on passengers trying to escape the brutality of the Nazi regime. Jews and the disenfranchised from all over Germany were scrambling for tickets and the German authorities were extracting a terrible cost for those wishing to escape. There was no bartering, no pleading of special circumstances for those oppressed and wishing to leave their native country. No one cared of their plight, those with that kind of power rarely do. In fact, cost of passage on the *St. Louis* was increasing daily, sometimes twice in a day.

Theirs was a desperate journey. Hans told no one at work of his secretive plans, even his most trusted Jewish co-workers. The risk was just too great. An atmosphere of mistrust and paranoia had engulfed the facility. Many Jewish and Polish scientists talked of this ship and its potential for escape to freedom, but no one talked openly of it. The Reich had its spies imbedded within the workers. They would need to be very cautious.

Fredrick began his efforts to secure passage for the Mueller family on the *St. Louis*. He had his contact within the government immigration office, but things were changing rapidly. An atmosphere of suspicion had settled into the workings of the now tyrant led regime. Everyone's actions were closely watched. Passenger names were submitted and researched. No one of any value to the war machine would be allowed to leave. Several days had passed before Fredrick met with his contact at a little restaurant. They sat at a little outside table and his agent was on edge. His forehead was beaded with sweat and his hands trembled. He gulped at his glass stein of beer.

"Things are very tense at the facility; the SS knows that highly valued people are trying to escape Germany. Every move, every decision is being scrutinized. People are being removed from their jobs for the slightest infraction. Your clients will pay dearly for their counterfeit visas and passports."

"Yes, yes I know. My friends have liquidated everything they own. Their jewelry, watches, furniture, old family possessions, Mrs. Mueller sold her family Steinway. I have a trusted friend who can take the passport photos. Shall I begin that process?"

"Your trusted friend is not my trusted friend. I will handle it all or it just won't get done. That's the way it is. Do you understand?"

"Of course."

In the end Fredrick was told to have the Mueller family ready for pictures at their own apartment on Saturday afternoon. They would need to dramatically change their appearance. Hans cut his hair very short and removed his beard. Mrs. Mueller bleached her hair blonde and it too was trimmed and curled. They were not to leave their flat until it was departure time for their vessel.

Fredrick picked them up with freshly altered pictures on their forged passports and he drove them to the city wharf.

"There has been a last-minute change. Your passports have been stamped with a Cuban entry visa," he told his nervous passengers.

"We are supposed to be going to America," Hans nervously stuttered.

"I know, I know. The US is trying to remain very neutral with global matters like this. They are temporally restricting entry visas from Germany. Just go with the flow, tell people you are visiting relatives in Havana. Once we get to Cuba, things will change, strings will be pulled, I promise."

Fredrick purposely parked away from the wharf and helped his passengers with their belongings. "This is as far as I go, I will wait in the shadows to watch you board. Walk to the boat like you own it and do whatever the Gestapo asks of you. God go with you."

The Gestapo was everywhere, the Muellers' paperwork was carefully examined at the numerous checkpoints. Passports were held up next to their faces and comparisons were made and satisfied. No words were ever exchanged, just a piercing stare that seemed to last for eternity and then a quick nod of the head and their passports returned. Their hearts pounding in their chests and stomachs about to empty their contents. Hans and his wife struggled to maintain an air of composure. Finally, they were allowed to board to the *St. Louis* and they hurried up the gangplank on wobbly legs.

They reached the promenade deck and turned to search the bustling crowd on the city pier below for their good friend Fredrick. There was a blast of the vessel's departure horn and wharf personnel began the process of removing the heavy lines that kept the *St. Louis* tethered to its pier. They found Fredrick immersed in the throng and waved to him. He did not return their wave, only nodded and turned to leave. There was a sudden commotion below, a dark sedan with its horn blasting sped down the pier and came to a screeching stop by the last gangplank that was about to be pulled back. A middle age couple with an adolescent child jumped from the car and rushed to the footbridge, they carried only light bags. Gestapo personnel already retreated from their checkpoints were unprepared to stop the dash of the tardy passengers and the remaining dock workers made no effort to stop them as they raced up the now moving ramp. With his wife pushed ahead, the father of this delayed family leaped from the teetering catwalk with his child in his arms. Passengers and the horde below screamed in horror as the gangplank collapsed beneath them, but they had made it and strangers hugged and comforted them. Gestapo officers with their whistles screeching and nightsticks raised rushed the departing vessel with vocal threats and orders to stop. But it was too little too late, the *St. Louis* with all its mass was underway. There would be no stopping her.

Now all attention was directed to the mystery family and their dramatic entrance. Passengers welcomed them and were delighted that they had thwarted the hated SS. However, ship security personnel soon had them in custody and they were taken to the captain's office. After meeting with the captain, the couple and their child were restricted to their cabin. Hans, his family, and most of the passengers anxiously waited for their release. The unknown family's dramatic entrance was all the passengers could talk about.

It soon leaked out that their last name was Hoffman and they had lived in Berlin. Two days into the ship's travel, after it was determined that they were not a security risk and the *St. Louis* would not be pursued by German officials, they were allowed to leave their rooms and given freedom of the ship.

People warmly greeted them. Heartfelt hugs and handshakes welcomed them. They became instant celebrities; everyone wanted to hear their tale. Mrs. Hoffman and her young daughter were hesitant to talk about their exaggerated arrival, the sudden attention overwhelming, but the father was all too willing to relive the events of the bizarre day. He was not shy or hesitant of his hatred of the Gestapo and what Hitler had done to his people and their country.

His name was Peter, Peter Hoffman, and he had been a dentist in Berlin. He had established a successful practice and a loyal following. His wife was the record keeper at their practice and their little girl had just started first grade at the nearby grammar school.

Hitler's plan of persecution soon took its toll on the Jewish orthodontist. People became fearful to visit his office and his patients stopped coming. Their income stream steadily disappeared and soon they were forced to close their doors. Yellow six-pointed stars became the required moniker. Going out in public became a risky adventure. They became captives in their own home.

Word of the *St. Louis* reached them and they knew it would be their only chance at freedom and they began to orchestrate their escape. Trying to stay ahead of Hitler's secret police was an everyday challenge, as was evident by their last-minute leap on board the *St. Louis* as it pulled away from its slip.

A clear, cool, early spring morning, the Muellers sat in the warmth of the indoor dining hall. They finished their hot breakfast and Hans and Emma sipped at their coffee. The ship's dining area was a mishmash of strange shaped tables and odd colored chairs. The Hoffmans entered the large arcade and looked for a place to sit. They approached the Muellers and inquired if they could join them.

A common theme on this ship, the two families soon talked of their own tale of persecution and flight. Hans insisted that some of the specifics of their plight should remain a guarded secret. He was still a very valuable fugitive. When asked about his background or where he was from, Hans provided a false narrative.

"Well, I can only speak for ourselves," Mrs. Hoffman said, and she became melancholy. "So many of our friends, Jewish friends, started to be mistreated. Rocks were thrown through their windows late at night, swastikas painted on their doors. Nobody did a thing. And then people were moved out of their homes, relocated to some unknown place with little notice, their property and possessions confiscated, and then some families suddenly disappearing completely. Simply abducted off the street."

Hans and his wife felt a spontaneous bond with all the passengers on this ship of freedom, but a special link had quickly developed with the Hoffmans. Peter Hoffman's optimism for the better days that lay ahead was infectious. The two families began to dine together during the evening sittings. Much of the late morning and afternoon hours the Hoffmans remained in their quarters. Important paperwork required for entry to Cuba was incomplete. Their panicked, hasty boarding had secured that outcome. Peter's days were spent involved in hectic communications with Cuban officials as well as with the US State Department.

Often during their evening meals, people would stop by their table, introduce themselves, and plead with Mr. Hoffman to recount the tale of his family's leap to freedom and of hoodwinking the Gestapo. The *St. Louis* carried a people who had long endured the exploitation Germany's secret police was noted for. To see and hear the details of how the Hoffmans had deluded the mighty SS was simply uplifting and inspired them all. Peter was an instant celebrity.

The weather was becoming warmer and the sun was setting later in the day. Everyone was excited about beginning their new lives in America. In three days, the *St. Louis* would be docking in Havana, Cuba.

The US State Department had not officially given the *St. Louis* permission to dock at an American port, but most thought it was just a given formality. They would dock in Havana, wait the few short hours before permission was granted by the American government, and then they would complete the short voyage to Miami. They might even be granted permission to sail directly to Florida before arriving in Cuba; their vessel was in constant contact with the State Department and influential people were trying to get things done.

The final evening before arriving in Cuba, Hans and his family were bursting with excitement; their bland menu that evening could have been a culinary delight. Their anticipation would not be dampened by canned ham and brown rice. The Hoffmans' mood, however, seemed low and without spirit, and they picked at their food. They offered little conversation and were quick to retire to their cabins. It was a complete turnabout from Peter's jovial temperament and his engaging dialogue. Hans was taken aback by Peter's new dark persona. He grabbed Peter's arm as he left the table and inquired.

"Peter, what has come over you?" Hans searched his eyes. "Last night you could not wait for our arrival in Havana and this evening the mere mention of that city appears to horrify you."

Peter turned and looked at Hans, was about to say something and then checked himself, said, "I'm tired that's all," and looked away. "Didn't sleep all that well last night. The seas seemed to be rolling all night long."

Hans could not remember a calmer night since leaving Bremer. "Peter, what's going on, last night was like an ice mill pond," he said, and he once again grabbed his friend by the forearm.

Peter stopped, looking all around as if fearful someone might overhear their conversation.

"Hans, I hope I can trust you, but I just found out last night that there is a member of the SS posing as a passenger, perhaps more than one, a spy Hans."

Hans was stunned with the disturbing information, his insides turned with disbelief. "A Gestapo spy, what in god's name for?"

"Apparently there is a highly regarded scientist stowed away on board this boat. He did not show up at his job at some research facility and they believe he made his way onto this ship with fake documents and changed appearance. I am so fearful for my family, we also secured some false papers, my wife dyed her hair and I shaved my beard. God knows if I have jeopardized my family with my boasting of how I tricked the stupid Gestapo."

"How is it you know so many details?" Hans asked, stunned with the news.

Peter told him of an old friendship with the captain; it was through his help that he got them last minute passage on this ship.

"He learned of the spy last night and told me to keep a low profile. He does not know who the infiltrator is but whoever he is, he probably does not appreciate my vocal condemnation of the Gestapo." Peter's hands began to shake and he was near tears. His voice cracking with fear he whispered," I'm afraid I will not be allowed to disembark in Cuba."

Hans knew it was time to reveal his identity. They were all Jews trying to begin a new life. He could no allow one of his own to suffer such anguish.

He leaned in closer to Peter and spoke softly. "I am that stowaway, that scientist the SS is searching for. It was a decision my wife and I made quite easily. It was just a matter of time before the SS would have taken my family hostage to secure my commitment to Hitler's war machine. Leaving would not be so easy. Fake passports and changing our appearance were required and the trauma it brought to our young daughter was beyond anything you could imagine."

Peter was stunned. "You are a very brave man." And he shook his head in disbelief. "I will assume Cohen is not your real name."

Hans told him of his real name and that of his wife and daughter. "Please keep this information to yourself. Now, more than ever, I need to protect my family's identity."

"We both need to continue our charade," Peter said. "Obviously the Gestapo has not identified their target; no one has been taken into custody, although I was told they have begun questioning some of the passengers."

"Ahh," Hans whispered, and realized that their escape was now in jeopardy. The tension was ratcheting up. Arriving in Havana and departing the *St. Louis* could not happen soon enough. He did not relish sharing this new disturbing news with his wife.

The two men said goodnight and shook hands, now knowing they shared a secret pact and would talk more tomorrow.

HANS

ST. LOUIS

"God in Heaven, Hans what a torturous trip it must have been," Klaus justly replied. "I am in awe that you revealed yourself to Peter. It must have been quite nerve wracking."

"At that time, it seemed like the obvious thing to do," Hans replied. He began his tale again.

The *St. Louis* docked at the large wharf in Havana. Tankers and freighters from all over the globe were secured to its massive concrete wharfs all around the terminal. Other vessels waited offshore for their turn to offload or take on cargo.

Passengers were charged with optimism. At the first early morning sighting of Havana's harbor, people began to gather along the rails of their freedom ship. Some gestured with their hands, pointing to

Havana and looking back to family and friends and shouting with excitement. Their first step towards deliverance awaited them.

Bow and stern lines were tied off and the center gangway was about to be put in place. Two wearied, official looking men in wrinkled white suits stood below where the walkway touched down. Four soldiers in combat dress stood nearby, bayoneted rifles crisscrossing their chests.

The older of the two officials stepped forward and yelled through his megaphone that the captain and his first mate would be needed for a meeting; in the meantime no one would be allowed to leave the ship. He turned and signaled to a nearby building. A company of fifty rifled sentries hustled out from the shadows within to take positions alongside the *St. Louis*. The mood on the vessel suddenly turned somber, their lives once again invaded by armed guards and their independence threatened.

The *St. Louis's* captain returned to the vessel in about two hours. He brought discouraging news with him. They met with Cuban officials at the capitol building in Havana and were told their passengers would not be allowed to disembark. America and Cuba were trying hard to remain neutral with regards to the growing unrest in Western Europe. Allowing these German refugees safe harbor might be seen as a provocative gesture. There were heated exchanges between the captain and Cuban diplomats. The *St. Louis's* skipper demanded where they were to go from here, they would need fuel and provisions. Frantic communications between US officials at the American consulate in Cuba and Washington began in earnest.

Hans, his family, and the rest of the passengers thought they had been granted asylum in Cuba long before the *St. Louis* left Germany. Now the German SS mole hidden among the passengers would have ample time to discover them. The thought terrified the Muellers. Bewildered passengers huddled in groups seeking answers that no one could offer. The possibility that no country would provide safe harbor drained their optimism. The fear that they might be forced to return to Germany now consumed them.

In the early morning hours Washington telegrammed officials in Cuba that they would pay for needed fuel and supplies. Cuban dock workers delivered the required provisions and government bureaucrats insisted the vessel be outside Cuban waters by daybreak tomorrow. After refurbishing was complete, lines were hastily cast off and the *St. Louis* was nudged by sending tugs out into the Havana waterfront. Word also came that the *St. Louis* should proceed to New York; diplomats were trying to facilitate their entry into that city's marine terminal.

An unknown Gestapo agent was on this ship and Hans would have to continue his masquerade in plain sight. His anxiety was dialed up. The sooner he was off the confines of the *St. Louis* the safer he and his family would be. Cuba had turned their back on them and now they sailed towards America. Perhaps safe harbor waited for them there.

That evening the Muellers and Hoffmans gathered around their dinner table, their mood submissive. The reservations and fears that were their daily lives in Germany had chased them across a vast ocean and had cornered them in Cuba.

"I wonder what choice we have but to sail towards America," offered Peter his, voice low with little energy. "Is the man that helped you escape onboard, what does he think of all this bizarre diplomatic posturing?"

"He's not on this ship, why would you think he would be?" Hans asked, somewhat startled by the question. "I assumed he returned to Peenemunde where we both worked, maybe to help with other escapes," Hans replied

"What a kind and brave man he must be," Peter said. "If he was ever captured, the outcome for him and his family could be very ugly."

"I suppose it would, but what about your friend the captain," asked Hans, wanting to change the subject. "What does he say about all this last-minute course change, the chaos in Havana?"

"He is as much in the dark as the rest of us," Peter said. "He has accepted that we have no other alternative but to travel on to New York, he wonders if we will be well received. Right now, America is trying desperately to remain out of a war that the whole world sees as inevitable."

That night they steamed on to New York, a tropic sunset reflecting off all the port side portals.

HANS

ST. LOUIS

A new day, and closer to New York City and perhaps freedom. Last night they had tossed and turned in their restrictive berths. Praying for a fresh start, a new beginning, sleep had been elusive. Weary, they left their cabins and joined others on the promenade for the short walk to the dining area for breakfast. Many of the passengers had gathered along the rail and were pointing out towards the early morning sun. There were grumblings and looks of puzzlement on their faces. Something was wrong.

Hans stood with his family and searched for some clarity. There was no panic, but an uneasiness had spread throughout their ship.

Peter Hoffman was suddenly among them. "Hans, we turned around early this morning, now they say we're heading for Miami." His voice was filled with anticipation. "Maybe this is good news."

Hans knew immediately why travelers were pointing towards the morning sun. They had seen the sunset on the port side and now a sunrise was visible on that same left side. The *St. Louis* had indeed reversed its travel.

"What does your captain friend say about this?" Hans questioned.

"He can offer nothing; I think he's afraid to say anything," Peter said, his voice now quiet with suspicion. "Perhaps he too is being watched."

"What has happened to our world?" Hans's wife interjected; her voice close to tears.

"You know Hans, I never asked if there are other passengers like yourself trying to escape the hell hole that is now our Germany," Peter inquired.

Hans was puzzled be such a question. "I would think this whole ship would be full of people like that."

"No, I mean important, gifted scientists such as yourself, perhaps there is someone or some group that is trying to facilitate their escape. A person similar to your stature would be a worthy addition to any country's defense sector. Did anybody assist in your flight from Germany? Perhaps there is a way to reach out to them; maybe they know what is really happening here. I would imagine all sorts of things are taking place behind closed doors right now."

"I did have help, a good man named Fredrick, he never revealed his last name, and some other very decent people, not Jewish either, but their help was critical. There were so many components. But I'm sure there would be no way to contact them. That all ended when the *St. Louis* left Bremen."

The two men tried to envision a way that would land their ship in the safe haven of Miami or any American harbor. They could only desperately wait while someone else decided their fate.

"I can't imagine they would have gone to such length to get you out of Germany just to leave you floating on a ship in the middle of the Florida Sea. Right now, I would think there are important people in America who are lobbying quite aggressively to get you off this ship. If we only knew who they were, perhaps they have a contact on this vessel."

"I wish I could tell you more, I just don't know how my contacts in the old country could possibly help and I know of no one in

America. They purposely withheld people's names; I was told someone would contact me when I landed in Cuba."

"This hasn't been easy for my family either, must be insane
for everyone on this ship," Peter said, his distress obvious. "I'm not
sure how much more of this uncertainty my wife can take. She was
so critical of my boasting about the incompetence of the SS."

"Try to calm yourself. Maybe this whole conversation will
be pointless if we dock in Miami later today," Hans said.

"My god, I hope you're right," Peter said, and he walked off
to find his family, his shoulders slumped and his walk slow.

The *St. Louis* steamed slowly in a large circle just outside
Miami's commercial wharf. They were again in a holding predicament and passengers became irritable in the heat and humidity. Little
information was shared with them, other than they were trying to secure a docking. Intensive negotiations were ongoing between the
State Department, Cuban, and German authorities. Finally, they were
told that discussions had been fruitful and they would be docking at
around 10:00 pm. Travelers were told to have all their belongings
packed and ready. They were being advised to make their dis-embar-
kation as speedily as possible. Representatives from the State Department would be there to assist.

A tropical front had moved in late in the afternoon, a light
drizzle would welcome the immigrants to America. They stood in the
light rain, a mass of desperate asylum seekers gathered at the single
gangplank that offered freedom. There was little conversation, suspicion had checked any optimism. They would wait quietly in the Miami mist, fearing any outward sanguinity might jinx this last and final
step. They shuffled along like drips from a leaky faucet. One by one
they stepped away from the *St. Louis*, their movement slow and trying. A police car pulled up close to the gang-plank. Two uniformed
officers in rain gear and an older man in a suit and carrying a briefcase
emerged from the car. One of the policemen held an umbrella for his
suited friend. They joined the other officials at the base of the

walkway. Passengers were stopped from leaving the ship. Documents were pulled from the briefcase of the new arrival and were examined under the umbrella with a flashlight. The drizzling rain and the faded lighting provided by random wharf lights gave the setting an unnerving and macabre feel. People sensed no good would come of this sudden gathering of officials.

A murmur slowly worked its way back along the gangplank; something was wrong, people became uneasy and they began shouting their concerns about the sudden delay and pleaded with the officials to let them disembark. Children became unnerved and their pleas to their parents for clarification went unanswered. It only escalated the situation. The men at the base shined their flashlights up along the gangway and insisted that everyone should remain calm.

Hans and his wife knew that panic was close. People were beginning to jockey for position, soon there would be a dash for freedom at the base of the gangplank.

Suddenly Peter Hoffman was next to them, his family not with him. He leaned in and whispered to Hans, "You and your family need to come with me right now," his voice full of warning. "The authorities down below are here to arrest you. My captain friend can help."

Fear took possession of Hans's thoughts; escape became his first instinct. He grabbed his wife and scooped up their daughter. "They are here to arrest me, Peter can help. We should go with him."

His wife gasped with the sudden dread. They slipped away from the crowd and hurried to the upper decks. They entered what appeared to be the captain's quarters. Peter quickly closed and double bolted the door behind them. Breathless and dripping with rain, they began to remove their hats and outer clothing. Across from them stood three imposing figures dressed in full Gestapo regalia with their evil red swastika armbands proudly displayed.

Hans and his wife were stunned; they looked to Peter for resolution. From within his overcoat Peter produced a luger; he stepped away and pointed it at them.

"Do you really think we would let you escape, how stupid of you, but then again you are a Jew." One of the Gestapo officers also drew his weapon while the other two placed handcuffs on Hans and his family.

"Peter what have you done?" Hans said, his voice full of hurt. "You have deceived us all."

"My name is not Peter and I have only sought to protect the Deutschland from traitors such as you, but then again you are a Jew."

"This has been a ruse this whole time, what a godless man you are. I hope you and your family rot in hell. But these people are probably not your family, are they?"

"Yes my Jew friend, it has been a scam," he said with a little apathy and complete disdain. "We were expecting defectors aboard this ship, and then we learned through our contacts at Peenemunde that a critical scientist might also try to flee."

He walked about the stateroom, a king in his throne room. He stopped to light a cigarette, inhaled deeply. "Ahhh, these American cigarettes are quite good." He exhaled.

"Quite an entrance on our part you must agree, although leaping from the gangway to this ship was closer than I wanted. It took a while to zero in on you and your family; cutting your hair and shaving and your wife bleaching her hair threw us off a bit. But we uncovered you. I tried to extract more information about those that helped in your escape. However, you only revealed a single name. The traitor named Fredrick is now imprisoned and his family is in work camps."

Hans stood there in suffocating sadness, staring at the floor. "I suppose that will become our fate." His wife began to cry as their daughter clung to her side.

"Oh no, my Hebrew traitor. You are too valuable a researcher. You will go back to Berlin, this time they say your work will be on the V-2 rocket. But your family will be held within a compound and will be guarded night and day. Things will not be as restrictive for you, but your family's well-being will be determined by your behavior. Work hard and your family will live. We don't expect you to be a problem."

He turned to his Gestapo underlings. "Take them to their rooms, Mr. Mueller in his own room, his wife and child in another. They are not to leave their rooms." And then to Hans, "Oh by the way Hans, that commotion just now on the wharf below, they were your potential rescuers, people from the American State Department looking for you. People that report to me told them no such person was aboard this ship. They would not risk forcefully searching the vessel; it could become an international incident they did not want. We will be underway in a few hours, just as soon as we offload the rest of your fellow sinners. America can have them." And then with choking sarcasm he added, "Welcome back home Hans."

"Oh, Hans these stories of yours are so wrenching, how terrible this must have been for you and your family," Klaus said, his voice despondent.

Hans only nodded his head. There was more to his tale.

USS *ELDRIDGE*

AFTER GERMAN SUB

Petty Officer Bruno was the lead NCO on the damage control team. After any incident on the *Eldridge*—if it was weather related, accidental, or the result of enemy fire—it was his responsibility to examine, evaluate, and report his findings to the lead officer on the ship. Twenty-two years of navigating the oceans of the world had taught him a lot. Valued by his superiors and admired by his subordinates, he did his job well.

Now he was evaluating personnel, a responsibility he was never really trained to do. Horrible injuries and deaths were occurring on his ship, to men he liked and respected. It was beyond anything he had ever seen and, he was horrified by the butchery of it all.

One man was killed and another seriously injured after their brief encounter with the German U-boat. Bruno, along with the ship's corpsman, rushed to their aid. Finding Seaman Bud Robinson, his first discovery, shocked him. Robinson's body was tortuously implanted at mid-section into a steel partition near the forward ammunition magazine. His body hanging limp on either side of the metal

54

wall. Flesh, muscle, and intestines grossly suspended. His torso appallingly burned along its middle. The smell of burned flesh was nauseating. The concept on how such a grotesque event could happen mystified and sickened Petty Officer Bruno. It appeared as if Bud had somehow briefly gained the ability to walk through walls, and then in mid-stride had lost that capacity. The young sailor's body would later be separated from its steel trap with the use of a cross-cut saw. Cutting through flesh and hip bone was sickening and exhausting. The entire ship was horrified by the event.

The screams of agony from Lieutenant Richards directed Bruno to the other injury; the shrieks echoing along the ship's passageways horrified the crew. The lieutenant's right arm was embedded and divided just above his elbow. The ship's surgeon was once again forced to separate a sailor from his limb with a carpenter's saw. Lieutenant Richards would survive, his right arm amputated and the scarring extensive.

Captain Van Noy arrived at the gruesome scene as they were removing Lt. Richards on a stretcher, his arm a bloody stump. Petty Officer Bruno gave Van Noy the gruesome update. "The Doc just gave the lieutenant another shot of morphine. It's the only way we could cut his arm off." Van Noy nodded his head and turned to the ship's physician.

"How's the lieutenant doing?" he asked.

"He'll be OK, his arm I mean, the burns he got will take a lot to get over. Infection is the biggest challenge with those things. Horrible burns, almost like his flesh was eating itself. I got to head down to the other man; I've been told it's pretty ugly. Guess we will need a few men to cut him away from the wall."

"I just came from there," Van Noy said, his voice despondent. "It's not pretty at all; we have sheets draped over either side of his body. Do what you have to do to prepare him for burial at sea."

"Starting to see some grisly injuries, and now a horrific death on this ship." The doc's tone was more challenging than just a simple observation. "This special device may end up killing us all, you sure it's worth the risk?"

"Does seem a little dangerous, I mean sort of self-inflicting. Don't you think, Captain?" added Bruno.

"Doctor Bellows, Petty Officer Bruno, you need to keep those kinds of observations to yourselves," the captain barked, suddenly confrontational. "Do you understand me on this? We are at war and these types of things happen." He stared momentarily at each man, briefly locked eyes with the doc, and then was briskly walking away. The two men were stunned with their captain's apathy.

The *Eldridge* sailed on towards its south Pacific destination. The fallout from Seaman Robinson's gruesome bisection and the amputation of Lt. Richards's right arm unnerved the crew of the *Eldridge.* The screams of Lt. Richards when his arm was embedded in the bulkhead and then when it was cut away were haunting. They seemed to echo throughout the ship. Some sailors said they could still hear his screams in the night, days after it happened. Lt. Richards was on a steady dose of morphine and he drifted in and out of a deep slumber, only to awaken when the morphine wore off and the intolerable pain returned.

A growing fear had taken root in the *Eldridge*. The crew wondered if their captain's quest for confrontation had become his dangerous obsession. He cared little for the harm inflicted on his crew by their special weapon. Their secret weapon had turned deadly. Every sailor on the *Eldridge* wondered when it might be his screams echoing through the passageways.

HANS

ST. LOUIS

"Now my narrative becomes more familiar to you Klaus, this is where you and I were re-united at Peenemunde to toil together, more like slaves for Hitler's war machine, my God, I absolutely despise that goddamn animal.

"We traveled back to Germany, with only the suspicious, ever present SS officers for company. I, my wife, and my daughter endured the miserable, lonely return trip to Germany. Gestapo officials met the *St. Louis* when it docked at Bremen. I was handcuffed and quickly driven to a location near my new work assignment at Peenemunde. There I was beaten and interrogated for five days. The Gestapo wanted the names of other people involved in my escape. I had already unknowingly given up the name of Fredrick, who I learned later had been shot only days after my return to Germany, but there were no other names that I could provide, names were purposely withheld from me. Nevertheless, it took numerous poundings and days without sleep before my tormentors finally accepted that there was nothing left within me. I believe some of my persecutors actually enjoyed their sadistic acts. It's hard to imagine how a person could sink to that level of the depravity and then delight in it." The tale continued...

Hans returned to his work and was reunited with his old friend Klaus Bjurman. His bruised and swollen features were difficult for Klaus to look at. It was a clear reminder to the other Jewish workers that their world had turned ugly and their day to day existence was extremely delicate.

Things had turned oppressive at Peenemunde prior to Hans' arrival. His beating and forced immersion back into the work force only strengthened those fears within the Jewish ranks. Klaus waited for Hans' bruises to heal and with it, his sense of self-worth, before he told Hans how bad conditions had deteriorated. Management had become much less tolerant of the Jewish researchers at Peenemunde, always accusing them of little effort and minor progress. They implemented unrealistic guidelines and goals and instigated bizarre punishments, sometimes not allowing them to see their families for several days.

There was trepidation in the work place, work became difficult and they brought their concerns to those in charge. The top-secret research center was under the tight control of Germany's new secret police, the SS. The scientists were told their fears were unfounded and to focus all their energies on the V-1 program, their fuhrer and country demanded it. Attempts to further discuss their worries were abruptly dismissed and they were instructed to return to their work stations.

No one's reservations had been eased, the callous dismissal of their fears only reinforced the horror stories they were hearing from the home front. Jewish researchers began to gather covertly in small groups, their conversations very guarded, and they talked only of escape from their hellish workplace. Most of the men had families and it only complicated their predicament. Fear for their families stopped many of them from any further talk of escape.

Approaching the SS senior staff with their concerns raised the suspicions of their superiors. Now they were watched constantly. Their automobiles were confiscated and they were bused to and from work. Their families' travel became very limited and outside contact with extended family was closely monitored. Mail delivered to them was opened and obviously read.

Klaus approached his good friend about escaping from Peenemunde. He knew Hans would not be receptive to the notion.

"You want to talk about escape," he hissed, his tone quite bitter. "You're talking to the wrong man about that, and I should think you knew that. I traveled back across the Atlantic locked away from my wife and daughter. For six days a thin steel wall stood between me and my family. We would knock on the bulkhead at certain times of the day. It was our only form of communication."

"Hans, we can't stay here, our time is running out." Klaus was pleading.

"Oh yes we can. You saw what they did to me; I know what the SS is capable of. There are parts of my body that still have bruising. My feet will never be right. You see how I walk. Be a good Jew and build good rockets for the fuhrer and you and your family will survive."

Klaus understood his friend's skepticism and bitterness. He hoped time might change his old friend's mind.

Months later Eric Schultz, a trusted associate of theirs from their time at the university, was transferred to Peenemunde. He became the assistant director for the project and was a close associate of Albert Einstein, although Hans and Klaus were the only scientists aware of that. Eric brought disturbing news with him and would only share it with Klaus and Hans.

"Things have become very dark, more terrible than you can imagine. Horrible things are happening to Jews all over Germany. Hitler has become a tyrant. He has shown that he is capable of truly horrific acts. There are reports of death camps all over our country. Hitler plans to eradicate the Jewish people. I am here to get you and your families out of Germany."

There was stunned silence. Finally, Klaus broke the stillness. "We knew this day would come; Hans was not so sure." And he looked at his colleague for redemption. Hans could only nod his head; old feelings of dread came rushing in and checked his voice.

Klaus continued. "I suppose we hoped the stories were exaggerated, foolish of us it now seems. How do you propose to get us out of this fortress and then Germany after that? We will do whatever you need."

This time Hans nodded his head. "Yes, yes, of course."

"The plan is not elaborate," Eric explained. "There are those among us who are not Jewish, but see the terrible path our country is on. The Americans with your associates, Professors Einstein and Tesla, are trying mightily to extricate those with a background in this new science of jet propulsion. Einstein knows who those talented minds are and he has put the two of you near the top of his list. The Allies have their network of trusted contacts; when they have things ready, we will make a dash for the Switzerland border. It could be in the next week or two, maybe sooner, maybe later. Just be ready to go at a moment's notice. You will only have the ability to bring the coat on your back, perhaps not even that. Just have your family ready to go at any time of day. Do not talk to anyone but yourselves and your family. You are being closely watched; some of Germany's best scientific minds are disappearing and showing up in the west. They will shoot you under the slightest suspicion; we have heard that families of Jewish researchers are being held separately as hostages. That hasn't happened here yet. That's why we will have to move fast. I will know more in a few days, just always stay within easy reach."

Time seemed to crawl and the days were stressful. Hans and Klaus never strayed far from their desks. Whenever Eric Schultz entered their work area, they would search his expression for a sign that their time for flight was here. His eyes wide with intent, he would always give a subtle shake of his head. Their stomachs would drop and they would return to their tasks. The SS posted guards in the work area; there were sentries on their buses. All of their research was examined and evaluated. One day, two of their constituents were forcefully removed from their work place. Secret police in their black woolen outfits with the bold red swastikas on the upper arms were suddenly upon them. Forcefully shoved and beaten with clubs, they were quickly put into a waiting open truck, where members of their families sat waiting for them. They huddled around the dazed, bloodied men and tried to comfort them. The truck quickly drove off and they were never seen again. SS officers said they were guilty of crimes against the Reich. No other explanation was given.

Each day the same torturous, anxious wait and each day they brought disappointing news home to their families.

The new restrictions were even harder on the families; children were no longer allowed to attend school and they were confined to their small apartments. Home schooling became their only option. Travel was extremely limited. Sleepless nights and exhaustive days became blurred.

And then the time for their escape to freedom arrived. A simple nod of his head when Eric Schultz entered the laboratory that morning put their senses on edge. He casually made his way over to Klaus's desk; he pointed to some calculations on his desk and feigned interests in their accuracy.

"Your time is here, no questions please. Just listen carefully! When you leave at the end of the day, there will be a distraction as you prepare to board your bus, an explosion near the south gate. A man will direct you to the back of this building, a hole in the wire fence will allow you to escape a few hundred feet into woods; a car will be waiting for you there. You will meet up with your families at another location. Do not try to contact them. Let this run its course. Share this with Hans. Do what the man tells you to do! Good luck!!" Eric turned to leave and Klaus tugged at the side of his suit jacket with a secreted hand.

"You?" he asked under his breath. Their eyes met briefly and they bared their souls.

"I will stay, there are others," he whispered, and then was heading for his office.

Klaus told Hans of the message delivered to him and the two men never ventured far from their desks. The morning and afternoon dragged by, and then finally the guarding corporal told them their bus was there, time to leave. They walked together out of the laboratory and down the long hallway to the big outside doors where the bus was waiting for them.

There was the sound of an explosion and the floors and walls reverberated with the concussion of the blast. SS officers were quickly shouting orders and soldiers were already scurrying about when they reached the outer doors. Chaos was everywhere in the open yard. A small older man dressed in worn woolen pants and a patchy, filthy brown sweater was quickly at their side. His long thin hair and patchy beard were gray and unwashed. They had seen him before; he was part of a work detail that was there to do the menial tasks of the SS, always there to clean up after their horrific acts. They were terribly mistreated, continually underfed and under clothed.

He grabbed Hans and Klaus with a powerful grip and tugged them around the corner of the building and they walked briskly to the rear of the structure.

"Hurry, hurry," he told them quietly as he forcefully folded back the chain linked fence he cut in the early hours of the day. They scrambled through the metal barrier on their bellies and dashed through the woodlands to where a parked car sat idling. Covered with brush and vines, another man stood leaning against the driver's front door, but was quickly scrambling to discard the camouflaging debris when the three men ran out from the woods. Hans and Klaus were quickly in the car and soon were bouncing along a barren, seldom used road. They looked back to where the car had been parked and their saboteur had already disappeared, probably back into the compound to help others to escape. Their lives had been saved by a man whose name they did not know. They were stunned by the humanity of the gesture.

"What was that man's name?" Hans asked their young driver.

"Karl," he replied

"Is he Jewish?" Klaus asked tentatively.

"No, neither am I," he answered flatly, never looking at them. "One of you should get in the back seat; we've got a long drive ahead of us."

HANS

PEENEMUNDE

Klaus could remember, as if it was yesterday, their panicked escape from Peenemunde and the very sad ending it brought for Hans. He would have the rest of his life to reflect on it and wonder if he too might have become the same angry man his good friend now was.

After escaping the research center, their young driver Gustaf drove straight through the remaining afternoon and into the night, stopping only for gas where containers had been hidden. They traveled along back wood roads and trails, trying to avoid all the known checkpoints. Miles and miles of their journey were traveled without the use of headlights. Often, they became lost, and would sit in open fields or on overgrown and rarely used roads. Hans and Klaus huddled with their young driver using a fading flashlight and map, desperately searching for a recognizable landmark. Their travel had been chalenging and riddled with anxiety. Headlights in the distance terrified them and a thousand SS shadows chased them all along the way. Both scientists thought constantly of their families and were impatient for their reunion. The plans had been to reunite with their families at another location close to the Swiss border, but when they arrived at the rendezvous point, only Klaus's family was there. An instantly, visibly shaken Hans was told the SS had visited his family's apartment only minutes before they were to leave for their meeting with Hans. They were taken into custody and hustled off. People in the underground felt that the SS had been tipped off

The news was devastating to him. They had driven hundreds of miles to escape the Nazi war grip, the whole lonely, torturous ride made endurable only by the knowledge that his family was waiting for him on the other side of freedom. Now, Hans was livid with everyone; twice he had been swayed that escape from Germany would be he and his family's salvation and twice he paid a terrible price. The reality that he would never see his wife and child again and thoughts of where his family might be and how they were being treated consumed him. The possibility that they could already be dead pressed in on him. In an instant he became a bitter, angry man.

He paused from his story, the pain swallowing him, his eyes red with tears. Hans turned to his old friend.

"You see Klaus, every time you look at me and wonder how I became this angry person so consumed with hatred and desperate for revenge, remember these stories I told you. Everything that I loved dearly has been ripped from me and I only have my pain to keep me company. Thank god I have my research. It's the only thing that gives me purpose now. Always remember that, Klaus."

"I know your work has sustained you Hans. I'm not sure it would have been enough for me if our roles had been reversed. But I think you're stronger than me."

"I'm not sure stronger is the right word, I just think I am capable of a deeper hate. Never thought I would be proud of such a quality. Do you remember our ship ride to America after we got to

Switzerland; I did not think I would survive that journey. My hatred had not yet become a strength.

"Like a ghost, I boarded the vessel that would bring me to America. I could not be around you and your family, it brought too much pain. I hid in my cabin. It was the wrong thing to do for many reasons, but I just wanted to hide from the world. I'm sorry for that."

"Hans, you do not need to apologize, my wife and I understood completely. However, when we learned you were very ill, it scared us."

Hans went on to finish his tale.

This was his second long ocean journey to the United States, both trying for different reasons. The first: an attempted escape with his family on the *St. Louis*, only to be denied by a ruthless, conniving SS officer who had played him like a fiddle. The second: a lonely and incredibly painful journey without his family. The thought that his family were struggling daily to survive in a death camp tortured him.

This time he became prone to the nausea that rolling seas can generate. Because Hans rarely left his cabin it only aggravated his seasickness. He became quite ill and the ship's doctor was concerned the already acutely depressed passenger might not survive the journey. They docked in Philadelphia Harbor and the next day were introduced to their new center for research. Hans's mood change was sudden and complete; before him was the finest and most advanced laboratory and equipment he had ever seen, all in abundant supply. Other researchers from Germany and around the world were there; all gathered to collectively end this horrible war. They were told all theories would be entertained and if deemed credible would be one hundred percent funded.

Hans immediately saw purpose to his existence. In Peenemunde, he and Klaus were forced to discuss their theories in secrecy; supporting calculations on torn sheets of paper were exchanged and reviewed during lunch and work breaks or on bus rides to and from work. Now they could openly discuss their new strategy with capable colleagues. Hans hoped the promising theory he developed in Peenemunde would lead to a technological breakthrough and from there to a new lethal weapon. He would use it to soothe his inner anger. He would make them pay.

Hans would bring terror to the Germans and Japanese. They would pay for their acts of genocide to his people and the brutality inflicted on his family.

Again, he spoke to his colleague's concerns about Project Rainbow. "I am convinced our weapon testing is progressing forward, perhaps not without its risks and sometimes unforeseen dangerous consequences. That element of the testing saddens me, I assure you, but we are not moving backwards with this process as you are trying to suggest." Hans was emphatic in his conviction.

"I will not allow you to derail this process and I am sure our Captain Van Noy will not support your observations. He is very committed to this project."

Klaus Bjurman had witnessed the transformation of his colleague from a gifted scientific mind to a man obsessed with revenge. Hans had been a steadfast, but innovative researcher; always challenging conventional science. Always full of optimism and energized daily by his work and the overflowing love of his wife and child. They had taken his family from him and they would pay a heavy price for such a monstrous act. That day at the Swiss border when they had told him that his family had been taken into custody by the SS, Klaus had seen the life instantly drained from his friend. For days he had cried, rarely eating or bathing.

USS *ELDRIDGE*

O530, duty officer Lieutenant Estrella took the last sip from his coffee cup as he scanned the horizon. He had drawn the early morning watch. A cloudless, vacant dawn was beckoning a new day. A windless, calm ocean seemed appropriate for the rather plain sunrise.

"Lieutenant," radar tech William Hanes broke the doldrums of the weary morning bridge watch. There was alarm in his voice. "I have radar contact at 090 degrees, about twelve miles."

"Hansey, any idea?" the lieutenant asked.

"No not really, according to naval intelligence. No Allied shipping should be in the area, but that relates only to wartime vessels. Could be a freighter or tanker."

Lieutenant Estrella did not hesitate in his action, the captain's directive had been explicit, any radar contact or otherwise was to be treated as hostile and threatening. He turned to the bridge lookout.

"Seaman Mullins, sound general quarters," his voice boomed, loud and committed.

A blaring, pulsating alarm engulfed the *Eldridge*. The ship was suddenly alive. Sailors sprang from their berths, floppy bottom pants were stepped into in seconds. Scurrying like mice in an upended grain cart they raced to their stations. Helmets and flak jackets were soon donned. Gun crews stood ready. Firefighting personnel gathered quickly at their stations. Engineering was standing by.

Captain Van Noy was quickly on the bridge; his uniform looked like he had slept in it because he had.

"Tell me what we have Lieutenant." His voice was crisp and mechanical.

"Hansey's got radar contact, 090 degrees about 12 miles, Sir."

"Bring Hansey on the bridge speaker." Switches were flipped and the radar tech responded.

"Yes sir."

"What's the update on your contact?"

"Sir, he's at eleven miles at 090 degrees, he's steaming, got him at 28 knots, good size, my guess a cruiser, no tanker or freighter is gonna do that kind of speed. Looks like he wants to tangle, he's coming dead on."

"OK Hansey, good work. Get a firing solution to our No 1."

Off in the distant horizon a flash of light, like a thunderbolt in a line squall and then the sound of something large being propelled through the air. Suddenly the water about a quarter of a mile to port erupted. An enemy salvo pushed huge towers of water skyward. It crested high above the bridge of the *Eldridge* and it shuddered with the concussion.

"Hard over to starboard," Captain Van Noy shouted to the helmsman. "All ahead full."

The young helmsman pulled mightily on the huge ship's wheel, his biceps bulging and his eyes wide with fear. Bridge stanchions were dialed to full speed and the engine room was responding. The ship was going hard over and her bow, driven by the added speed, pushed a wall of water ahead of her.

"That had to be at least a 14-inch salvo," Commander Preston observed. We've got a cruiser or heavy cruiser just over the horizon trying to range in on us."

"I agree Commander," Van Noy offered. He picked up the phone that connected him to the Rainbow Room. He knew at least one of his German scientists and Professor Kincaid would be there.

68

"Ensign Williams, I need our cloaking mechanism working right now."

"Engaging as we speak," the nervous ensign replied. Van Noy could hear orders being shouted, a thick German accent sporadically interjecting additional directives.

Abruptly the ship's forward speed was reduced by half as power was diverted to the huge cooling pumps and generators. The ship shuddered and the feeling of heat began to emanate from below. Those near the secretive room began to experience dizziness and nausea.

Another salvo exploded, this time 100 yards to the stern of the *Eldridge*, its wake still smooth from the broad beam of the destroyer. The ship shuddered and bulkheads strained under the percussion of several hundred pounds of high explosives. The huge wave it created forcefully lifted the destroyer's stern out of the sea and pushed its bow down so that it was awash with ocean.

"Helmsman hard over to 170 degrees." The captain once again picked up the phone for the Rainbow Room. "Ensign Williams, is our system engaged?" Van Noy screamed into his receiver.

There seemed to be confusion and indecision in the Rainbow Room. Van Noy could hear his young officer asking the same question. Finally, Professor Mueller had the phone.

"Captain, this is Professor Mueller, our cloaking device is fully engaged. There was some hesitancy among the staff. But the system is performing as needed."

Van Noy hung up his headset. "Let's hope so," he muttered to himself, and then through the intercom he addressed his radar specialist. "Hansey, where is our kraut?"

"Still at bearing 090 degrees, 9 miles, still at 28 knots, no doubt about it sir, he wants to engage."

"Let's not disappoint him. Bring us dead on to him." And then he turned to his fire control officer. "I want to be clear on this, no one fires until I give the command, understood Mr. Lapierre?" Lt. Commander Sinclair Lapierre was his lead gunnery officer. "I want to crawl right up this guy's ass before we open up."

"Understood Captain."

PRINCE BADEN

GERMAN HEAVY CRUISER

Captain Helmit Schnieder and the heavy cruiser *Prince Baden* had been running from their own shadow the last several weeks. The German navy was a weak reflection of what it used to be; their submarine taskforce, which coordinated with its surface fleet, once instilled fear into any and all Allied shipping in the north Atlantic. But now their sub wolf packs had been decimated and the once invincible battleships *Bismarck* and *Scharnhorst*, along with two of their sister ships, had been sunk by the British Royal Navy.

Now they were forced to carry the fight to the Americans as lone vessels of war with no escorting destroyers or refueling ships. They had wandered around the mid-Atlantic the last few days, dangerously low on fuel and food. Twice their refueling tanker had missed its rendezvous. Morale was at a low point, information coming out of Germany was also not encouraging.

But two days ago, their tanker finally arrived with fuel and provisions. The *Prince Baden* once again was a lethal warship and her 14-inch guns could bring terror from the heavens.

Their radar operator with his radar dome mounted nearly 100 feet above the water line had detected an enemy vessel 16 miles out at 285 degrees. Captain Schneider had gone to battle stations and lethal charges were loaded into her main battery. His radar officer determined that it was probably an American destroyer and surprisingly was alone. Schneider knew he outgunned his enemy and would open fire as soon as they were in range, miles before the American would be in effective range.

The first salvo had strayed to port; the second salvo had just missed the stern of the destroyer, its explosion no doubt terrifying all those onboard. The next barrage would be deadly.

"Captain, I have just lost radar contact."

"What?!" Captain Schneider exclaimed, his surprise real.

"Captain, I have no idea what happened. He was there and then he was gone."

"Check your instruments," he bellowed, and then turned to the gunnery officer. "Have the forward mount fire to the last bearing but bring it in 800 meters, Schnell! Schnell!!"

The information was relayed to the forward battery and soon the whole shipped recoiled from the blast of its forward arsenal.

"Find out what happened to that American destroyer, we did not hit it, there would have been an explosion. He's out there somewhere."

USS *ELDRIDGE*

"Hansey, what's Heinie's bearing and distance?" Captain Van Noy asked his radar tech.

"Still bearing 090 degrees, distance 8 miles, sunrise in about 5 minutes. Should see his profile on the horizon just about now."

A third salvo exploded about 500 yards off to starboard, again with its impressive aquatic display, but harmless in its effect.

"He's lost us." Van Noy squealed with delight. "God Damn I love this device. Now to get up close and personal. Helmsman, maintain bearing and speed."

He picked up the phone to the blue room. "Ensign Williams, please have Professor Mueller report to the bridge."

PRINCE BADEN

Alarm and indecision had suddenly handicapped the men on the *Prince Baden's* bridge. They had acquired a strong, clearly defined radar contact and had confirming visual on the American destroyer from their men aloft and with that they had provided a firing solution to their big guns fore and aft. With two salvos they had zeroed in on the enemy vessel, the third barrage would send it to the bottom and then the US warship had suddenly vanished. The radar technician was immediately under intense pressure, but ranking officers were also demanding feedback from their subordinates in engineering, the gun crews, the fire and damage control teams. No training had ever prepared them for such a bizarre scenario as this.

Captain Schneider sought to rein in the dread that had quickly engulfed his bridge personnel.

"Beruhigt euch alle, everybody calm down," he shouted. "We have an enemy destroyer out there. Let's find him."

Every man on the bridge stopped in their places, their voices suddenly still. They waited for their captain's next words.

"I want extra men aloft with binoculars," his directions calm but focused. "We know his last bearing and distance. Let's focus on that. I want every available pair of eyes searching that area of water."

Next, he turned to his radar officer. "Ensign Schmidt, check your equipment and fast. Start looking for any kind of a return. Report to the bridge anything that shows up on your screen, I don't care how faint or insignificant you think it might be. If you think it's a goddamn seagull, I want to hear about it. Maybe the Americans have something that helps them hide from our radar."

USS *ELDRIDGE*

"Captain Van Noy, the enemy cruiser is at 120 degrees, distance 4.5 miles, well within range." The intercom screeched Hanes's update.

"We'll do this the same as the U-boat," Van Noy told his officers and crew. "I have complete confidence in our cloaking device. When we are within one mile, we will engage with everything we have and I mean everything. Our opening salvo must be devastating. This is not a sub with a single deck gun. You all saw what this cruiser's rounds did when they hit water. We're ready; just have your teams do what they have been trained to do. Gunnery officer, make sure your teams wait for my command. We've got about five minutes. Get word to Lt. J.G. Gomez, he needs to be ready to put a couple of fish up Heinie's ass when the time comes."

The *Eldridge* was indeed ready; they had practiced this maneuver countless times. The philosophy of engaging hostile ships had become simple. Their cloaking device would conceal them from the enemy and would allow them to achieve a lethal nearness. But once they fired upon their adversary it must be with as much fire power as they could muster. Captain Van Noy had once joked that he wanted the cooks to throw hot cooking grease at their enemy. No one was sure how long an engagement could last, and although they could not be seen by their opposition, there was concern their adversary might trace an incoming round back to a general area of ocean.

PRINCE BADEN

"Does anybody have anything?" Captain Schneider demanded through the ship's intercom. With binoculars pressed to their foreheads, panicked crewmembers of the *Prince Baden* searched the water in front of them.

Heads shook and shoulders shrugged, nothing was returned on the intercom. Some sailors hoped the American warship had broken off its engagement. They were just a destroyer; it made no sense to engage a heavy cruiser like the *Prince Baden*. Perhaps they had seen the folly of their intent.

"Captain, I have something at 265 degrees, a very faint return, not really sure it's anything," the radar tech offered.

Everyone in the bridge turned to the bearing given and raised the field glasses in unison. Nothing but an empty ocean filled their eyepieces.

"Schimdt, do you have a distance on this faint return?" the captain demanded.

"That's my concern sir; everything tells me this is our American destroyer. He's about 1.5 miles off our port side amidships. If that's him, we're fish in a barrel right now."

"Get a firing solution to our gun crews right now. Have them open fire immediately after that."

The foredeck area suddenly exploded; a fireball shot into the air. Steel decking tore open as if it were cardboard. Sailors were thrown into the air with fury. Some shells detonated on impact, destroying 40 mm gun stations and killing their crew, other rounds penetrated bulkheads and exploded within. The damage was severe and the carnage extensive. Thirty and fifty caliber machine guns as well as 20 mm deck guns traversed up and down the cruiser's port side. Fires were soon ravaging the warship inside and out.

"Where is that fire coming from?" Captain Schneider demanded. His subordinates, distracted by the bloodbath and destruction all around them, once again brought their spyglasses to bear on the sea before them. Tracer rounds seem to appear out of a fog, except there was no haze. Some of the junior officers lowered their binoculars and stared blankly at their commanding officer.

"Did our batteries receive a firing solution?" Schneider demanded.

"Yes, they did, they're coming around to port now."

Schneider looked below and watched as the huge muzzles slowly turned to port.

Machine gun fire now ripped the bridge. Plate glass shattered and bullets tore through steel bulkheads and the men behind them. The killing had finally found the command center of the *Prince Baden*.

Those still alive or with minor injuries began to seek out the dead and the dying. Captain Schneider would have none of it. He bellowed his indifference. "Leave them where they lie, we can do nothing for them now. The ship is coming apart. The *Prince Baden* is your priority." And then he was directing his remaining officers.

"Can we still communicate with our gun crews?"

A junior officer picked up the bridge phone, its mouthpiece was shattered and its cord severed. No words were needed.

Collectively they stared at the forward turret as it slowly turned to port. They knew their survival rested on its explosive potential.

Two eight-inch holes suddenly appeared in the foredeck turret, and then it exploded from within. The munitions within its steel enclosure only multiplying its destructive force. Flames shot out the long barrels of their armament.

The heavy cruiser rocked from the explosion. Captain Schneider wondered if the blast was perhaps fatal. Fires seem to be everywhere and secondary explosions were occurring throughout his vessel. Machine gun fire continued its deadly path up and down the length of the *Prince Baden*. Engineering had received several deck piercing rounds; one had hit their no. 2 boiler. High pressure steam exploded, killing many of the machinists in the area and destroying numerous controls and instrumentation. Up on the bridge the loss of power was sudden and complete. No response to the ship's wheel was apparent either. Officers and crew knew their situation was dire.

But the *Prince Baden* had begun to fight back. Some of its crew had returned fire from anti-aircraft mounts and 30 caliber machine gun platforms, although their return fire was indiscriminate and haphazard. A brief sense of pride encouraged their search for a way to turn the tide.

The *Prince Baden's* rear bartizan was now their only hope. Schneider turned to face its aft deck 14-inch mount; it too was slowly turning to port. If they could return one lucky salvo, they might save their ship. The rear turret stopped its slow turn, briefly paused, and then all six rifles erupted. A cheer went up from the battered crew. Her 14-inch salvo was impressive; it moved the vessel 12 feet back in the water.

Perhaps that broadside would be their redemption. Captain Schneider began to rethink his strategy, and then four rounds of high explosive TNT turned what remained of his bridge into a huge fireball. There was no "perhaps," only a finality that comes to us all. The command structure of the *Prince Baden* was gone and with it all sense of order. No senior officer was needed to issue the "abandon ship" order; common sense dictated there was no other alternative.

The *Prince Baden* was rapidly taking on water, she was listing heavily to her port side foredeck. Chaos had engulfed a once proud ship.

Another incoming round pierced the ammunition magazine deep in the lower midships of the heavy cruiser and the explosion was devastating. Flames and debris shot hundreds of feet into the air. The *Prince Baden* was split across her beam and sinking fast.

USS *ELDRIDGE*

"**G**ood that you're here, Professor Mueller," the captain declared, charged with optimism. The professor left the Rainbow Room when the captain had requested his presence on the bridge.

"This will be the true test of your device. A German frontline cruiser is right there in front of us and he is completely unaware that we are close enough to see the color of their eyes." In a few minutes we will open fire on these poor slobs. It should be a fine show."

Before leaving for the bridge, Professor Mueller and his team engaged their device and the now familiar oppressive heat and humidity began to emanate out from their room. After the engagement with the sub, they had tweaked the cooling pumps to provide additional cooling to the machinery. Hopefully that might minimize the serious and escalating side effects, but bulkheads began to heat up, and piping once again started to sweat extensively with condensation. Men became dizzy and nauseous.

"I suspect it will be," Hans replied with guarded optimism. He would not mention that the serious side effects of their device were again present, but they became secondary the moment Van Noy and he formed their surreptitious pact.

Captain Van Noy picked up the phone to the ship's P.A. system and addressed the crew. "Gentlemen, on my command, the *Eldridge* will open fire. Your actions need to be lethal and committed. We will break off our engagement when I give the order. You may commence firing."

The USS *Eldridge's* starboard side erupted. The distance between the two ships was so close that there was little distinction between shots leaving the *Eldridge* and their impact on the German warship. Their salvos, at this range, were accurate and deadly.

This was not a deadly destruction from afar as most naval engagements are; ships' batteries from miles away firing on each other, flame and smoke the only indicator of damage done. With this engagement, every round that struck the *Prince Baden*, its destruction and killing, were all very visible to those on the *Eldridge*.

Men were dropping where they stood from machine gun fire. The German cruiser and crew were being punished. Large explosions all along the warship's port side, bulkheads exploding and sailors on fire jumping into the sea. Outboard the destruction deadly and visual, inboard the horror had to be just as deadly. Smaller explosions seemed to be everywhere as 25- and 40-mm anti-aircraft weapons peppered the heavy cruiser.

The onslaught continued unabated. On the bridge, Captain Van Noy and Professor Mueller looked at each other. No words were exchanged, none were needed, only a vindictive nod of their heads. Their shiniest trophy yet with more to come.

The staccato fire of a machine gun, suddenly, somehow found the *Eldridge*. Two sailors were hit and they wondered if the ship's ability to camouflage itself had been compromised. But then the spray of the automatic weapons trailed off into the waters aft of their ship, and then the bullets returned along a different path. Most of the *Eldridge's* company took a collective sigh of relief. The German cruiser had become desperate in its attempts to return fire; pure chance had allowed gunfire to find the *Eldridge*.

Captain Van Noy was not so sure, the enemy's big turrets fore and aft were beginning to turn to port and then its forward mount erupted in a huge fireball. His destroyer's big guns had found their mark. There was no need to continue the bombardment.

"Hard over to port, all ahead full," he barked at his helmsman. "Commander Preston, we will disengage from the enemy ship, all guns cease fire, but maintain fire from the number 5 battery. This German cruiser is about done, but let's put a couple of fish into him, just to be sure. Have Lt. Gomez launch two of his torpedoes."

The *Eldridge* was hard over and putting distance between the two warships. Moments later two separate massive explosions ripped the German heavy cruiser in two. She was rapidly losing her bow to the green blue of deep water. The carnage extracted from another German warship was complete, the crew of the *Eldridge* had done their job well; again there would be no need to search for survivors.

On the *Eldridge*, one crewman had been killed and two seriously burned. The sailor's manner of death just as horrific as the others, but not the result of any exchange with their opponent. Something terrifying had again been released in the bowels of their ship and had sought out its victims. An ugly twist to the definition of friendly fire.

USS *ELDRIDGE*

HANS AND KLAUS

Hans sensed the complete betrayal of his friend Klaus was near. The engagement with the German cruiser and the testing of the device before that had revealed the deadly instability of their mechanism.

Speaking in their native dialect, the two German researchers sat in their confined quarters aboard the *Eldridge*. Both were exhausted and strong coffee had become their sustenance these last eight days. The application of their device was no longer predictable. Events that in the beginning had been subtle notations had now developed into severe side effects with lethal results. In fact, Bjurman was astonished that there weren't more deaths and more pushback from the Americans.

"It's time we told the Americans that our experiment is becoming more and more unstable," Professor Bjurman plainly stated, "although I think it's fairly obvious to most of the officers and crew that something is quite wrong." And he once again reviewed the precarious events and conditions that had become the new normal on the USS *Eldridge*.

Each testing brought about intense heat and sailors were slow to recover from the heat exhaustion, dizziness, and nausea that seemed to accompany the high temperatures. Sickbay was overwhelmed, which was easily done; aspirin and trying to get some rest were all that Doc Bellows could offer.

When activated, the cloaking device made simple activities challenging and potentially dangerous.

Navigating the passageways became difficult. Sailors complained of a strange force pulling them inward towards the center of the ship, often causing them to stumble along overheated gangways, sometimes resulting in second degree burns to their hands and forearms. Seamen began to wear gloves during the testing and when at general quarters. Frequently, they depended on their shipmates to pull them away from the mystifying grip of overheated bulkheads that drew them in.

All valid points, Hans conceded to himself. Nothing presented by Professor Bjurman could be questioned or trivialized. However, the twisted pact between Professor Mueller and Captain Van Noy must survive and it would. This feeble challenge by his colleague would go no further than the confines of their cabin. Bjurman was never the one to aggressively press his argument forward; that just wasn't his makeup.

"I simply cannot agree with your assessment," Professor Mueller offered. "We have had some problems with our beta testing, that's true, but did you think our sea trials would be without some issues?"

"Oh, come on Hans, 'some issues?' Men are dying, others horribly injured," Klaus countered. "All because of our invention. If you won't go to the captain with these concerns, then I will."

"Again, Klaus, I cannot and will not support these baseless accusations. We have had some regrettable consequences with our invention. We put a futuristic device on a navy destroyer, an extremely powerful one at that, and we expect it to perform flawlessly. That's a little naïve of us, don't you think? We're at war; we just don't have the luxury of a lot of time to do the extensive testing we'd like.

Captain Van Noy has voiced his concerns to me and we believe a large proportion of these deaths and injuries are the result of poor training and ignoring specific safety guidelines. You go to Captain Van Noy with these issues and he will throw you out of his cabin. I can almost guarantee that." The betrayal was now complete. What little trust that remained in their friendship was gone. There would be no going back.

As Hans expected, Klaus reluctantly back away from his idea of approaching the captain. "Perhaps you're right, Hans. But this is becoming a festering problem with the crew. They might be the ones that make this a bigger issue, one their captain cannot ignore."

Klaus moved to his upper bunk, his anguish over this issue and lack of sleep pulled at him. "Think I will get some much-needed sleep. We'll talk some more on this later." He lay down and his thoughts raced; every instinct told him his argument and logic were sound. Sleep would not come easy.

SIMON

eaman Bruno, Vincent as labeled on his navy fatigues, had invaded Simon's dreams again, his burned and charred body pushing its way into his peaceful slumber. This was Chief Gunner's Mate Vincent Bruno's fourth intrusion into his nighttime. His tortured body was difficult to look at. He must have been a powerful man in his earthly presence, a barrel-chested man with powerful biceps and bulging forearms, supported by legs that might have been tree trunks in another life. A thick neck now supported a disfigured head and face. Dark brown eyes were swollen wide as if being squeezed and pushed from behind; they were blood shot and something had terrified them. The skin around those shadowy Italian eyes was burned and peeling. His squared-off chin had been laid bare and only a charred jawline remained. It was as if his face had been forced into an open hearth, held there, and allowed to burn. The pain must have been tremendous. What clothes remained were burned remnants and hung loosely from his suffering body. Singed and raw patches of skin were everywhere. A large heart shaped tattoo with 'Lynette' in the middle was visible on his right forearm. He entered Simon's dreams and wandered about before finally walking off into the darkness, beckoning, almost begging him to follow with a gesture of his left hand.

Simon struggled to understand the significance of Seaman Bruno's visits and his pleading to follow him to some unknown and mystic destination.

It was his gift again, or curse, fleeting at times, that allowed the dead to communicate with him. They would reach across that strange barrier that has separated the living from the deceased for as long as there has been birth and death in this world. He was helpless to know when a wandering soul might reach out to him. He had been free of these inexplicable intrusions for almost three years; his last taxing experience was at a troubled home in Jamestown, Rhode Island.

Madame Alice, his old friend from New York, had helped him bring closure to a desperate and anxious woman who lost her entire family to a deadly hurricane in 1938. The experience had been confusing and exhaustive.

These last few weeks Seaman Bruno had randomly entered his sleep, but the last two nights he had arrived with what must have been one of his younger shipmates. A thin, youthful lad with the same terrified look as his older mentor. His clothing and skin too were burned and charred, similar to that of his senior shipmate. His hair scorched from his scalp, the young seaman appeared timid and terrified in this new dimension he was in, never venturing off, always hovering close to Petty Officer Bruno. Simon sensed that Bruno had been a nurturing, protective figure in the young sailor's brief naval career.

Bruno seemed to be reaching out to Simon, a sense that there was so much more attached to these nightly visits. There was desperation in his garbled speech and gestures, his young counterpart reinforcing the distorted narrative with frequent, exaggerated nods of his disfigured head.

They had been difficult nights, and Simon woke tired and troubled. He knew his disturbed visitors were desperately trying to tell their heartbreaking account and their frustration had only added to his exhaustion.

SIMON

A Monday morning, the beginning of a work week, and Francis Simon Bouchard kissed his wife goodbye and forced his tired body down the stairs of his south Philadelphia apartment and boarded the bus that would convey him to his job at Barber Publishing. The bus was full with the usual passengers; war time gas rationing and the diversion of steel and sheet metal away from the automotive industry in order to meet military demands had guaranteed crowded, rush hour buses.

The country was tired of the global conflict and the war in the Pacific was not going well. The numerous damaged ships that were being repaired were evidence of that costly engagement. The shipyard in Philadelphia was straining to stay ahead of the repairs and retrofits. All three shifts were working at a demanding pace. Simon's bus traveled past the shipyard in the morning and early evening. Shipyard entrances were always a bustle of activity with thousands of workers and the hundreds of new recruits that moved in and out of the gates. The new enlistees stood out in their navy-blue pea coats and white Dixie-cup hats.

Today, a slight drizzle seemed appropriate for the Monday morning commute. Simon sat in his usual seat near the front of the bus and stared out a window frosted from the many passengers and the cigarettes most of them seemed to be smoking. Naval Shore Patrol personnel stopped Simon's bus to allow shipyard traffic to navigate the dockyard entrance. Simon leaned against his window and rubbed his cotton coat sleeve across it.

His heart stopped. There, standing among the hustle and bustle, was Petty Officer Bruno and his young companion. They were oblivious to the commotion around them, and their apparel seemed absent of any moisture despite the rain-soaked setting. Seaman Bruno, his eyes now sad and his look despondent, gently pushed his fledgling shipmate towards Simon's bus. The spectral young seaman, his anxiety visibly escalating, took small tentative steps forward and then lifted a burned and battered life ring for Simon to see. Even with its tattered presence, the name USS *Eldridge* DD-628 was clearly visible and despite the physical distance and being seated in a crowded lorry, the young recruit's simple words "Please help us," were plainly whispered in Simon's ear.

Unknowing, scurrying shipyard workers suddenly were upon the two phantom shipmates, passing through them as if they were a thin low-lying fog, and the two navy men quickly vanished.

His heart pounding in his chest, his palms suddenly sweaty, Simon knew he had been commandeered for a mission that would demand his participation. It had all the identifiers of the previous unworldly recruitments he had experienced. They would begin with incursions into his nightly imaginings; tortured spirits would wander about his dreams and would offer anxious gestures to demonstrate the torment of their predicament. Often horrifying images of their tragic passing and the deep sadness connected to that event would be shared with him. Difficult for him to witness, but all done so as to convince Simon of their worthiness. They knew he had a gift, much like their living counterparts recognized. On rare occasions those that had moved on would vocalize their pleas, the sadness and desperation in their voices was difficult to ignore.

This time he sensed a collective, distressed calling from beyond and there would be no diverting them, these shipmates had chosen Simon to deliver a plea for help from a very desperate crew of an American vessel called the USS *Eldridge*. He knew he would help them, much like a parent knows they will defend a not-so-innocent child.

Simon began his rescue efforts that evening on his way home from work. He got off his bus at the shipyard stop. A simple inquiry with a young ensign at the shore patrol office into the history of a potential naval vessel named the USS *Eldridge* had been met with unpretentious bewilderment—no such vessel had ever been docked at the shipyard. When Simon pressed him on the matter, the ensign obligingly consulted his logs and documentation.

"Sorry Mr. ahh. I didn't get your name."

"Bouchard, Simon Bouchard."

"Ah yes, Mr. Bouchard. Our records do not show a vessel of that name ever being based here. Perhaps you've confused it with another vessel, in 1937 we had a USS *Evert* dry docked here for repairs; she was a mine sweeper. Could that possibly be the ship you're thinking of?"

"No, it was definitely the *Eldridge*," Simon answered, his face an expression of misgiving.

"I'm afraid that's all I can do for you right now. I'll ask my C.O. what he might know, if you leave your name and address, I'll let you know if something pops up. I have some paperwork to do, so if you'll excuse me..."

Simon left his name and his address in south Philadelphia then caught the next bus home, a little disappointed with this unproductive start.

MADAME ALICE

Wednesday and it was baking day at the Prudence Inn. Madame Alice was preparing her special summer dessert of peach cobbler for her special guests, two couples all the way from Chicago, Illinois. Clarisse Duffle and her husband Stanley found Madame's clairvoyant abilities remarkable and would make the annual journey for her gifted insight. This year they brought Clarisse's sister and her husband.

This was the sixth consecutive year they made the yearly pilgrimage. Their wealth encouraged such trips and obviously made the decision to travel that much easier. Her husband's company had developed the duffle bag two generations ago. Now World War II and all branches of the military were keeping his factories straining under the demand.

It was a busy seasonal weekend and there were other guests visiting their seaside inn. The long hot days and cool evenings of summer had settled in and their guests seemed relaxed and full of good cheer, the goal of any well-run boarding house.

Madame Alice ran the Prudence Inn with her husband Milton. Years ago a middle-aged man, deeply troubled by the sudden death of his parents in a boating accident, brought her future husband, Milton Post, to Madame Alice's doorstep in Island Park, Portsmouth,

Rhode Island. He hoped she might provide some insight into the tragedy that left him so hollow on the inside. There were several visits; she held his hands, read his cards, and she probed his thoughts with uncomfortable questions. In the end she told Milton there was no intuition she could offer on his parents' sudden and tragic passing. They must be content where they are, they had moved on, perhaps he should do the same. Madame Alice could no longer take his money when she could not provide a service. She would not attach herself to such a reputation.

Something about her character, her honesty, a pleasing smile and her deep blue eyes pulled him in. On a hunch, he asked her to dinner on his last visit to her quaint little living room. She accepted, and within a few short months of quiet, relaxing times together open and honest talks reinforced what they both quickly sensed; they were perfect for each other.

Nearly twenty years ago Madame Alice, or Sarah Sheppard as she was known back then, experienced a very painful loss when her first husband unexpectedly left her. The wound was deep and the pain awful and lasting. But the curing had begun and now Milton's love would complete the healing process. Madame Alice never once doubted that.

A small private wedding followed, and she joined her new husband on Prudence Island where Milton ran a small inn that desperately needed a woman's influence.

Madame Alice quickly settled into the quiet and peacefulness that was Prudence Island. A small island in the middle of Narragansett Bay, Rhode Island, it offered its own unique life style to only those that treasured its subtle nuances; private sandy shorelines, brash black beaked wood thrushes, bold and ravenous whitetail deer that devoured everything but the yellow and white daffodil and rose of sharon. There were summer days measured by countless heartfelt smiles, seasonally tanned bodies, old grateful friends and new budding comrades, witnessing, knowing and unknowing, the bonds they were building and would share for the rest of their lives. Madame Alice welcomed that warmth and the stability that it brought to her soul.

A feeling of dread nudged Madame Alice this morning, a sensitivity she hadn't recognized in several years pulled her from a restless slumber. There had been a brief disturbing image in her dreams. A young officer, she thought, possibly a navy lieutenant, it was difficult to say, had appeared to her. His uniform was singed and burned in so many spots. Face and hands were horribly blackened, the hair burned from his scalp. He appeared to be a young man that had fallen into the fire pit of a Fourth of July barn fire and been too slow in his leaving. Two blue pupils outlined by bulging white blood-shot eyes reached out to her and he whispered "Please bring us home," and then was gone. The whole event lasting mere seconds.

Sprinkling flour on her cutting board and rolling pin, she began to work the pie crust for tonight's peach dessert. The intrusion to her early morning dream by the ghoulish visitor had left her feeling uneasy; she knew there would be other visits from the wandering, tortured lieutenant. Too many years and too many misguided spirits had taught her that once they knew that the Madame could help them reach across a barrier that was believed to be impenetrable, they would not leave her alone until a resolution was reached, and not always the outcome they may have hoped for.

A late morning sun brightened her pantry pastry board. Her fingers covered in flour and dough, she paused to massage her arthritic hands and looked out her east facing kitchen window. A tired, bygone oil barge pushed its way north, against wind and tide up Narragansett Bay. Loaded with emollient, it would soon be making its turn east under the Mt. Hope Bridge and up into Fall River Harbor where a small refinery was located, and then she saw him. On the field below, out near the lighthouse. Tall, thin, his clothing and flesh charred, an unholy sight. He stood there among the scrub pine and cattails; a lonely figure lost between two worlds. His stare was piercing despite the distance and it briefly paralyzed her, then suddenly he spoke to her.

"I speak for all of us." His words were clear and soulful despite the distance. "You must find us and then bring us home; it is so wrong what they have done to us and it is against God's law how we have been left for eternity."

He took a step towards her and slowly raised his burned right hand as if he were about to salute, she thought, and then he was gone. The wind rushed in, as if it were held at bay by the ghostly lieutenant's presence, and the dwarfed pines and seaside flora swayed back and forth as if confirming his departure.

The lieutenant had entered her late morning dream with a plea for help and now showed that his visits were not restricted to her dreams, he could move all about her property. Always with the same petition, help for a crew that had experienced something unholy When pleas from beyond reached these levels, Madame Alice knew participation would be her only option, ignoring these desperate pleadings was not her reality. She had been given something quite unique, ignoring it was futile. Another crusade, much like Jamestown, awaited her.

SIMON

Simon spasmed in his bed. Deborah, his wife of only eight months, screamed and turned into his protective embrace. Someone was pounding on their apartment door. "Mr. Bouchard!" a male voice shouted through the door and then yelled again, "Mr. Simon Bouchard!"

Simon turned to his wife. "This sounds serious, you stay here," he said, and he kissed her quickly. The pasting of his door never stopped. Opening his door, he found two burly sailors from the shore patrol with their fists poised to continue the thrashing of his door. With them was the young ensign he spoke with several days ago at the shore patrol office. In the background stood a Philadelphia policeman.

"Mr. Bouchard, my apologies for our loud and early visit," the navy ensign said. "But you need to come with us. We'll wait for you to get dressed."

Rubbing his eyes he demanded, "Go where? What the hell time is it?" His irritation obvious.

"Sir, it's 0430. My commanding officer, Admiral Robert Carlson, needs to ask you a few questions at the shipyard. You really do not have an option with this." He turned to the policeman and, as if he had waited for his cue, the constable told him he should go with these navy personnel, that his captain at the precinct had been told it was a matter of national security.

"Seems the navy thinks you're a pretty important guy right now, best do as they say," he reiterated.

Simon nodded his head and asked for a few minutes to get dressed and explain the situation to his wife. He retreated inside. Somehow, he had sensed this early morning visit and the sudden disruption to his life. Two nights after his visit to the shore patrol office, Chief Bruno and his young apprentice again visited him in his slumber and communicated that this first step had been the right one.

"This is about that sailor named Bruno, isn't it?" his wife probed once he had returned to their bedroom and explained the bizarre, early morning visit. Simon had shared with her the incursions into his dreams by the sailor called Bruno and his visit to his bus at the shipyard entrance. Only two years ago he had told his fiancée of his strange ability to converse with the dead and it had challenged their romance.

"No one has said a thing as to what this is all about," Simon told his nervous wife, "but I think you're probably right, this has everything to do with Seaman Bruno. It seems a little odd that just a few weeks after I visited the shore patrol at the shipyard they're knocking on my door at a rude time of day. I have to go to a location in the shipyard and speak with someone who is probably much higher in rank than the young ensign outside."

"This frightens me, how do I reach you, when will you be home?!" Deborah pleaded, close to tears.

"The navy officer will leave you an address to where they're taking me and a phone number. But the ensign believes you should not expect me home before noon." He kissed Deborah goodbye and once again assured her that everything would be okay.

They drove through the deserted early morning streets of south Philadelphia and on to the shipyard. A snippet of light on the eastern horizon signaled the start of another day, and soon layers of red and yellow slowly began to turn back the night. No one said a word. It was a mystifying, lonely ride for Simon. They entered the dockyard through a gate used only by high ranking naval personnel. I.D.s were examined, phone calls were made, and they were finally processed through. A short drive brought them to a square building painted a dull off-white. They were met at the entrance by two shore patrol personnel. Simon was thoroughly searched and led into a large gathering room, where a collection of naval officers and two civilians were gathered to his immediate right behind a small row of folding tables. A log fire burned in an impressive stone and mortar fireplace at the opposite end of the room, too far for Simon to feel its warmth. He was directed by his navy escorts to a single hard wooden chair about 15 feet in front of the tables. There was nothing comforting about this, and he could feel his stomach turn and his heart rate surge. He was told to take his seat, and the seamen stood to either side of him. Navy brass quickly took their seats at the lined-up slabs. All eyes were now focused on Simon. Beads of sweat began to attack his collar and he pulled at it.

The least decorated but highest-ranking officer at the center broke the silence. "Mr. Bouchard, my name is Admiral Carlson and this Lieutenant Commander Morrison," and he nodded to the officer to his immediate left. "Right now, you don't need to know the rest of the gentlemen to either side of me," he said, as dry and as impersonal as he could. "I imagine it was a pretty rough start to your day, but let's get to the point, what do you know about the USS *Eldridge*? Please don't dick us around, we both know you have information about that ship."

Simon knew it would come to this. A wandering soul from another dimension had reached out to him and had shared a highly guarded secret with him. It was a secret that Simon knew he must share, but he soon discovered the sharing would be challenging.

"Admiral Carlson, I know very little about the USS *Eldridge* and the brief amount I do know was shared with me by a Chief Vincent Bruno and a young seaman friend of his. They told me only that they were unhappy where they are and others in their crew feel the same way. I believe they are dead."

And then the same looks of disbelief and doubt as before, the skeptics were always quick to challenge anything beyond their understanding. There was a shuffle of paper by an officer a few chairs to the admiral's left and then a line by line search, a pause, his eyes frozen on the parchment, then a slow rise of his head, a look of bewilderment at the admiral, and then a nod.

"It appears you know the name of at least one of the *Eldridge's* crew." He paused and thought for a while, "and now you say he is dead." He shook his head slowly and searched for the next words. "Why don't you tell us how you know that name and why you are convinced that Seaman Bruno and possibly others are dead?"

Simon began his bizarre narrative again. The skepticism and sarcasm always made it difficult. It was always there, a barrier to those that did not believe or trust. He told his audience of his lifetime experiences with his unique ability, his own early doubt of his own sanity. How could these strange visions and visitations of complete strangers, all very sure of their own deaths, be happening to him? Why had they chosen him? How could he possibly tell anyone of these experiences? His sanity was sure to be questioned. But then he had discovered others that had the same gift and he found comfort and support in their close circle, and with that confidence he accepted his gift and no longer doubted his sanity. He began to share it with the world.

"Admiral, I communicate with the deceased, I know that is very difficult for you to accept, but Chief Vincent Bruno has been reaching out to me, which tells me he is indeed dead."

"How did he die, when did he die?" Admiral Carlson rattled off. "How do we know you are not someone with knowledge of a classified operation shared with you by someone, say, like a Seaman Bruno, who compromised his own integrity and his nation's security?"

"Admiral, I can assure you I knew nothing about Petty Officer Bruno before he invaded my dreams and then my daily routines. Your security inquests will bear that out, our paths simply never crossed. How he died and when, I cannot answer, but I can tell you it was an agonizing death and it occurred on the USS *Eldridge*."

"Oh, this is just freaking marvelous." The admiral's voice was thick with sarcasm. "Now we've got Edgar Cayce in the room with us." Snickering and whispering dialogue drifted up and down the conference table.

A Lieutenant Commander Morrison, as indicated on his shiny name plate, suddenly entered the conversation. "Admiral, I wonder if I could have a private word with you, perhaps we could take a few steps away from this table." He hesitated and then nervously pleaded, "You should hear me out on this sir, please." Admiral Carlson seemed surprised by the sudden request. He studied his young officer's face and then scanned the expressions of his attending board of navy brass. "This appears a little strange, Commander. But we can step away for a bit. Gentlemen, if you'll excuse us."

They rose from the table and retreated to the other side of the room and stood near the fireplace, its crackling and spitting of logs helping to shield their intimate conversation.

"I did not see this one coming, Brewster." The admiral inquired, "Where's this heading?"

"Admiral, my gut tells me this guy is on the level and I don't think embarrassing him in front of your staff will serve any purpose. Allow me some one on one with this man; I'll explain more of what's behind my hunch later on. Trust me on this, he has something to offer on this and we need to respect that. My gut is telling me to listen."

Admiral Carlson checked himself, studied Brewster Morrison's face, and then looked back at Simon Bouchard, who had turned back and was watching the two men. Both men had an air of confidence about them. "All right Brew," he said, and he rested his hands on his hips and nodded his head several times. "I'll give you the time you want with this guy." He paused again and then continued. "Your gut is telling you this guy can help; mine is telling me this man's a fool."

Admiral Carlson turned back to his staff. "Gentlemen, let's excuse ourselves from this meeting for just a bit. I am going to allow Commander Morrison some one on one time with Mr. Bouchard."

There was some low grumbling and discourse up and down the long table.

"Gentlemen..." the admiral reinforced his directive and headed for the door, his subordinates soon followed like ducklings to the water's edge.

99

"Mr. Bouchard, can I call you Simon?"

"Of course."

"Why don't we get a little comfortable?" Morrison pointed to the stuffed chairs near the fireplace.

The notion was quickly supported and they soon settled into the warmth of the fireside. "Simon, I apologize for my fellow officers' snickering and doubt."

"I have heard this type of skepticism all my life, it no longer offends me," Simon replied with conviction. "Why do you want to talk to me alone?

"Simon, I have a strange tale to tell you." He told a bizarre account of his mother-in-law and her chance encounter with a very gifted woman many years ago in Portsmouth, Rhode Island. The gifted woman ended up saving her life.

"I am married to a very beautiful woman, even more attractive on the inside. We met in Newport, R.I. where I was attending classes at the Naval War College. But we would never have met, her life never a reality, if her mother had not had that fortuitous meeting with a woman of unique abilities. I am not sure what value I place on the capacity to see the future, 'clairvoyance' I believe is what you call it. But my wife and her mother will swear by it."

Commander Brewster continued his saga of a time long before he was born, when his mother-in-law had been a troubled young woman, unsure of the path she should take. A young man had asked for her hand in marriage, someone she loved with all her being, but her family disapproved of him. There was another young suitor in the picture, the son of some old and close family friends. The two had been friends since childhood and never anything more than that. She could never envision those intimate moments in a marriage; in fact the mere thought of it repulsed her. There was only one young man that could ignite her passions, a single person that connected with her soul.

However, he was not the man her parents approved of, a wild spirit from the other side of the tracks they called him. Her parents and future in-laws pushed the wedding plans along. Now, her true love had proposed to her and she was slowly suffocating.

Desperate, she sought out a woman known throughout Newport County for her ability to see the road not yet traveled. The savant had confirmed her instincts were right: she should follow her heart and not the expectations of others, but what the skillful sage revealed beyond that had stunned her. There was a hidden tumor in her colon. The psychic pleaded with her to follow up with their family doctor. She did, and the physician confirmed the presence of a festering and obviously symptom-free tumor, waiting to reveal itself when it had taken its toll and offered only a deadly outcome. Surgery was performed and the young woman's life had been spared. She was profoundly grateful to this woman and learned of others who had also been blessed with her gifted foresight.

Simon was stunned by the tale told to him. "As strange as this might seem to you Mr. Morrison," he said with disbelief, "the last part of your story is something I have heard before. I believe the clairvoyant your mother-in-law sought out years ago was a woman named Sarah Sheppard, or perhaps she knew her as Madame Alice."

Lieutenant Commander Morrison was astonished, the silence between them was revealing. He stared at Simon in disbelief. "How could you possibly know anything about this?"

"That gifted woman is an old and close friend of mine." Simon told of his early life in New York City where he worked at the *New York Journal*. Madame Alice did not exist then; she was still Sarah Sheppard, a young woman deeply in love with a talented reporter for that same tabloid. Simon was a friend to both of them. Sarah would soon be married to her sweetheart journalist and would feel blessed in their marriage until the tragedy of the RMS *Titanic* invaded their happy life and tore it apart.

Sarah's gift of clairvoyance had warned her of the tragedy attached to the *Titanic*. The family of her sister-in-law's fiancé was traveling on that fated ship to attend their son's wedding in New York. Sarah's attempts to dissuade them from traveling on the *Titanic* were met with cynicism and distrust. Then the whole tragic event unfolded, most of the immediate family drowning, just as she had predicted. It caused irreparable harm to her marriage. The man she loved so deeply suddenly abandoned her. Life had quickly become without purpose. She soon left New York to live in Portsmouth, RI near to her father's business and home in Newport. There, for several years she licked her wounds before she allowed herself to help those that sought out her gifted insight.

It was these simple life events that had triggered Commander Morrison's mother-in-law and Madame Alice's paths to cross; in fact, she had given Madame Alice her new name and title.

"My God, this tale has become stranger and our connection stronger. I believe you and your other gifted friend will help us find the *Eldridge*. Too many bizarre events now linking together. We just need to convince Admiral Carlson, and I'm not sure what I can tell him or not tell him," a truly perplexed Lt. Commander Morrison confided.

Simon replied simply and confidently. "Tell him the truth."

SIMON

S imon was home from his sudden abduction by the US Navy; his wife at wits end cried and hugged him deeply when he opened their door and called her name. He sat on the living room couch, Deborah with her head and flattened hands nestled into Simon's lap. He stroked her soft dark hair, her feel and her perfume comforting him. Simon told of his visit with Admiral Carlson and his staff at the shipyard. The tale was bizarre; even more strange the triad that Simon, Commander Morrison, and Madame Alice now shared. Some mystic power had brought them together, the reason and its impact on all of their lives still to be revealed.

Deborah was unnerved by her husband's bizarre tale. A different sensation gnawed at her, a feeling of dread and separation. She had hoped that they might escape the tragic global war that had invaded everyone's lives, but some higher force had intervened and she knew that Simon would be leaving her for a greater cause.

"What does these mean for you and I, something tells me the navy is not finished with you and that this is all connected to your unique ability, and I know this goddamn war takes precedence over us and everything else. Will you be leaving me?" she asked softly, tears now in the corners of her eyes.

"The navy has not revealed its next step, but I too sense some strange events are about to dictate where our life goes from here and I believe my old friend Madame Alice will be caught up in all this craziness."

"Oh," Deborah said, "I forgot to tell you, Madame Alice called this afternoon, she introduced herself, a very nice woman, she told me a little about your friendship. Wants you to call as soon as possible."

The strange forces from beyond were aligning things, every instinct within Simon confirmed it. Of course Madame Alice called while he was being questioned by Admiral Carlson and his staff. It was meant to be. Commander Morrison had probed and he had shared his experiences and connection to this woman. The mystic plan was being weaved.

Finally, she had called. A letter penned long ago, still unanswered, was now upsetting to Simon. He had written to his old friend Madame Alice just two days after Seaman Bruno and his young understudy had invaded his nights. His instinct told him his old friend was connected to these bizarre intrusions.

Petty Officer Bruno from the USS *Eldridge* had found his way into Simon's evening visions, but Simon knew it was not a random act of the cosmos, these invasions from beyond rarely were. The tortured crewmen of the *Eldridge* were here for Simon's help and it was clear that this task was again beyond his abilities. Madame Alice's assistance would be needed.

Something tragic had happened on a United States destroyer and Simon was confident the disturbing events aboard the frigate were still being played out. Seamen Bruno and his young friend were there to save their shipmates from a horrible fate. Crewmen of the USS *Eldridge*, those that had passed on, were reaching out to Simon.

Fatigued from his long day with navy intelligence, Simon would call Madame Alice first thing tomorrow. Tonight, he would sleep with his wife, his arms around her. They would comfort each other.

Milton Post had just finished sanding four of the road facing shutters of his hotel; that left eight more to do and then the painting. Closing the shed's door, he started up the slight incline to his inn. He heard the phone ringing back in his work shed. Six months ago, they ran an extra phone line to the outbuilding. Numerous, sometimes important calls were being missed. Madame Alice, for some time now, was sleeping later in the morning and taking more naps, often dug in like a tick. No phone call, regardless how many times it clattered, could roust from her rooted sleep.

He did his best about-face when he heard the phone's piercing ring. Milton slid the shack door open and grabbed the phone on the tool bench just inside, its receiver already spotted with paint of different colors.

"Hello," came a gruff, impatient greeting.

"Hello, Milton, this is Simon Bouchard."

"Oh yes, hello Simon, Sarah told me you might call. She's napping right now; I'll have to go wake her."

"Let her sleep, she can call me back or I can call later." Simon knew the emptiness of his words; he hoped his tone had not given his insincerity away. He desperately wanted to talk with her.

"No, Sarah insisted that I wake her the minute you called, she was quite emphatic about that." Milton hesitated; Simon sensed there was more he needed to share.

"Simon, I know you and my wife are old friends from a long time ago and the last time you visited you took her on a very trying journey. Now, she talks about another possible pilgrimage, just know that she is not a healthy woman. Actually, her health is quite poor. She would never tell you that but I will. Please do not take advantage of her desire to help. She's just incapable of turning her back. I don't think she has another journey in her."

"I am sorry Milton; I did not know she was feeling so poorly," Simon said, his voice sad with news of his old friend's ill health. "Please tell her I called and perhaps I will call at another time."

"No," Milton said again, this time with added emphasis. "Please hear me out. Simon. My wife is quite ill, although she will never agree with that assessment. Her appetite has almost vanished; she has the craving of a sparrow. Sarah's energy is very low and she is easily out of breath. I am convinced there is a something wrong with her heart. A doctor could reveal so much more, but she refuses to see one."

"Hello," a raspy, sleepy voice joined the conversation. It was Madame Alice.

Anticipating Simon's call, Madame Alice placed the phone on the end table next to her rocker, but a warm late morning sun and her *Reader's Digest* had lulled her to sleep. She was in a tender dream of a time long ago when she was with her first husband William, lying naked, wrapped in his arms on a tropical beach on the shore line of North Carolina. It had been their honeymoon and she would hold onto that loving and happiest time of her life, if only in her dreams.

Now the phone's piercing ring was slowly fetching her back from those sultry memories. William's sensuous touch, his smell, and gentle smile were slowly fading into the gray of her dream. There would be other dreams, visits again to those blissful days of when her first husband and she shared a life overflowing with happiness and warmth.

Her first marriage had been a storybook romance. A chance encounter on a wintery day in New York City had magically blossomed into a blissful love story. Sarah and William Lowe, the tall handsome reporter for the *New York Journal* were smitten with each other. They dated, and as their relationship intensified, she told him of her ability to see the future and reach beyond the grave. It was of no consequence to him. They were shortly married and their days became idyllic. Sarah found her sleep an annoying but selfishly comical daily occurrence, it was time stolen from being with the man she deeply loved.

They believed nothing could ever breach the solid foundation that was their picture-perfect marriage. But then the RMS *Titanic* struck an iceberg and its deadly and sorrowful impact suddenly fragmented their love for each other.

Her name was Sarah Sheppard then, her birth name. Years later she would become Madame Alice, a name her passionate clients had deemed appropriate. Friends soon accepted her new identity

Her young sister-in-law was to be married and her fiancé's family from England would be traveling to New York to participate in the happy event. They would be passengers on the fateful RMS *Titanic*. They had been dining at the posh restaurant, Delmonico's on the East Side when the happy couple shared the news with Sarah and William. An immediate sense of dread overwhelmed Sarah and in the weeks leading up to the wedding, she was tortured with the vision of a disastrous event in the north Atlantic. She knew a terrible fate awaited her in-laws' trip aboard the *Titanic*. Unable to hold the horrible vision to only herself, she approached her sister in law and her fiancé with her disturbing vision.

"You must stop them from boarding the *Titanic*," she told them in desperation. They instantly questioned Sarah's stability.

The change to their relationship was immediate and deflating. The happy couple would not entertain such distasteful lunacy, and then when the tragedy as foreseen by Sarah was visited on them, there was an instant, frightened withdrawal from her. It was as if a Sarah carried a deadly plague with her and to be near her or even see her meant sudden death. Even William, the love of her life, quickly changed the dynamics of the relationship. A soul-destroying divorce shortly followed and shattered her identity.

It had been a terrible time in her life and she left New York City in haste. She moved to Portsmouth, Rhode Island and slowly over the years her deep wound began to heal.

She fumbled with the phone, unsure of her grip. "Hello Simon," she said, knowing completely it was him.

"It's Simon," Milton said, blunt and to the point. "You weren't answering, so I picked up out here."

"Thanks, honey. I was napping."

"Remember what I said Mr. Bouchard." His tone was more asking than threatening and he abruptly hung up.

"Oh, Simon I am so sorry I did not answer your letter, but I had misplaced it and only just read it yesterday. I called the very minute I finished reading it. It's good to hear from you. How are you?" Her voice was soft, almost whispering.

"Good to hear your voice again, Sarah," he told her. "I'm okay; I didn't hear back from you and I was fearful its content and this challenge I now find myself in would be too much for you. I didn't know what to do. I knew you were the only one that could help me. If you don't want to involve yourself in this, especially now that Milton told me of your poor health, I would understand completely."

"Simon, Milton dotes on me, the slightest sniffle and we're off to the doctor's. Please take everything he says about me with a grain of salt. He loves me deeply." And then her tone changed; a sudden eagerness. "Things have happened up here too, things that I believe are intimately connected to what you are experiencing in Philadelphia."

"Tell me what's going on, Sarah," Simon anxiously demanded. And then added, "Can I call you Sarah? I know you prefer your new name Madame Alice, but it's hard for me to forget that I knew you all those years as Sarah, it's so deeply ingrained in my subconscious. I will try though."

"Sarah is fine; you are an old dear friend."

She told him of the tortured navy lieutenant that first visited her in her dreams and now wandered the grounds adjacent to the inn.

"I believe he experienced a very painful death, but with a heavy burden, a huge emotional weight attached, pulling at his character. I believe he brings a message, perhaps a pleading from others and many of them that have suffered the same fate. A twisted reality was forced upon them and it imprisoned them in a strange dimension, one that has isolated them from their loved ones and offers no closure or any hope of it."

Simon then told Sarah of Seaman Bruno's visits in the night and the bizarre encounter in front of his bus at the navy shipyard: the young sailor with horrible burns, holding the ship's life ring that displayed "USS *Eldridge*." He told her how he inquired at the shore patrol office about such a vessel, told no such vessel existed, and then two burly petty officers hustled, almost kidnapped, him yesterday in the early morning hours.

"I was abducted from my apartment by armed guards. It terrified my wife; we've only been married a short time. You'll like her Sarah. They drove me to an admiral's office and conference room and I was grilled about a ship that several weeks ago, I was told did not exist. I believe they thought I was a spy. I was kept there until the early hours of the next day and the interrogation never stopped. By the time they returned me to my apartment, I was exhausted and hungry. My wife was a wreck. It made no sense to talk to you in the agitated state I was in. I hope you understand."

"I understand completely, I just needed to reach out to you. Something is amiss within our country's navy, something truly terrifying. This ship whose existence they deny is in some sort of serious jeopardy and the two of us are being pulled into that dilemma. The fact that you are being interrogated at such a high level seems to suggest that they are desperate. Your interactions with the navy are far from over and when they do call upon you again, tell them what I also know. We have both been chosen by the crew of the USS *Eldridge* for a truly moral reason."

Madame Alice knew a voyage was being crafted for her and Simon. A long journey lay ahead, waiting for them. She wondered if she had the physical strength.

The last several months had seen a shortness of breath, and a plaguing fatigue tested her daily activities. Simple tasks were now more challenging, her garden and baking on Wednesdays required more commitment and energy than she seemed to possess. Milton discovered her napping in the late afternoons, something she had never done before and often found it difficult to wake from these late day siestas. Her loss of appetite concerned him and mealtimes became confrontational. Madame Alice would not concede that she was eating less, although she did privately acknowledge most of her clothes were not as snug as she remembered. Something was wrong with her body's inner balance and she knew that her exit from this human tragedy called life was being crafted by her God. She would take great care to hide this reality from her friend Simon.

Just last night, the young *Eldridge* officer with other shipmates stood confidently before her in the hotel's living room. All of them beckoning her to follow, their burned and damaged forms difficult to look at. She sensed these heroes, now discarded like used, worn out machines had sacrificed everything for their country. They pleaded for the closure only she could provide.

The phone was now trembling in her hand, the uncertainty of things to come. "Simon, they will not leave me alone, nor can I ignore them, I sense a powerful calling. They will visit again. You and I know that."

USS *ELDRIDGE*

They assembled on the foredeck to commit two more of their own to the depths, both men victims of the deadly device located in the lower depths of the *Eldridge*. This time a simple test run had delivered the deadly consequences. Other sailors with missing limbs and serious burns stood among the ship's company, all victims of a cruel mechanism and a captain's twisted obsession. The crew of the USS *Eldridge*, an elite American destroyer with special abilities, was spiraling slowly into a dark abyss, and their commanding officer was oblivious to their pain.

They left their home port in Philadelphia on June 9th, steamed south-east across the Atlantic, sinking a German U-boat and heavy cruiser as they traveled. They voyaged around Cape Horn of Africa, through the Indian Ocean, and were now deep in the South China Sea. They rendezvoused with their re-fueling ship and mail was taken on board. Letters from the home front was always a special event. Correspondence from wives, girlfriends, and family made the lonely days at sea tolerable.

But Captain Milton Van Noy would not allow any outgoing mail. It was a shock to the crew. Their mission was too classified, the security risk too great. Morale, which had been suffering with their captain's ruthless command, plummeted. Most of the crew put little

111

stock in his reasoning. Their captain had become obsessed with control of the ship. Captain Van Noy began to micro-manage all of the vessel's activities. Seamen Clarke and Capron were restricted to their bunking area for not wearing their hats while on watch. The tiniest infractions maddened him, and his punishment was always immediate and excessive.

And now as they gathered to pay their respects to their dead shipmates, Van Noy chose this moment to address the crew for their lack of commitment and dereliction of duty. This was their fourth assembly since leaving Philadelphia and these musters had become a raw annoyance. It became Van Noy's mechanism to berate the entire crew at once. It only deepened their hatred of the captain.

"Gentlemen," Captain Van Noy began, holding the microphone, he stood on the decking just outside the pilot house, his voice echoing off the steel walls and superstructure. "We have paid our respects to two of our fallen comrades. May God have mercy on their souls." He hesitated, his voice turning confrontational, "But it seems gentlemen, that we still have not grasped the seriousness of our mission. You may not feel that this is the appropriate time for what I am about to say, but I am not of that opinion. This is a highly classified undertaking; you knew that from day one. You are a hand-picked crew. Everything you do on this ship, every single task, no matter how trivial it might seem, is critical to the success of our mission. Two men were lost because of carelessness, a loss of focus. We were already a reduced number the day we left port. We cannot afford the loss of personnel. I will not tolerate any lack of commitment, nor should you. I ask you now to police yourselves; you know what defines good seamanship on an American destroyer. Report any dereliction, however minor, to your senior officer. We will deal with that person swiftly and harshly."

Well it has finally come to this, Lt. Estrella thought to himself, *now we're supposed to spy on each other. The captain is slowly unraveling.*

"And gentlemen, do not think for one moment—" and then the general quarters alarm screeched across the vessel. Everyone froze in their place, the ship's speaker carried Commander Preston's voice. "Captain, we have radar contact at 060 degrees, about 16 miles, moving pretty fast, Hansey thinks it's a Jap cruiser."

Captain Van Noy picked up his mic, his voice once again booming throughout the ship. "Mr. Preston, contact the Rainbow Room, have them engage our device ASAP." The crew, stung with sudden terror, did not move; fear at what was lying across the horizon and dread of what lay within their own ship froze them where they stood. Van Noy screamed above the battle station alarm. "GO!"

MYOKO

The emperor's heavy cruiser, the *Myoko,* at nearly 12,000 tons, was traveling at 32 knots. Her attending 1,700-ton destroyer, the *Natsugumo,* was struggling to keep up. Ensign Tanaka, the radar officer aboard the *Natsugumo*, had picked up the echo return of the American destroyer.

The *Natsugumo* was one of the few Japanese naval destroyers equipped with the new technology called radar, something developed by the English. Military commanders at the top were unsure of its capabilities and were more concerned that its use might give away their position; the flawless and undetected attack on Pearl Harbor had proven that radar had done very little to give the Americans an early warning. Their secretive and hostile mission had never been compromised by their lack of this new technology or their enemies' use of it. Stealth, meticulous planning, and ruthless tactics had ensured total victory on that December day for the land of the rising sun.

However, there were still enough influential people at the naval command center that would not bury their heads in the sand. Perhaps there was something to radar, and to ignore its potential would be foolish. Two destroyers and one destroyer escort would be equipped with this infant technology and Ensign Tanaka had attended six months of intensive schooling to learn its intricate workings and potential. More ships were scheduled for this update.

The *Natsugumo* had gone to battle stations and had alerted her larger sister ship the *Myoko*. Firing solutions were dialed into the destroyer's forward guns, but the enemy vessel was beyond their range. Coordinates were shared with the heavily armed cruiser, but her captain had elected to secure visual contact before engaging. Radar was still new to him and he mistrusted its effectiveness. He ordered the ship to battle stations.

Ensign Tanaka studied the distinct blip on his radar screen. The echo was strong and he was confident of the enemy's location. The reality that a deadly surface battle was only minutes away gripped him with anxious anticipation. Would they come within range of the hostile destroyer with their own arsenal? Or would the *Myoko* obtain a visual and erupt with her own big rifles? Time ticked by. The dilemma the two ships shared was nerve wracking. It was only a matter of time before the American ship opened up with its own broadside. The first accurate salvo often determines the outcome of a naval engagement. And then the blip suddenly disappeared, his radar screen blank.

"I have lost radar contact, Captain!" he shouted, and scrambled to troubleshoot his instruments. The captain on the bridge waited impatiently for his junior officer to restart his scan or explain his dilemma. Finally, he could wait no longer—hesitation and indecision in battle can be deadly.

"I want men aloft with glasses," he barked. "Ensign, what was your last bearing and distance on our target? Contact the bridge of the *Myoko* and share that information with her. Let her know we have lost radar contact with the enemy vessel and we are unsure why. Ask Vice-Admiral Kobayoshi for permission to fire on our last known position of the enemy frigate, recommend they do the same. Also suggest we change our course and speed. Get those coordinates to our own gun crews immediately."

"Bearing 265 degrees, distance 22 kilometers," Tanaka revealed, his voice strained with nervousness.

The captain and several junior officers raised their binoculars to the coordinates given and gazed out at the open vista.

They watched as the *Myoko's* forward and aft turrets rotated ever so slightly. Then they exploded, their 16-inch salvos outgoing towards a location where a blip on a screen said the enemy should be. The concussion was deafening and forceful. Crew members on the bridge of the *Natsugumo* covered their ears.

Firing orders were quickly given to the gun crews of the *Natsugumo* and within seconds her salvos became part of the assault.

USS *ELDRIDGE*

"Captain, our Jap cruiser is not by herself, think she's got a destroyer as an escort," William Hanes announced to the bridge.

"How sure are you Hansey?" Van Noy asked.

"Oh, there's an escort alright, this is no echo. I got two very distinct blips at 16 miles and they just went hard over. They know we're here, which is a little strange. We're beyond the horizon. They couldn't have gotten a visual on us yet. My guess, one of those nips has radar, which I thought the Japs didn't place a lot of confidence in."

"Well, I guess they do now."

In the past Captain Van Noy would have contacted the Rainbow Room to get confirmation that their technology had been activated. That was the odd thing about their cloaking device: after the initial activation and the brief adjustment interval, there was little indication that they had entered into another bizarre dimension. Their ship and all her personnel were visible to each other, but just a short distance away from their ship. To all other creatures, human or mammal, they appeared to have vanished into some foggy abyss.

Now the strange 60-cycle vibration would emanate from below decks. An unnatural, sometimes dangerous heat would spread throughout the ship, and nausea and dizziness would engulf almost a third of the crew. These were now the indicators that they had vanished, invisible to all others, but at a price that was ever increasing and quite discernible to them.

"Bring us to 060 degrees, steady as she goes," the captain ordered, and then the ocean suddenly erupted several hundred yards to their stern, starboard side. One mile forward, the same starboard side, several plumes of sea water, not as big, heaved skyward.

Van Noy pointed aft and said "Cruiser," and then brought his index finger forward. "Destroyer. That's rather obvious. Probably fired at our last known position. All our firepower should be directed at that cruiser. Have the torpedo crew starboard side stand ready. Do our gun crews have a firing solution?"

"Yes, they do, we should be in range in a few minutes," Lt. Estrella, their firing control officer, responded. "We're closing that gap rather quickly."

Once again Professor Mueller, the German scientist that was key to the development of their top-secret weapon, had joined the captain on the bridge; their excitement about the battle soon to be joined was almost juvenile. They exchanged demonstrative handshakes; they wore broad smiles that barely contained the exhilaration within. They paced about the bridge with nervous energy, anxious for the battle to begin.

"Lt. Estrella, let's get a lot closer, I want to make sure our salvos are deadly accurate. They have no idea we're right in front of them. I think Professor Mueller can wait the additional few minutes."

The two men turned to each other like two children that had stolen apples from a street vendor, and this time soundly patted each other on the back and snickered. Those on the deck were stunned by their interaction. Men were about to die on both sides and yet their captain and his German accomplice were overjoyed with its eventuality.

The *Eldridge*, its oblique V-bow slicing through the South China Sea, was a ghost ship about to bring death and destruction to an unsuspecting enemy, a sneak attack so incredibly ironic and rewarding to Captain Milton Van Noy.

They had closed the distance and Van Noy gave the order to fire. A sudden starboard broadside moved the *Eldridge* 10 feet in the water to port. Within seconds the afterdeck of the Japanese cruiser erupted in flames. Each turn of the destroyer's twin props brought her closer to their Japanese foe. Short seconds later another full salvo left the US destroyer and erupted amidships on the *Myoko*. A large secondary explosion deep in the bowels of the enemy cruiser sent bright orange flames, pitch black smoke, and wreckage high into the heavens.

Where to attack and how to defend were causes that the Japanese cruiser would never participate in. They were ducks on a pond, vulnerable and pathetic.

They were attacking a ship that had little chance of defending itself. There was no honor in such lopsided slaughter. What they were doing now resembled simple target practice, except these targets were living and about to die.

The *Eldridge* continued its onslaught. Round after round exploded all along the topside of the enemy cruiser. The stern was already below its water line.

"Captain Van Noy, the destroyer escort has broken off its defense," Commander Preston informed. "Hansey has them at 35 knots, still at 060 degrees. They're making a run for it."

"Noted, Commander," Van Noy responded, his voice dry, mechanical, without feeling. "Let's finish with his big sister first, we can hunt them down later. Fire torpedo tubes 1 and 2, all other weapons cease firing."

Professor Mueller was suddenly at the captain's side. He had just hung up the phone that connected directly to the Rainbow Room. Concern was written all over his face.

"Captain, we have problems in the Rainbow Room." For the first time there was doubt in his voice. "It seems our pumps cannot maintain the required temperature control. Professor Bjurman believes our cloaking may have been compromised."

There was a sudden explosion near the stern of the *Eldridge*. The whole ship shuddered. Those on the bridge turned to look aft but there was no visible sign of a hit, no smoke or fire, no shattered hull or damaged super structure. And then a hit to their midships, the round penetrating through bulkheads and exploding in the radio room.

"Damage control report." Petty Officer Bruno was already running, on his way aft. But feedback was already being provided to the bridge.

"Captain, communications room reports a direct hit, minimum two dead, still working on the injuries. No fires!!! We also have damage in the after steering compartment, possibly our rudder has been damaged. Up here, the helm is not responding. There was no direct hit but it was close enough to do some damage. We have no control of our heading."

Van Noy's face turned red with rage and complete frustration, he slammed the ship's wheel with his open hand. Looking in the direction of the fleeing escort and then back at the burning wreck of the Japanese cruiser before them, he cursed through gritted, snarling teeth, "God damn those fucking animals, continue firing on that cruiser. I want every one of those beady eyed bastards on the bottom of this ocean."

NATSUGUMO

Both Japanese warships had just fired their opening barrage at an enemy craft they could only hope was there. Radar officer Ensign Tanaka gave his best estimate of the last location of the enemy vessel. Tanaka and most of the senior officers knew it was folly. The distance to the American warship was beyond their range. The cruiser had visual and was well within range of her big guns, but the enemy had suddenly vanished into a fog bank. Requests to her escort for updated radar coordinates went unanswered. The enemy destroyer had disappeared from their radar screen.

High atop the *Myoko,* a lookout spotted the plumes of water, vertical to the flat distant horizon. But no enemy vessel near or far was evident.

Despite all their years at sea and all their training, both Japanese commanders were broadly unprepared for the dilemma they found themselves within. Simplistic orders were shouted and rapid follow through was demanded. Heading and speed were changed. All done in an effort to defend their complete vulnerability.

Agonizing minutes dragged by. Ensign Tanaka, with senior officers huddled around him, checked and rechecked his equipment. He finally stood and faced them, his arms close to his side; he bowed stiffly, apology visible in his every move. There was nothing more he

121

could do. The American destroyer, clearly visible on his screen short moments ago, was gone.

Lookouts posted on both vessels could find nothing. Crew members and junior officers began to think the American destroyer had turned tail when they realized they were outgunned and over-matched. The old salts knew that was not war time reality. When the enemy is before you, always engage

They waited, only a clear and empty seascape before them. Perhaps the Americans had fled the battle scene after all. Then the aft turret of the *Myoko* exploded, the suddenness of the blast and its frightening visual terrifying them all. A large steel housing with men and machine within was now a mound of crumbled, twisted, and jagged steel. Huge flames rose up from the wreckage, killing and injuring those that might have survived the initial explosion. Bodies or sections of them littered the stern deck. Seamen with their torsos on fire ran screaming insanely into the arms of fellow shipmates, others threw themselves into the sea around them.

Although no order was given, smaller weapons on the *Myoko* began to fire randomly into the empty ocean around them. Another barrage from the American warship struck amidships. Men and ship's plating suddenly gone, replaced by flame and toxic smoke. Some of the enemy rounds pierced through the outer bulkheads and exploded within, the carnage and destruction had to be extensive.

The men of the *Natsugumo* watched in horror; their countrymen were being slaughtered and a proud symbol of the Japanese navy was being destroyed before them. They were appalled with the bloodbath and consumed with guilt, there was nothing they could do to aid their compatriots.

Salvo after salvo detonated all along the deck of the *Myoko*. No shot ever off target, no explosions in the surrounding ocean. It was as if the terror originated from a vessel at point blank range, where a miss is just improbable, yet no enemy destroyer was visible.

Captain Saito of the *Natsugumo* was shocked with the quick and deadly obliteration of a once powerful war ship. His instincts told him to flee from this already lost engagement; he ordered his destroyer hard over to starboard and directed his engine room to squeeze every bit of horsepower they could muster. Hopefully they might survive to fight another day.

As the *Natsugumo* raced away from the lopsided sea battle and their doomed sister ship, Ensign Tanaka continued to stare at his radar screen. Each sweep of the dial revealed an empty ocean. Yet somewhere out there a confident phantom ship was releasing unchallenged death and destruction. The whole concept of an invisible enemy and the hopelessness it represented filled him with dread. The scenario in front of them seemed as if it should be a passage from a science fiction novel and not this horrific reality before them.

Tanaka looked back at the once expansive cruiser and saw the *Myoko* was already losing her stern to the sea. Then two large explosions amidships at the water line sealed her fate. "Torpedoes," he said quietly to himself. The *Myoko* would soon vanish from the nearby eastern horizon.

Suddenly another image, and not of the *Myoko,* appeared on his screen, it indicated the presence of the enemy vessel. Tanaka plotted it to be about 2800 meters to the west south west. The image then briefly faded, only to return to a defined shape and location and then faded again. The duplicate now floated in and out on his display.

"Captain, I have radar contact," Tanaka shouted above the turmoil on the *Natsugumo* bridge. "I think it's the American destroyer, I can give you firing coordinates."

Suddenly there was silence on the bridge. His captain and those on the bridge immediately turned to him. The fear and the panic that had engulfed their ship's bridge loosened its grip.

"Then do so!" the captain barked, and then picked up the phone to the aft battery. "Number three, four, and five, Ensign Tanaka will give you bearing and distance to the enemy vessel. Be quick and be accurate."

Tanaka gave the coordinates to the stern mounts and moments later its turrets exploded. Those on the bridge shouted with jubilance. They were fighting back. Off in the distance they saw the plumes of water from their exploding shells, but no indications of a strike to the American destroyer.

"Tanaka, can you update your last location?" his captain demanded. But Tanaka's locator screen was once again blank. He turned to his commander, again a lifeless look of complete frustration was all he could offer. This new age technology had failed him again.

"Cease firing. Continue heading, all ahead full," the captain quickly ordered, his words firm, but with little resolve. "Ensign Tanaka, you need to get your instruments working again, until you do, we will be at the mercy of the American *funa yurei*."

Captain Saito's battle report to naval command in Tokyo would be reviewed with skepticism, but overall would be sobering and alarming. Captain Saito and Ensign Tanaka were hurriedly ordered to back to Tokyo. A seaplane quickly facilitated their return.

Their flight to Tokyo was long and uncomfortable, they slept little. It was an intensive briefing. Japanese naval command wanted to review any and all information surrounding the disastrous engagement with the American destroyer, although there were several senior officers that felt it may not be an American vessel, perhaps a Russian vessel. Military intelligence shared information that the Russians were researching a whole new technology, perhaps this was it. Tanaka was not swayed, something within told him this was an American plot. Regardless of who developed the hardware, Japanese brass collectively agreed that it was a game changing weapon. Additional ships should be included in this search and destroy mission, but the battle for the Pacific had turned against the Empire of Japan. No vessels could be spared. The *Natsugumo* would be the lone vessel responsible for this demanding challenge.

Captain Saito and Ensign Tanaka were immediately returned by that same seaplane to their destroyer still stationed in the East China Sea. Their orders were to intensify their search for the enemy ship. It had crept up on one of their most feared battle cruisers and had vanquished it in mere minutes, and the *Myoko* was helpless in defending itself. The concept was chilling to the Japanese navy. The American destroyer had to be located and destroyed.

Japanese naval intuition suggested that this lethal destroyer would seek out and engage all other Japanese vessels. The further it traveled into the East China Sea, the better the chances of confrontation. The *Natsugumo* plotted its course for that area of ocean and zigzagged its way to that destination.

USS *ELDRIDGE*

Convinced the Japanese destroyer that had caused the damage to their rudder and after steering might reappear at any moment, Van Noy stationed himself at the stern of the *Eldridge* and oversaw the repair efforts. The repair of the communications room was left to the XO, Commander Preston, although there was little that could be done. The damage to that room was severe, simply not enough spare parts, communication to the outside world was forever gone.

The fact that a seaman had been killed by the forces released from the Rainbow Room and another terribly burned had little impact on the captain; that would be another unpleasant responsibility Van Noy could pass off to his subordinate.

Van Noy continually moved from the stern deck to deep in the aft section of the ship. He second guessed all directions given, micromanaging the slightest decision, pushing the men, demanding they work harder and faster.

He was alone in that reasoning. The ship's company was confident that the enemy destroyer, after seeing what had happened to their formidable sister ship, was making good speed away from the scene of the costly engagement and thanking their God for a fortuitous escape.

125

The near miss from the Japanese destroyer had bent the rudder, and below in the far aft steering compartment, one of the big hydraulic pistons that moved the tiller had been slightly warped, and its mechanical flanges cracked.

Fortunately, they had the ability to make the repairs at sea. Several men at a time were lowered into the water, all wearing masks and oxygen lines. As evening approached, nighttime lighting was provided and they worked around the clock. Pneumatic hoses were dropped over the side to operate the necessary equipment. The work was tedious and exhausting; each three-man team would labor for an hour and then a new trio would replace them, and they alternated like this for the entire project.

Below decks, in steering, the confined space hampered their work. Men worked feverishly to remove the damaged piston and flange. The machine shop toiled just as hard to fabricate a new flange. Large gas torches were used to heat the damaged piston and com-a-longs were used to straighten it. Temperature in that confined area hovered at 120 degrees. Inside and out the work was exhausting.

Just after 1300 hours in the afternoon, Seaman Paul Graves was attacked by a shark, a black tip they thought. His lower left leg was a mess of torn flesh and exposed bone. The other two men drove the shark away with pokes from their flat bars. The rear deck was alive with commotion and panic. The young sailor was screaming with pain and orders were shouted for his treatment. The remaining men were ordered to leave the water immediately.

Reports of the shark attack quickly found Captain Van Noy in the after steering section. He scrambled up the metal grate stairs and arrived just as young Graves was being carried to sickbay. The ship's doctor walked along next to the injured sailor. Van Noy grabbed the doctor's shoulder. "How is he?

"He's lost a lot of blood; his leg is torn up pretty bad. My guess it was a good-sized shark. Good thing he wasn't by himself, he'd be another unintentional fatality on this ship," he added with pointed sarcasm.

Captain Van Noy stared at him with complete contempt. He quickly turned to his attending yeoman. "Mr. Clemens, please go to my quarters and retrieve my holster and side arm." He returned to the doctor. "Mr. Bellows," he growled, his voice filled with disdain, "you should see to your patient." And then was off to address the men at the rear of the ship.

They had gathered around the two sailors that had just left the water. Still in shock, they sat on weathered stools. The deck around them was covered in Seaman Graves's blood. Sitting in stunned silence, they slowly rose to salute their captain. Others in the gathering made halfhearted attempts to extend that courtesy to their captain.

"Who's in charge here?" Captain Van Noy barked at the gathering. The men, briefly startled, turned to face him. "I will assume that would be you Ensign Hughes."

"Yes sir," Hughes sheepishly answered.

"Then why is no one in the water?"

"Sir, we just retrieved Mr. Graves from the water. It was very unsettling to the men."

"I suppose it was, but Seaman Graves is on the way to sick-bay. There is nothing we can do for him right now, let's get your men back in the water. I will not sit here, dead in the water, for a single second longer than I have to."

"But maybe there are other sharks, Captain."

"There probably are, all this lighting has probably attracted them, and now the smell of blood will pull them in. Regardless, we need to push ahead here."

"Are you sure that's a wise thing to do Captain?" Ensign Hughes challenged.

"Ensign, how do you think we can get this ship underway? We need our rudder and we won't have it until you fix it. Seems pretty simple to me."

Yeoman Clemens returned with the captain's side arm and holster. He attached the side arm to his waist, and after adjusting its fit, he looked directly at Ensign Hughes.

"Mr. Hughes, let's get your men back in the water." His voice was calm but firm.

A sailor in the water during the shark attack suddenly jumped up from his stool, his eyes wide with disbelief. "I ain't going back in that fucking water," he shouted at his commander. Others stood and gathered around him, demonstrating their support.

Van Noy calmly turned to his attending petty officer. "Mr. Clemens, please escort Seaman Moretti to his berth and handcuff him to his bunk. Let him think about his loose tongue for a bit."

Ensign Hughes was stunned. "Captain we nearly lost Graves, the men are a little uneasy right now, maybe if we waited till morning."

"Ensign Hughes you have your orders, I strongly advise you follow them."

Another sailor spoke up, not as challenging as his previous shipmate. "But sir, you just said there are probably more sharks in the water."

Captain Van Noy suddenly pulled his forty-five from its holster and fired a shot in the air. The group of men, startled, took a step back. Van Noy took several quick strides to the edge of the ship and fired his gun blindly and quickly into the surrounding sea.

"That's how you deal with sharks." His voice was forceful and full of anger. "Get more men along the rails with M-1s, put men in a dory with the same, get more lighting if you want; I don't care what you do, just get it done. I don't know how I can make it any clearer. If you are not up to the task, you can get cuffed to your bunk too. Ensign Hughes, we need to get this ship underway."

He locked eyes with his subordinate for an instant, then turned and walked briskly away.

It was late afternoon when Ensign Hughes informed the captain that the restoration was complete and they could get under way. They had worked around the clock for the last 34 hours; they were a weary and troubled crew. Numerous shots had been fired at some of the more aggressive sharks and two had been killed. Their carcasses were removed from the water to prevent a feeding frenzy. Each shot fired sent ripples of dread up and down the *Eldridge*. Sailors were on edge and they feared for their comrades underneath the ship. Men that emerged from the dark hell beneath the stern of the ship were visibly shaken. They trembled with fear, often disoriented, sometimes unresponsive to those around them.

Watching the ghostly lifeless eyes of the too many to count black tip sharks paralyzed many of the workers with terror and hindered their work. The lights from above and below the waterline illuminated the white eyes of these predatory monsters. They would move all about, always on the fringe, and then there would be a sudden rush; deadly bleached eyes would close in on them and then silvery rows of jagged teeth would reveal themselves. Lifeless eyes and life taking tines, it was too much for those men in the water. Three more men were attacked and bitten; luckily the wounds were not severe. But more blood had been spilled, terrorizing the crew and exciting their killers.

After getting his ship underway, Captain Van Noy addressed the crew through the public address system. Most of the men were seated in the galley, it was their evening meal. There was already a gathering consternation of the way the captain handled the whole shark incident, a topic of conservation at every table. Did he have to harass them so soon after the terrifying event and in the middle of them eating? It only deepened their dislike for him.

"Gentlemen, we have finished a rather difficult and unpleasant task. There should be some sense of a job well done, but it was not a job done well. Those of you involved with the repair to the rudder lost focus of the larger picture; sometimes duty requires sacrifice for the larger, common good of the ship. Those in the aft steering section seemed like every move they took was hampered by a lack of confidence in our mission. Rather childlike from my perspective. Why not have every E-1 second guess the strategy of every admiral? I'm sure that'd be a real shit show."

He again emphasized that they should indeed be grateful that the enemy destroyer had not returned; they could have been easy prey. He promised more drills and tighter control of the ship activities. They listened in complete apathy. The crew of the *Eldridge* had moved past the point of caring. Too much damage had been inflicted on them. The shark attack had become their defining moment. They despised their captain. Mutiny was not such an improbable recourse.

USS *ELDRIDGE*

MUTINY BEGINS

60,000 horse power turbo engines at flank speed could push the sculptured hull of the *Eldridge* through Pacific waters at about 45 miles per hour, but the demand for fuel at that speed could consume near 100,000 gallons per day. Flank speed had its thirsty mandate. Today she steamed at twelve knots. The rolling rhythm of the sea, the soft winds along her decks, a warm tropical breeze and sun belied the tempest that grew within their ship. A disturbing reality was descending on the *Eldridge*. On their ship, a secret fuse had been lit and no one knew when the bomb would go off.

Lieutenant Estrella had heard the rumblings from crew members of the *Eldridge* for the last seven days. He was not numb to it. It was a threatening and escalating concern to most of the crew, officers and enlistees. Collectively, confidence in their special weapon and their captain was long gone.

They shared their concerns with two of the junior officers on board, Ensign O'Donnell and Lt. J.G. Gomez. They were well liked and trusted by the crew. They moved those concerns, with their own

131

support, up the ranks to Lt. Estrella. The lieutenant had likewise begun to doubt the worthiness of their mission and that of Project Rainbow, the secret weapon they now knew was not ready for practical use. The project had been rushed, not enough testing in actual battle condition. Hell, even within the secure boundaries of the New Jersey shore line, a final testing took the life of Seaman Galuska, his body never found. But pressure from the war department pushed them out to sea and the gory incidents only intensified. Most of the ship's company was convinced it would bring about their own demise.

Lieutenant Robert Estrella was headed aft; he had been asked to attend an early morning gathering in the No. 5 rear turret. It was 0330 hours, sunrise was still more than two hours away and on the big ocean it was dark, lonely dark. He climbed the small access ladder to the turret and opened the hatchway. A lone red light bulb illuminated the cramped quarters. Five seamen were squeezed into the compartment. They stood around the artillery piece. He nodded his head and saw that Petty Officer Bruno was the ranking member of this gathering.

"Mr. Bruno, I will assume you are the spokesman for your mates here?" he gingerly asked.

"No sir, Ensign O'Donnell is the spokesman for this group," he answered, his deep voice a statement of fact. "But this ain't all of us; practically the whole crew is with us on this. Something's real wrong on the ship. We all know it."

Lieutenant Estrella looked around the gunnery room. He didn't see the young ensign. "Where is Mr. O'Donnell?"

There was a clang of an opening and closing hatchway and Ensign Hughes stepped into the crowded rifle turret. There was a sigh of relief from the sailors; their voice, their concerns could now be better organized and expressed. Two of the sailors stood and shook his hand and offered a pat on the back. He was a thin man with bright red hair that seemed ever more present in the dark quarters of number five gunnery mount.

"Sorry I'm late Lieutenant Estrella." He offered his hand. "Thanks for coming. The men have approached me to voice their concerns. We all know meetings like this carry serious consequences.

You and I talked earlier about the bizarre activities occurring on the *Eldridge*. Six men are dead and nine injured in pretty horrible ways."

"I'm here for a gun inspection," Lieutenant Estrella plainly offered. "I penciled it in a couple of days ago on the ship's activity log. Officially, that's why I'm here. Unofficially I'm here to hear you out, but be careful what you say," he warned. "You are on very thin ice."

"Ah, come on Mr. Estrella, there's not a man in this turret who doesn't know what we're about to discuss could be considered insubordination, maybe even mutinous." His voice strained with the tension of their potential actions. "You know like the rest of us, that fucked-up, deadly events have been happening, and it's not just the death machine in the lower level of this ship. The whole thing with the after steering repair, the shark attacks, the captain's approach to the whole thing was nuts."

The ensign walked the lieutenant through some of the events that had befallen the *Eldridge*. "This has taken a toll on us, that's the truth and you know it. Each day we all wake up and wonder if it will be our last. Just three days ago, Quartermaster Hillman just up and vanished. Some of his buddies think he jumped ship, all the deaths and injuries maybe just too much for him. He talked about the crazy dreams he was having and was convinced he was next on the list, or maybe he really was next on the list. Who the hell knows?" he shrugged.

USS *ELDRIDGE*

The nausea and dizziness became the signature side effects of their futuristic weapon. Extreme heat would radiate from the bowels of the ship, bulkheads would heat up to dangerous levels, and piping and conduits would drip with humidity. Men would burn their hands and forearms on partitions. Then crew members began to suffer gruesome injuries. Men appeared to melt, their physical forms no longer sharply defined, almost floating in the heavy air. They were pulled towards the center of the ship, sometimes moving down stairways, Jello-like in their form. Sometimes when confronted by a bulkhead or hatchway, they would merge into the barrier itself. There would be horrible screams from their pain. When the mechanism was de-activated, their bodies would solidify within those same barriers. Their screams of torture were horrific. Intestines and jagged bones would protrude at disturbing angles. Blood would splatter all about. The bodies of the dead and injured all with terrible burns.

Seaman Tirelli's severely charred left leg had to be cut away from the steel wall it was rooted in. All that witnessed it would never forget his agony, nor would they erase from their memories the sawing action of Doc Bellows as he worked with the carpenter saw. Several of his shipmates held Tirelli in place during the gruesome ordeal.

"How long is this going to go on, Mr. Estrella?" asked a be-wildered Ensign O'Donnell. "Why is the captain driving us so hard?" All the tired faces in the room searched, almost begged, for an answer from the lieutenant. He had always been their friend within the upper ranks. Always the officer that would make the difficult demands, share the awkward, sometimes sad news, but always with concern and caring.

He too had been slowly heading towards this same point as these men in this steel enclosure. Privately he had questioned his superior's decisions. He was indeed pushing the crew to excess. They were exhausted and emotionally fragile. Too many injuries, too many horrific deaths. The captain of the *Eldridge* had become a man possessed by his mission. His focus so intense he was extracting a terrible toll from his ship's company, and he was oblivious to all of it.

The enthusiasm shared by the crew of the USS *Eldridge* when it began its journey was gone. No longer was there a collective excitement of a brave new challenge with a weapon that possessed the capacity to bring a horrific war to a speedy conclusion. The brutal deaths and crippling injuries within a very close ship's company had reaped its ghastly toll. They were engaged in a global conflict. War-time casualties are to be expected, but the *Eldridge*'s wounds were self-inflicted. Engagements with German and Japanese ships of war had demonstrated that their weapon operated with horrific and lethal efficiency. Not a single deliberate round from an enemy vessel ever struck the *Eldridge*, but shipmates, close friends, were dying. It all seemed wrong; their captain's actions, his blindness to his own twisted acts were criminal even in this time of war. Service men hope to survive the rigors of war, now the crew of the *Eldridge* prayed they might survive their own captain's madness; their innovative lethal weapon simply an instrument of his psychosis.

Lieutenant Estrella searched the cramped gun turret. The faces of these exhausted men deserved an answer, they had sacrificed so much already.

"I know this has been tough; we've lost some good men, our friends, and I am at a loss to justify or attach any meaning to their deaths. The captain does appear to have become misguided in his actions. But where you or I go from this point is a treacherous path. Just meeting like this carries some very real risks. Even thoughts of mutiny can be treated harshly, because gentlemen, although no one in this turret has said it, the thought of mutiny has already crept into your heads."

The word had finally been spoken. It hung in the air, seemed to take on a new, more real presence. Ensign O'Donnell offered his insight. "Perhaps we should talk to the captain together, we could tell him of the men's concerns, their emotional state, so to speak."

"I don't think that's the way to approach this," he pondered, and he scratched his head in tortured thought. "No, I think I will talk to him privately, put it from a different perspective, maybe share some of my observations with him. Everybody here stays loose, don't do anything stupid." He turned to the grizzly petty officer, his stare piercing. "Mr. Bruno, this is not your first rodeo, be the calming influence I know you can be. Keep your men at ease. We'll get through this. I need to get back to my duty station before they start looking for me."

He shook their hands and exited the rear mount. He was leaving a weary, troubled collection of men and there was little he could do ease their concerns. He wanted to caution them more about the real dangers if they traveled the path to mutiny, but he already accepted its inevitability.

BREWSTER MORRISON

Just under a month later and the USS *Eldridge* is missing. Their top-secret vessel has suddenly disappeared somewhere in the South China Sea with two very important German theorists and their own American counterpart onboard. There was a lot of brain power on that vessel and losing it would be crippling to this priority one project and his career. The *Eldridge* had missed her last two radio check-ins. The president and the Pentagon were dialing up the heat.

Lt. Commander Morrison had watched the *Eldridge* fade into the eastern horizon when she steamed out from Philadelphia. He had done his job well; expectations had been met and even exceeded in some areas. Navy brass was grateful, even Roosevelt's special envoy stopped by personally to express the president's appreciation. Brewster was exhausted; rest and time with his wife and infant son were all he could think of.

Panicked petty officers from the shore patrol found Lt. Commander Morrison thigh deep in the Jersey shoreline surf, his casting rod working the nearby shoals. His wife stood nearby on their cottage front porch with their baby son in her arms, a suspicious look on her face. She knew their vacation was suddenly over.

Admiral Carlson quickly renewed their friendship and again his orders were crystal clear. "Find that God damn ship," and with that edict, the familiar, "You will have whatever resources you need."

Brewster had been reviewing the daily central Pacific reconnaissance reports since the *Eldridge's* disappearance. The gathered intelligence was disappointing. Two destroyers, four destroyer escorts, and one escort carrier were scouring the area surrounding the South China Sea and points north, the last known location of the *Eldridge*. There was no sign of her, no debris, no oil slick, and no bodies recovered. Earlier in the war, the US Navy had broken the Japanese code and earlier today enemy radio traffic revealed that a possible engagement with a US destroyer had occurred in that very area. Details were sketchy; the Japanese frigate had opened fire on the enemy ship and had possibly inflicted damage. The American vessel had never returned fire and had inexplicably disappeared into a nearby fog bank. Two American bodies along with some debris were recovered, but the seamen's bodies were void of any identification, which seemed quite puzzling to the enemy. The captain, as well as a junior officer of that ship, was quickly ordered to return to Tokyo Bay by seaplane. Apparently, they had more critical information worthy of analysis.

Morrison knew this had to be their missing ship. The *Eldridge* had last contacted Admiral Halsey's Pacific fleet on July 13th, her scheduled check-in. Indications were that they were beginning to experience problems with their shrouding device. The complications were deemed minor, they were still trying to assess the implications and would provide more details at their next scheduled check-in, two deaths and four injuries had been documented. Per directives no names were provided over the air. Brew wondered how two deaths and four injuries could be considered minor.

And now her last two scheduled check-ins were missed, naval command knew the implications. The *Eldridge* was missing. The navy had implemented strict guidelines to track her progress. Critical updates with validating data were deemed necessary for their mission to be allowed to move along. How far she traveled was irrelevant in respect to the results of her on going sea trials. Navy brass only wanted to hear that Project Rainbow was continuing to be a wartime success. Here and now, she had inexplicably disappeared. Naval command was unstable. An extensive search of her last known position had been directed. Planes and ships were scouring a 100,000 square mile area around her last known location. Their search efforts continued to be discouraging, no sightings, only empty ocean.

Lt. Commander Morrison was about to walk into an emergency briefing and would report that no additional intel had been secured, but that he had directed Halsey to commit three additional vessels to the search and rescue efforts.

Quickly rising from his barren desk, a young ensign in his crisp dress whites greeted him in the small outer office of the admiral's command.

"Good morning Lt. Commander Morrison; Admiral Carlson and Mr. Friedman from the State Department are waiting for you in the conference room." He nodded to two burly representatives from the shore patrol who stood at ease before two impressive oak doors. "Gentlemen, please show Lt. Commander Morrison to the conference room." One of the petty officers opened the heavy doors; the other led the way through a small waiting room and opened another set of identical hardwood doors. Admiral Robert Carlson and President Roosevelt's representative David Friedman were leaning over one end of the long conference room table and were reviewing a map of the south Pacific. Several junior officers stood nearby and were engaged in quiet conversation. The table was clustered with paperwork, coffee cups, carafes, and navy broad hats. Carlson again would be the hard ass, second guessing every move and thought involved in locating the *Eldridge*. Brewster should not expect anything less.

"Lt. Commander Morrison, please join us," Admiral Carlson said briskly, and waved him towards the meeting table with a right hand that held a cigarette about to burn two very nicotine stained fingers. The action now made him aware of the searing sensation in his fingertips. "Damn," he angrily stubbed out the cigarette in a nearby ashtray and began again. "Lt. Commander Morrison is the lead officer of a very ambitious program that if successful could change the tide of this shit-ass war—we are all hoping you have some good news about the *Eldridge*'s disappearance or perhaps a strategy for going forward. Gentlemen, let's have a seat and hear what Mr. Morrison has to say." They settled into the long table with Admiral Carlson at the far end seated in his cushioned Winchester.

The spotlight was on him, actually had been for some time. But now the light was a lot brighter and with it some added heat. Seeking relief, he loosened his collar and twisted his neck.

"I'm afraid I don't have much to offer," Lieutenant Commander Morrison shrugged his shoulders and lifted his hands out from his sides. "Search efforts have been unproductive. Prior to this meeting I requested Admiral Halsey to commit two additional destroyers and another escort carrier to their search and rescue efforts and to expand the search area based on ocean current and wind conditions."

"What do we have committed to air reconnaissance, the more planes we have up the better the results, I would think," offered a lieutenant commander fresh from his paper pushing, wide ass, wide chair assignment at the recently dedicated Pentagon building in D.C.

He wanted to challenge the suck-ass, *No! I assigned two carriers to the search area, but ordered them to keep all their aircraft on deck,* but he checked himself. "We've got as many planes in the air as possible, but remember we're looking at an area about half the size of Texas."

"However, we did gather some information from decoded Japanese radio traffic." Admiral Carlson was focused again. "It seems one of their ships, the destroyer *Natsugumo* we believe, was involved in a skirmish with an American vessel. We believe it was the *Eldridge.* The transmission alluded to an enemy vessel that could easily slip in and out of fogbanks and the *Natsugumo* recovered the bodies of two sailors with no identification, i.e. no dog tags. Which goes along with our directive on this classified mission. No personnel were to wear any dog tags. The ship itself had been stripped of its identification number."

"Two dead seamen recovered; this may sound morbid, but I hope they were indeed deceased. I would hate to imagine what the Japanese are doing to them right now if they're not," Admiral Carlson interjected and then added, "Captain Morrison, let's review what we know about the events leading up to the disappearance of the *Eldridge.* I also want to review the logs of the sea trials. We had six weeks of beta testing; most of it looked very promising. But when the *Eldridge* went online in the south Pacific, that all went to hell in a handbasket. What happened between the sea trials and arriving in the Philippine Sea? You had several weeks of information regarding where they were, how the testing was going, problems they were having. Maybe there is something there, something we're missing?"

"That's an awful lot to cover," Brewster answered bluntly, overwhelmed by the task. "Where do you want me to start? I really should have my team here to present the complete analysis."

"We can talk with your team later, but for now, let's go back to square one." Some frustration was showing. "Give us the condensed version. This table of officers is here to pick your brain, but it's not meant to be confrontational. We need to work together on this. Later we can get into the minutia. We have a very important ship that is missing and we will do whatever it takes to find it. Gentlemen, I am feeling a lot of heat from the top and I will not disappoint. If you got personal plans or commitments, forget about them. If your wife is about to deliver triplets or if your mother and her mother just died, I don't care. Your ass belongs to me right now, now Lt. Commander Morrison, one more time, let's start at the beginning."

SIMON

Five days later Simon was again hastily summoned to the shipyard. This time they approached him at work. The same burly seamen cleared it with his employer and allowed him to make a quick call to his wife and tell her of another abduction. It was the same quiet car ride to the shipyard, this time meeting only with Lt. Commander Morrison in his small, but spotless office.

"I'll make this quick Mr. Bouchard," Morrison offered. "Desperate times require desperate action. Admiral Carlson has ordered your conscription. You are now a highly valued advisor to the Pentagon as well as your friend in Rhode Island, Madame Alice, or whatever you call her. You need to reach out and tell her that her country needs her and you will do this ASAP. You will have all sorts of resources at your disposal. Your flight leaves Philadelphia for the naval air station in Quonset Point, RI tomorrow morning. Tomorrow evening you will be taken by PT boat to Prudence Island."

Simon jumped in at this point; his astonishment that Madame Alice would be brought into the fold was too much.

"You're involving Madame Alice in this bizarre mission," he blurted.

"You have boasted about her abilities, is there a more qualified person for this, although qualified is not my best word for this

142

scenario. You must convince her that her participation is critical and you must do it quickly. You're scheduled to fly out of Quonset at 1000 hours the following day. From there, you will travel to San Diego, California where a newly commissioned destroyer will be waiting for you."

Simon's correspondences with Madame Alice over the years told of her declining health, painful arthritis in her hips, lower back, and hands, and the recent conversation with her husband only reinforced her failing health. Her last letter communicated a loss of appetite, delicacies that had always intrigued her no longer had the same appeal, and a continuing sense of complete fatigue caused her to no longer attack each day with her usual vitality.

"You do know that she is an elderly woman that has serious health issues," Simon said, his voice confrontational. "Such a trip, with all its physical and emotional burdens could simply be too much for her. It could kill her. You recently spoke how it was her special intervention many years ago that allowed you to meet your wife. Is that at all a consideration on your end?"

"I am aware of the unique connection I now have with your friend. It's a special gift, I guess. Although, would it be any different if I jumped into a pond to save a drowning boy and that same boy went on to become a senator or president? Guess it would make me a celebrity, but it would have been something any one of us would have done. I'm not sure I would use that analogy with my wife and mother-in-law. To them it was far more spiritual, divine intervention as far as they're concerned. But the bottom line is we need you and Madame Alice's participation. Imagine if you find the *Eldridge*, what celebrities you'll be. You're in the navy now Mr. Bouchard and you've been given an order. No discussion is allowed here. That's how it works."

Lieutenant Commander Morrison could not allow his empathy for a woman that had intervened in his life in a single remarkable way affect his mission. Madame Alice had saved his mother-in-law's life many years ago and the years had not lessened his appreciation of that, nor had it lessened his wife's indebtedness for the deed that had secured her very existence and a life full of bounty. But he knew he could never share these feelings with Simon or Madame Alice, not right now at least.

Simon sat there stunned, frozen in his chair. He had lost his voice.

Brewster Morrison sensed he needed more clarification. "Mr. Bouchard, I have my orders. I know the demands I am making are not without hardship and it bothers me. I'm not heartless, but my feelings are of no consequence." His answer was plain. "And now you have the responsibility of your orders. Do your best to follow them. You should contact Madame Alice ASAP." Morrison's voice and stare reinforced his words.

"Calling her will do no good, she will see right through my charade. No, I will have to surprise her with my visit. I surprised her once before and it worked out rather well. What do they say: if it works don't fix it?"

"Oh, and one more thing," Lt. Commander Morrison added. "I will be going with you!"

MADAME ALICE

They came for her in the early morning night, when barriers are at their weakest, when pleas for help are the strongest, and they brought her back to their sad and broken ship. Chief Bruno, Lt. Estrella, and others, their bodies burned and disfigured, pulled her from a deep slumber. They gently lifted Madame Alice from her sleep and she floated softly above her own body as if on a tender breeze.

Instantly she was rushing across the Pacific, her senses heightened by skimming, almost touching, the white tipped waves so near. Her own dark shadow streaked across the waters at unimaginable speeds, as if attached to the first ray of light at sunrise. Madame Alice knew she traveled without form; her body still cushioned a universe away on her feathered bed. No physical form, only her senses alive as they had never been. The sights, the smells, even the taste of the salt air overwhelming.

In the distance she saw the *Eldridge*, low in the water, the ocean moving quickly along her flanks, a simple fog appeared to grasp her form and then released its grip. She faded in and out. But Madame Alice could see the destroyer was a brutally damaged ship. Along her outer skin, there were the scars of war. Twisted metal with blackened steel spotted her profile. Portions of her super structure were ravaged, the impressive forward housings for her 8-inch guns were a shamble, what metal housing and steel remained was severely burned and distorted. It was almost unrecognizable.

They waited for her in the shambles that was once their ship's pilot house, its windows shattered, sheet metal and debris scattered about. She stood among them; they wanted to tell their story and she would listen. It would be a painful narrative, perhaps the last one she would have to witness. A lifetime of tragedies had worn her down. An inner message told her it was time to move past the pain of so many others.

But for now, she would hear them out. Their story would need to be retold and with it a message loud and clear; never again create and then release such a potential monster on a world that could not defend itself. They carelessly probed an unknown dimension with little understanding of its science. Learned people so desperate for revenge had foolishly set themselves on fire and prayed that their enemy would die from the smoke they inhaled.

Madame Alice understood her heavy responsibility.

SIMON

At 0600 hours the wheels of Simon's Douglas C-47 Skytrain left the tarmac in Philadelphia. Military flights were always on time. He had hurriedly packed his bags and almost as quickly made love to Deborah and tried to dry her tears. It was a tender moment, probably an event that was occurring millions of times all over the world. War only guarantees that single moment you are in, it needs to be cherished.

This would be Simon's second visit to Prudence. The first one, a challenging exploit six years ago to help an old friend. A devastating hurricane had ravaged the Rhode Island coastline, killing hundreds of people and destroying thousands of properties. A Jamestown woman had her entire family taken from her. Her navy captain husband, two daughters, twin boys, and her sister visiting from Philadelphia, all horribly taken from her in that storm. Some of their deaths she witnessed as her sister, her youngest daughter, and one of her twin boys helplessly clutched to the roof of one of their outbuildings as it was torn away from its foundation. They floated briefly like a cork in a saltwater tempest, and then their bodies were swatted away by a towering wave like insects on a church picnic table. The rest of her family perished shortly before that, but she had been spared that horrifying visual.

A loyal and longtime household servant that had also survived the hurricane asked Simon to help provide comfort and closure for her traumatized friend and employer. Claudia St. Louis, the devoted servant, and Simon were friends from long ago.

She was convinced that spirits from some of her deceased family were reaching across a barrier that was never meant to be penetrated and interfering with this woman's desperate struggle to survive. Simon traveled by train to Rhode Island and spent several weeks with Claudia and her tortured friend. Their once stately household in Jamestown was now home to wandering souls, trapped between the two worlds of the living and the departed.

Try as he did, Simon could neither provide closing or relief. He only knew that a spiritual tension existed in this house and it was beyond his expertise. Finding an old dear friend, the only one that might provide the relief that was required, would be challenging. He had not seen his old colleague in over thirty years. Returning to New York City where the friendship had blossomed, he began his search.

In time his pursuit brought him back to Prudence Island, just two short miles across Narragansett Bay from the fractured household in Jamestown. An early morning visit, he had surprised his close friend Sarah, who now called herself Madame Alice. Simon told his sad tale of a close family destroyed by a hurricane and his futile attempts to help the only surviving member of that family, a wife, a mother, and a sister, cope with that loss. Her pain was suffocating.

Madame Alice's compassion and her obligation to help those in distress was something she could not ignore. Her dedication to her craft should be respected. She and Simon left the next day for Jamestown. In the end they helped this empty woman find closure for the souls of her wandering family and rekindle, if only minutely, her own will to go on.

Now, again, he was about to surprise her with a new challenge. He hoped the same drive, the same sense of obligation for tortured souls, and this time for her country, would once again secure her much needed help.

SIMON

gentle wind out of the northwest, and a clear, cloudless early August evening had delivered cool temperatures. The ride from the Quonset Naval Base, across and up Narragansett Bay, had been smooth and uneventful. Wartime conditions demanded the officers and crew of their PT boat man their stations. They wore their woolen pea coats and watchmen hats. Lt. Commander Morrison and Simon had remained on the open bridge and enjoyed the cool, dry winds,;it had been hot and humid the previous four days and the change was refreshing.

Madame Alice heard the roar of its supercharged diesels as it cruised up the Narragansett Bay. PT-231 with its plywood hull cut through the choppy waters of the bay's east passage. Patrol boats in the bay were not uncommon sights in the ongoing war; after all, Middletown, RI is one of the training sights for PT officers and crew. Sections of the bay were cordoned off for the practice firing of their torpedoes.

The PT boat was quickly throttling back its engines, briefly reversing its prop action in front of the seaside inn, its wake pushing forcefully against its stern. They tied the 94-foot craft to a water-piling in front of Madame Alice's and her husband Milton's inn. Flood lights were turned on and began to search the Prudence Island shoreline. Circular beams of piercing light soon found the quaint hotel and illuminated the front living room where Madame Alice calmly sat, her privacy invaded.

With raised hands she shielded her eyes from the intense brightness.

The searchlight now moved to the beachfront and she watched as a small skiff was lowered into the water. Two men were soon rowing their way to the shoreline in front of the hotel.

Simon Bouchard and Commander Morrison stepped from the skiff onto the shoreline. Two men engaged in a mission that had now connected them to an old woman for very different reasons. But make no mistake; both men knew that Madame Alice's participation was critical.

Shaped by the stories repeatedly told to him by his wife and mother-in-law, Brewster had formed his own image of this savant. He had heard the story a hundred times.

On a cool day in early April 1926, Madame Alice, or Miss Sarah as she was called back then, had entertained a troubled young lady, Brewster's future mother-in law. She was engaged to be married, but her true affections were for another boy. This other young suitor had stolen her heart and occupied her thoughts daily. They would steal away for their heated rendezvous, their lovemaking hasty and passionate, and then the young girl's tears would conclude their trysts. Her young lover would beg her to run away with him, they would begin their life together.

But her family had long approved of the young man she was betrothed too. The two families had welcomed the engagement and were excited about its potential. Wedding plans were extravagant; each side would spare no expense to make this the most memorable nuptial event. As the wedding day approached, the young bride could not tolerate the corner she had been backed into. She sought out Miss Sarah, the clairvoyant that so many believed in.

Madame Alice answered the frantic knocking at her front door. A young woman, agitated and almost in tears, pleaded with her to share her special insight. They sat at a nearby table and she listened to the young girl's tragic tale. Madame Alice needed no cards, no tea leaves for the advice she was about to share. "How do I stop this tidal wave that has become my wedding? So many people will be disappointed, feelings will be deeply hurt."

"Follow your heart, my dear," she offered with the confidence of a thousand mystics. "Go to your young man and tell him what he desperately wants to hear from you. Then go to the nearest justice of the peace and make your vows to each other. After that there is nothing they can do to you. It will all work out; life has a way of securing the right outcome for all of us. Sometimes it just takes a while."

The young lady jumped up from her chair and hugged Madame Alice. "Thank you, oh thank you so much."

The sensation was immediate. Holding the woman's wrists, Madame Alice took a step back and looked deeply into her troubled visitor's eyes.

"You are not well," she said, the words bold and deliberate, a dire warning. The young girl's touch had conveyed a sensation of disharmony within her. The hair at the back of Miss Sarah's neck stood on edge. "You should see a doctor and quickly, something is very wrong inside you."

Now a whole new feeling engulfed the young lady, a sudden dark mood moved across her face.

"How can you be so sure?" she stuttered.

"Young lady, that is a question I have been asked countless times. I can't tell you how I know, I don't even know myself, but you are sick. Something has been festering inside you for a long time."

The young woman left Madame Alice's home with a burden removed from her shoulders, but now replaced with another pressing concern. She indeed had not been feeling herself lately, she had lost some weight and there had been a lot of episodes in the bathroom that had been rather unpleasant. She had shaken them off due to the stress of this unwanted marriage that had been thrust upon her.

She went directly to the young man that had taken her heart and promised her love to him for the rest of their lives together. They went to the justice of the peace at the Portsmouth town hall and were married. Two weeks later, a tumor was removed from her colon. Had it gone unchecked, the doctor had assured her, "the outcome would have been quite serious,"

Madame Alice had saved the young woman's life and had secured the lives of those to come. A gesture, a ripple in time moving forward, nurturing a family tree.

Simon and Lt. Commander Morrison made their way from the beach and now sat in the hotel's living room. Nearby was the large franklin stove, its doors open and within it, an ample provision of seasoned oak sat ready for the first chilly October day. All the windows were shut and Madame Alice sat wrapped in a heavy shawl. A lone tiffany light fixture hung from the ceiling behind them and they cast long shadows along the floor.

Madame told her visitors they could make their own coffee and help themselves to the lemon tarts she made a few days ago, they should still be good.

The visitors, comfortable in their rockers, sipped at their coffee mugs and sampled the pastries. Simon was stunned with the paleness of his old friend; her eyes were sunken and the flesh around them dark and deeply wrinkled. Her hands were bony, void of any sinew, and the joints of her fingers swollen from chronic arthritis. Simon struggled to find the right words to say. "Sarah, you do not look good to me. I have been searching for a more gentle way to say that. I suppose there is no charming way to convey it. I'm very concerned, are you ill?"

"Simon, this is the second time you have surprised me with your visit," she said. "Not an easy thing to accomplish on this far removed little island. I know I look rather pale, Milton is always telling me that, but I can assure you I am not as unhealthy as you might think. Last time you surprised me; we were soon off on a strange mission to help a troubled woman on Jamestown. Something tells me that another strange task awaits us."

"As usual you have stolen my thunder," Simon replied. "I should never be amazed by the capacity of your gift. But I need to ask, where is Milton, the two of you are inseparable. I hope everything is OK."

"This time it's more common sense than any special abilities I might have," she answered sarcastically. "The navy did not send you on a PT boat with a young officer in tow to ask about my health. And as for my Milton, his older brother suddenly passed away, heart attack they think. He left for Connecticut yesterday."

This time Brewster Morrison entered the dialogue.

"I am very sorry for that, please express my condolences to your husband, but Madame Alice, if I could get to the point, your country needs you," he said, his statement clear and to the point. "We have a highly classified navy vessel that is missing and its location and recovery has become as critical to our war effort as anything you could possibly imagine. It—"

Madame Alice interrupted, reading the identifier on his fatigue shirt.

"Lt. Commander Morrison. I know a little about your missing ship, the USS *Eldridge*. Some very troubled souls have reached out to me. I am still trying to understand the ordeal that they have been forced to endure."

"Madame Alice," he gasped bewilderment in his voice, "how you know the name of a very confidential ship is beyond me. But Mr. Bouchard has warned me of your unique abilities."

Lieutenant Commander Morrison told Madame Alice of their bizarre connection. The mere mention of his mother-in-law's name brought Madame Alice back to a time when she lived in Portsmouth, RI and was called by her birth name Sarah Sheppard. A vivid memory of long ago quickly formed of a very anxious young woman desperately seeking her counsel. In the end, it was her intervention and advice that saved the confused young woman's life. She and other indebted patrons of this gifted savant went to great lengths to bestow a title on her. They began to call her Madame Alice. The name stuck and soon people from all over began to seek out Madame Alice for her insight.

Lt. Commander Morrison returned quickly to the reason they now sat in her living room. The navy had lost contact with their valued destroyer and the search efforts had turned up nothing.

"The *Eldridge* is involved in a highly classified mission; it carries a secret weapon in its hold. Its potential for concluding this war is rather substantial. We need your assistance in finding it. I can't begin to understand how you might help. I will leave that to you and Simon. But if you can help, please do." Again, the lieutenant commander was pointed with his words.

They talked more about the ship and its mission; Brew Morrison was purposely vague about the technology aboard that vessel. Continually reinforcing how important it was to find the missing ship and not let it fall into enemy hands or it could tip the balance of the war in favor of the Axis powers.

"Will you be going on this quest?" she asked of Simon.

Simon told of his conscription into the US Navy and its traumatic effect on his wife, but acknowledged that the more he learned of this brave ship, the more he knew that he could not turn his back on its crew or his country.

"Yes, I will. The spirits of two very troubled sailors have reached out to me," he added. "And others have contacted you. You and I both know the significance of such collective actions. I think this is beyond anything you and I have experienced."

"Then I shall go with you," she replied, her voice soft, committed. "I feel as compelled as you. I will leave in the morning with you."

Again, Simon could not ignore the pallor of his old friend. Sitting there wrapped in her heavy throw, she looked frail, her eyes lifeless and her cheekbones sharp with edges. Her hands were cold and lean when they greeted. She had the appearance of a corpse.

"Sarah, I will say it again, you do not look well. Going on this trip, I believe, is foolhardy. Do you understand how demanding this will be? I don't believe you do. If Milton were here, he would not allow you to leave."

"Simon, I haven't been the poster child for a country doctor's office for many years. When we ventured out years ago on a challenge in Jamestown, you had a similar assessment of my well-being then. I believe we persevered through that without any impact on my health. Am I wrong?"

Simon shrugged his shoulders; for the most part, her recollection was accurate. She had looked tired, again her complexion dull. The ordeal was draining, and they had gotten through it. All of it true.

"Perhaps, but that was years ago, and time is no friend to any of us. I am still troubled. I will not try to fool myself and as I said, if Milton was here, he would not allow you to leave."

"My husband and I have some rather lively talks about that very thing. He raised his objections and we weighed them, but in the end, I am committed. I would not be swayed by him and I will not be swayed by you. Do you think I could leave Milton without saying a word? Have him return from his brother's funeral and burial and find me gone, only a note left behind to console him? Come on Simon, you know me better than that."

"You're quite convincing, as usual." He smiled, stubbornly accepting the finality of her decision to leave with them in the morning. "Something awful has happened on the USS *Eldridge* and we are both needed to help find it. That's been made quite clear."

"Oh, it has, Simon. I have felt a strong attraction to this task. It compels me like no other. However, if Commander Morrison believes I am not fit, and if I am not invited, then I suppose I can't go with you." She turned to face the young navy officer.

Lt. Commander Morrison had purposely stayed away from the two sages' delicate conversation, letting the two of them work through their concerns. All the while reading the validity of their characters. This was still a bizarre approach to locating a missing, highly valuable destroyer. It would always be. Mute acceptance along with the encouragement from his wife and mother-in-law to believe in the ability of this remarkable woman was all he could muster.

"You will find no objection from me," he acquiesced. "Right now, the two of you are the only hope we have and we must begin our journey quickly, but Simon is right Madame Alice, this will be a very demanding trip. We are racing against time, hoping against hope. I will do whatever I can do to make this as comfortable as possible. I'll make sure you have your own quarters, give you as much privacy as I can; starting tomorrow, you will be the only woman among hundreds of men. But make no mistake, this will test you. This is a journey of thousands of miles. Bouncing through the skies from here to San Diego in a military plane and then a long voyage on a navy destroyer to the East China Sea, a very volatile ocean right now. All of it, every measured distance, a toll your body will not enjoy."

"Well then, that's settled," Madame Alice surmised. "It's getting late, we should get some rest, we have an early start tomorrow, right Commander?" She turned to her naval chaperon.

"We need to be in Quonset by 0800 hours. We will need an early rise."

"You gentlemen should stay here tonight; you can take the two rooms on the right." She pointed to a corridor just to the left of the living room.

"I will speak to my men in the boat about that, your bed will be far better than the hammock that waits for me there. Goodnight folks." He tipped his hat and left.

"I'm glad we're doing this together; I sensed it would give us the best chance of bringing closure to something terrible. Just hope you're being honest about your health." He hugged his good friend, again feeling the coolness and frailty of her, and said good night.

"Perhaps this will be our final curtain call, so to say," she answered. "No other challenge speaks to me like this one. Good night Simon."

"I see you can't sleep either," Simon said. He had tossed and turned in his bed, consumed with the guilt of dragging his fragile friend into a difficult quest. Seeking the comforting seaside view of the east passage of the bay, he walked to the hotel's living room. Madame Alice was still there sitting in her rocking chair.

A bright full hay moon teased the water in front of the hotel. The navy torpedo boat tethered to its stay floated softly, the moonlight dancing along its dark gray top side.

Madame Alice raised her left arm and pointed down towards the shoreline. "We have visitors."

Staring down from the row of double hung windows that faced the near shoreline they saw the two spectral visitors from Philadelphia. Petty Officer Bruno and his seaman apprentice now paced the beach before him. Their burned, disfigured bodies awkwardly moving along the shifting soft sand. They dragged their feet as if huge weights were attached, each step a test of will.

Standing still in the foreground was the young lieutenant, the visitor to Madame Alice's world. His body charred like his shipmates. Two white eyes, a disturbing contrast to his blackened face, stared intently up at the inn, as if knowing that the two people within had decided to help them. He stood as before on his one sturdy leg, a jagged stick in his right hand, his support for a leg of that same side that was grotesquely missing from the knee down. He nodded his head and slowly extended his left arm forward, the palm of his hand vertical, perhaps a gesture of recognition and thanks.

The trio turned to the water's edge and began a slow walk into the rippling tide and towards the navy craft, their progress slow and painful to watch. Each step sank them deeper into the bay until only their blackened skulls remained above the surface and then a scream of pain and terror pierced the night. It echoed across the bay, no doubt bouncing along the opposite shoreline, and then just before reaching the hull of the PT boat they slipped below the waves and vanished.

Simon and Madame Alice watched as lights came on aboard the patrol boat and there was a scramble of men who began to search the sea around their boat with searchlights. It was obvious they had been jolted awake by the screams of tortured comrades.

Brewster Morrison came running into the living room, frightened and his guard up. "My God, what was that, is someone in trouble? It sounded like people screaming for help, I think."

Madame Alice answered calmly, "It was."

BOOK II

NATSUGUMO

"I have radar contact, bearing 285 degrees, 12 miles," Ensign Tanaka confidently informed the senior bridge officer, paused, and removed his head piece. "I think this is our American."

It was the same unique image as before; it began as an indistinct reflection on his radar display. Then its form began to lose its characteristics until disappearing completely from his display. This time, before vanishing from his screen, Tanaka detected a significant decrease in the enemy vessel's forward speed. It had happened in their previous confrontation but he had failed to make any sense of it.

The general quarters alarm was sounded and within minutes the *Natsugumo* was battle ready.

"Captain, just before they disappeared from my screen, I detected a dramatic decrease in their speed. The same thing happened in our last encounter. I just didn't connect it to anything. My guess is that when they engage whatever it is that gives them this special ability, it creates a tremendous load on their engines. Might explain some of the cavitation I've been picking up on sonar."

Tanaka knew the phantom destroyer was now bearing down on them. Within short minutes its full arsenal would open up on them and destroy his ship. They steamed on towards certain disaster.

161

"Captain we need to come about immediately." The words and his thoughts were coming together instantly. "We can easily out run this enemy ship; I believe its speed is reduced by half when they prepare for attack. If we don't do this now, Captain, we will suffer the same fate as the *Myoko*."

With his binoculars searching the distant horizon, Captain Saito lowered his field glasses and turned to his young radar technician. He had gotten to know the junior officer during their hurried trip to Tokyo, he recognized the young officer had a sharp mind and was accomplished at his craft. He studied him intently.

"Hard over to port, bring us about, all engines full ahead, begin evasive maneuvering," he shouted. "Good work Ensign Tanaka, perhaps we will live to fight another day."

USS *ELDRIDGE*

Carrying all the necessities for a shoreline picnic in their wicker basket, Milton and Vivian Van Noy hiked the secluded Koko trail on Honolulu to their sheltered spot on Halona Cove. They had spread their blanket, shed their clothing, and allowed the tropic elements to caress their nakedness. They made love, then swam in the vibrant blue waters and made love again. Vivian was five months pregnant and they talked of the happy days that lay ahead. They had decided on their baby's name, Max if a boy, Courtney if a girl. They savored their wrapped fried chicken, crackers, cheese, and fresh pineapple and mango. Their senses were alive with the magic of the tropics and the chemistry of their passion. Like two powerful lode stones they were pulled to each other. Lying on her stomach, her long brown hair, wet from her swim, lay across her shoulders. He leaned in and kissed the back of her neck. A soft purr escaped from her lips. His hands explored every inch of her form. The sharpness of her shoulder blades, the small of her back, the pliable firmness of her backside, down her tanned thighs. She opened her legs, barely realizing she had. Passion, harmony, and raw sexual attraction had taken control of her being. His fingers explored her intimacy and pushed her towards a precipice. She raised her buttocks and offered herself. He could have what he wanted and he desired all of her. He entered her, his hardness

163

and her dampness an erotic match. Deep, primitive throaty groans escaped from them both. Carnal desire took control, his thrusts were deep and forceful and she attacked his penetration with her own primeval appetite for more. With their moans and shortness of breath pushing them higher, they climaxed together. Collapsing on top of her and then regaining his strength, he rolled away from her then they turned to each other and fell asleep in each other's arms.

Short hours later, lying on the beach, head propped up by his right arm, he watched his young wife step away from the Pacific surf. Her abdomen slightly extended, her breasts swollen and nipples flushed. He wondered if it was possible to love someone any more than he worshipped this beautiful woman before him.

She stood before him, fresh ocean saltiness dripping from her naked form, sparkling in the waning sun. Like a Greek goddess, she had stolen his breath. Retrieving his air, he felt his loins pulse once more.

She leaned in and kissed his forehead. Her lips still wet with ocean. "We have radar contact," she said. Her words were a deep baritone, nor did they match the movements of her lips. What was happening? Her long beautiful hair retracting or falling away. Something terrible had suddenly invaded their moment and threatened their bliss. She grabbed his shoulders and shook him forcefully. "Captain, we have radar contact," she said again and then suddenly she was gone. His sadness suffocating and his fright crippling.

Lt. Estrella stood over him, his hands jostling him awake. "Captain, you are needed on the bridge. We have radar contact."

Stolen from his single love and only happiness, Captain Van Noy raised himself from his bunk. Revenge and anger were now his new affinity; oh they would pay for what they had done.

He donned his battle jacket and helmet and headed for the control room. Van Noy burst into the bridge, his sudden presence startling a weary crew. He grabbed the overhead mic.

"Whatta you got Petty Officer Hanes?"

"Captain Van Noy I have radar contact at 135 degrees, range about 12 miles."

Sensing there was more to Seaman Hanes's report he probed, "Tell me what else you got, Hanesy."

"My guess a destroyer, Captain. Might even be the Jap that took out our radio room. You know, the one that turned tail."

"Oh, this just made my day." A soft nod of his head and the same perverse smile as before. *Well I suppose it's payback time again. Thanks Mr. Hanes.*

He replaced the mic, turned to his bridge personnel, and raised his voice.

"Gentlemen, let's go to general quarters. Notify the Rainbow Room to come on line ASAP and to notify us when so."

All those in the bridge cringed, their stomachs turning sour when the directive to the Rainbow Room was given. Quietly, over the last few days, among the ship's company, a clear consensus had been reached; there was no clear victor in their past engagements, nor would there ever be in future ones. Hell was about to visit the USS *Eldridge* again.

Within minutes they were at battle stations. Now, awaiting confirmation from the secretive room in the bowels of his ship, Van Noy paced anxiously back and forth in the bridge room. They had all felt the sudden decrease in their speed, an indication that power had been diverted from the ship's drive to their high-tech weapon. The strain on the ship was obvious.

The captain stepped up to the communication panel, flipped a switch, and grabbed the microphone. "Ensign Williams, I need an update now!" he bellowed.

"We've had…had some problems, sir," the ensign answered, his voice choked with tension.

"What kind of problems—never mind put Professor Mueller on."

The next voice was the professor's. "Captain, our sea water pumps are not providing sufficient cooling. We almost experienced a thermal runaway; believe me you do not want that. It has been quite severe down here. We have injuries."

"Captain, our Jap has just gone over hard to port." The radar technician's update, annoying and a distraction to Van Noy. The tech continued with his finding. "He's turned tail again, making a run for it. I got him at about 35 knots. He'll be long gone in a short time."

Four rounds from what must have been the Japanese destroyer exploded all around the *Eldridge*. Fortunately, none of the incoming strikes found their ship.

Van Noy was furious with his radar tech's update. Their enemy was getting away. "Lt. Estrella, secure from battle stations," he hollered with frustration. "But stay on the nip's tail, when our device is disengaged, I want us at full speed."

He turned to his second in command. "Commander, I want a conference in the wardroom at 0600 tomorrow morning, have our scientists in attendance, I want engineering and the weapons officer there as well. Notify our corps men of possible injuries below decks. I have a brief meeting with Doc and Lt. Robinson in one hour in the wardroom. No doubt he will have a grim update on our injuries." He stormed out of the control room.

MADAME ALICE

AND SIMON

Their Gromman A-40 left promptly at 0900 hours from the Quonset Naval Air Station. The return trip from Prudence in the PT boat had been a little bouncy. The breeze had picked up out of the northwest and had challenged Simon's equilibrium, his stomach always on the edge of giving up its contents.

In her earlier years, a life now foreign to her, Madame Alice had often traveled the Fall River Line steamers between Newport, RI and New York City with her father and later her first husband. She had witnessed firsthand the effect that rolling seas can have on passengers and wondered how Simon would deal with the roiling waters of the Pacific. She saw no need to warn of the delirium that awaited him, she only hoped his adjustment would be speedy and his discomfort minimal.

They flew long hours, stopping only for refueling, rest, and bathroom breaks. The army had tried their best to make the flight as comfortable as possible. In an effort to soften the bolted in place steel and canvas wrapped seats, pillows, blankets, and comforters were in ample supply. With only two attending ensigns, the three travelers had the large plane to themselves. Short walks within the plane were possible, but not encouraged. Sturdy cots were set up behind temporary dividers for privacy. Madame Alice appeared to take the ordeal in stride, never complaining, always forgiving of the numerous apologies given for perceived inconsiderate gestures. The navy was simply unprepared on how to accommodate an elderly woman for a ten-thousand-mile journey, her frail appearance only amplifying their guilt. Madame Alice did, however, comment that she looked forward to the shifting seas of the Pacific. The rocking motion of the ocean had always been calming to her.

Worrying about his frail friend, Simon was constantly doting over Madame Alice, even insisting the flight crew give up on the concept of flying through the night. He reminded them of their precious cargo and they should treat it as such. Lt. Commander Morrison gave in and they located a small military airstrip in Waco, Texas. They touched down and after a hearty meal and a hot bath, the weary travelers headed for the cots in a small unused barracks building. Contributing little to their conversation and confiding in her fatigue, Madame Alice gathered specks of their evening meal into a cotton napkin and retreated to her room. She asked Simon to walk with her. A single cot with a folded blanket and pillow at one end was all the room offered. Several cautious steps brought her to the edge of the bed and she gently lowered herself.

"Simon, please have a seat." She patted the bed next to her. "We need to discuss something."

"Of course, what's on your mind?" he queried, his curiosity piqued. He sat next to her, like old friends on a park bench.

"Simon, you have to stop this incessant doting over me. It's becoming a distraction to me and an irritant to the others. Please stop it."

"I will try, but it won't be easy." He knew he had been a pest in trying to see to her every need. Her poor health, her frail look, and his guilt gave him no choice. "I'm sorry, I feel so responsible for where we are and for what potentially lies ahead."

"Please don't apologize; I'm a grown woman, capable of making my own decisions. Enough of this, now tell me about this new woman in your life, Deborah, right? You have talked very little of her. I want to know all about her. You and I were lucky, both finding someone new to travel through life with. Second chances don't usually present themselves so favorably. My Milton allowed me to thrive again. Deborah has done the same for you, hasn't she?"

"Sarah, you have always had the ability to connect with my thoughts and dreams, it's what defines our friendship. It's so odd, just last night I had a very vivid dream of her. Deborah was there on a nearby hill full of tall shifting grass, a rich blue sky around her. A breeze teased her hair, she pulled the hair from eyes as she waved to me and brought her fingers to her lips and floated a kiss to where I stood. It was a beautiful dream. Before I left on this journey, a long one we both knew, she told me that whenever I get lonely to think of her. Thing is I don't need to feel lonely for that, she's in my thoughts all the time."

He missed his wife dearly; Deborah had saved him, she was his rock. Losing his first wife to the Spanish flu in 1919 left him lonely and cautious. Sitting next to Madame Alice on a weathered old army cot, he would tell her his love story.

A new bakery, Covalesski's, had opened up not too far from Simon's apartment in the west end of Philadelphia. Simon loved the Polish *szarlotka* they made and frequented the shop. Deborah Covalesski, the owner's daughter-in-law, worked the counter and sometimes in the kitchen. She was a pleasingly stout woman with long, dark, wavy hair. Her piercing blue eyes offset her pale complexion and pulled Simon in.

A fiercely independent woman, she had lost her husband when some staging collapsed in the naval shipyard, sending the foreman and two other workers to their deaths. Moving in with her in-laws, she raised their only daughter by herself. Other relationships never seem to offer themselves; she believed her steadfast independence may have intimidated a lot of men. But she saw something different in Simon; her unconventional outlook on life did not intimidate him, it only represented strength and commitment to him. Small chats about the shop's assortment of tasty treats and special ingredients soon evolved into lengthy conversations about politics and philosophies of life. Having both lost their spouses to tragedy they soon found they had a lot in common, including the fear of another loving relationship. Only a deep hurt can cause a lasting dread like that. Where once before only the bewitching brown eyes of his first love Olivia could reach his soul, now the shining blue of Deborah's gaze began to touch him deep inside and he was alive again.

They were moving closer to a secure and lasting bond. A simple stone mounted on a gold band now concealed in his jacket's inner pocket would be his gesture of a lifelong pledge. But first there would be that awkward moment when Simon would share his unique ability and mystic past with Deborah.

They had rented a cottage at the Jersey shoreline in Point Pleasant. And now they walked that beachfront on a late afternoon. There was a stiff on shore breeze, almost tropical in its feel. Their bare feet kicked up the wet sand and a thin layer of ocean, leaving their footprints imbedded in the gray silt behind them. Simon told her of his gift, when it had started and where it had taken him. The bizarre interactions with those that had passed on, the relief and sometimes uncomfortable gratitude from those that he had helped. He told Deborah of his desperate trip to Jamestown, Rhode Island so he might help an old friend, and of its strange conclusion.

Her reaction was calm and reflective. It was a lot to take in. She told Simon she would need time to think it through. They continued their days in the sun. Simon saw no sudden change in her mood, always taking his hand when he reached for hers, their love making continually alive with passion. Sitting on the beach in their weathered Adirondack chairs, the summer sun retreating serenely behind them. It was their last night at the seaside cottage. Simon reached into the inside pocket of his windbreaker, retrieved the ring, and asked a question he had inquired only once before and never thought he'd ask again. He wanted to share the rest of his life with this remarkable woman. Deborah was stunned, she too had shared her deep thoughts and secrets with another and believed she had already used up her one chance at happiness, but now a new man had entered her life and she was waking each day overflowing with energy and optimism.

"Yes, I will marry you!" She clutched his hands between hers and pressed in on his searching expression, her blue eyes once again linking up with his depth. "I think I will have to adjust to some things when this strange part of who you are shows itself, but you are a very decent man. That has been quite clear from the day I met you. I can only see good intentions at the root of anything you do. I love you Simon Bouchard."

It was Simon's love story; everyone should have one. It all just tenderly fell into place, each conversation, each interaction building a bridge to something special.

"Simon, you are indeed a lucky man," Madame Alice offered when his tale was complete. "She sounds like a remarkable woman. I am glad you found her and her, you."

"Yes, I am." His thoughts were warm, his spirit at ease.

"Let's get some sleep," Madame Alice said, her eyes tired, nearly closed. "And remember, no doting on me."

Simon stood, hugged his old friend. "Goodnight," he said, and left the room, thinking only how frail and lifeless she felt in his embrace.

The next morning, an early rise and another grueling ten hours of flying. They finally touched down in San Diego in the early twilight. An anxious assembly of navy brass stood on the tarmac awaiting their arrival. Military greetings were offered and handshakes exchanged. They were soon speeding along connecting roads in open air jeeps. The cool early evening air rushing by, refreshing the tired pilgrims.

A newly christened destroyer, the USS *Reno,* a brief ten-minute drive away waited for them at her slip. Her crew was alerted to their arrival and were at their stations. Her engines were engaged and her stacks billowed with smoke. A shiny new superstructure with all the latest radar and electronic devices, attached to stanchions high above, was impressive. All in their striking dress whites, the captain and his supporting staff were waiting at the causeway. After introductions were made and pleasantries exchanged, Captain Joseph T. Bains, commanding officer of the *Reno,* welcomed his eclectic collection of passengers aboard and quickly reminded them they needed to be underway.

"Madame Alice, Lt. Commander Winslow and Lt. Poe have graciously given up their quarters for your convenience, you should be quite comfortable."

The officers tipped their hats and she thanked him for their kindness.

Captain Bains then addressed his second in command. "Mr. Winslow, cast off all lines, prepare the ship for sea. Let's get underway."

Madame Alice and Simon were escorted to their quarters. They were informed that a late dinner would be served at 2000 hours in the wardroom. More revealing discussions about the missing USS *Eldridge* would be shared and hopefully insight from Madame Alice and Simon might aid in its location. Finding the *Eldridge* and rescuing and returning all of its crew plagued the two sages.

NATSUGUMO

Ensign Tanaka had theorized a tactic that might change the odds or at least give them a fighting chance against the American ghost ship. He would propose his ploy at the captain's morning briefing.

"Captain, I think we may have a way to engage this American destroyer."

"Please explain, Ensign Tanaka."

"It seems that whenever this phantom ship engages its special device, it creates a tremendous power drain. Their speed is reduced by at least half. Twice now I have seen them transition from 32 knots to 13, 14 knots and the change is quick."

A senior officer inquired, "Is there anything to indicate that this destroyer can't resume flank speed once they've transitioned to whatever it is they do? How do you know what's really going on? We can't detect them with radar and we can't put any eyes on them."

"No, I don't think that's the case," Tanaka offered. "I am convinced that once they engage their device, their forward speed is very compromised. Twice now, we have broken off from our engagement and they have not pursued us. I can think of only one reason why, it's because they can't."

Captain Saito stared at his young ensign and then at the other officers seated before him. He saw only blank faces void of any alternative approach to their dilemma.

"All right Mr. Tanaka, guess we need to hear your strategy."

"Very well." The young radar officer leaned forward in his chair, placing his folded hands in front of him. "Gentlemen, I believe our radar capabilities are equal to or even slightly better than the American ship. The last few times I have located our enemy, it seems he detects our presence short minutes afterwards, sometimes less. That is when I see his speed significantly reduced. The image on my screen begins to fade in and out for maybe thirty seconds to a minute and then he's gone, and as you know we have no visual either. He's become a ghost. But for those last brief seconds or more I can still track him. I know his speed and course."

He looked around the room, he had everyone's attention, he had suddenly given them hope.

He looked directly at Captain Saito. "We need to be at battle stations or some elevated state of readiness at all times. I'll leave that up to you. But our window is small, quite small. When I make radar contact with the American, we will not have time to go to general quarters; he'll be long gone by then. We can't hesitate with our actions."

Lt. Commander Tahito, the number two exec, entered the strategy planning. "And what would those actions be?" he asked.

"I believe we should quickly open fire on those last known coordinates, perhaps even a few rounds ahead of the American, but several shots clustered together. Then we reverse our course, move away at flank speed. Again, with his reduced speed, we can easily outrun him. But if we can get lucky, put a shell or two into him, we just might change the odds in our favor, at least even them."

"Well done, Ensign Tanaka you should hold your head high," Captain Saito replied, once again impressed with the focus of his junior officer. "Your emperor will be pleased." He turned to his other subordinates. "Gentlemen, I want a plan prepared for my review in four hours. This ship must be in a state of battle readiness at all times. No doubt this will create other issues and will be tough on the crew. Gentlemen, I will leave, you have much to do. Make it so."

USS *RENO*

Calm waters and two days of much need rest allowed Simon to re-focus on their task. Madam Alice still wore her alabaster mask of complete fatigue, yet never complained of it. They sat in the cramped confines of the officer's mess. Simon had devoured his hearty breakfast of scrambled eggs, bacon, and toast. Madame Alice, like a frail chickadee, only picked at her morning brunch. They sipped their coffee.

Captain Bains and Lt. Commander Morrison entered the dining area, took mugs from the rack, filled them with black coffee, and joined them at their table.

"Lt. Commander Morrison, it seems as if our guests have no issue with rolling seas," Captain Bains offered with the reassuring smile of a salesman. "Two days out from San Diego and none of the issues that typically plague most navy tenderfoots. Good for you."

"Hearty old salts, the both of them," Brewster Morrison replied. "Mind if the captain and I join you?"

"Please do," Simon replied. Madame Alice nodded her head and extended her hand towards the seat next to her.

There was an awkward silence and then Captain Bains pressed ahead.

"We are about to enter some very dangerous waters, although all the world's oceans hold that potential right now." He continued on. "In two days, we will hook up with a resupply ship two hundred miles out from Pearl Harbor. Navy brass does not want this ship visible to anyone. We do not exist. Once we resupply, refuel, and get underway again, things could get very risky. The Japanese have employed a new desperate tactic. They are training pilots to steer their planes directly into American ships, a suicide mission, call themselves kamikazes. Effective and deadly."

The breadth and danger of their mission suddenly sunk in on the two clairvoyants.

Captain Bains offered his civilian guests some advice. "Stay close to your quarters and pay attention to all the updates that get put through our P.A.. system. We should have plenty of heads up if the situation becomes critical. We will do our best to keep you safe and out of harm's way. I have been instructed to offer all courtesy and consideration to the both of you. Admiral Carlson was very emphatic on this. For reasons he does not quite understand, nor do I, your participation in this search and rescue effort has been deemed critical. But I will tell you Madame Alice, I am a skeptic, I should ask you to tell me how this gift of yours is going to work, because quite frankly I am clueless. However, I will leave that responsibility to the lieutenant commander. He will keep me informed. If you will excuse me, I have a meeting with some of my officers." He stood, tipped his hat, and left.

"Captain Bains is a good man," Brew Morrison informed them. "He is extremely skeptical about this mission. You shouldn't judge him too harshly. It's only because of my mother-in-law's interaction with you, Madame Alice, that I've been given some insight, but to be honest there are just a few degrees of separation between the captain's and my own cynicism. Sometimes believing in something that has little substance is just too difficult for people. Guess that's what makes faith and religion so challenging. Can't have one without the other."

"Oh, I understand his cynicism, even accept it. But what you have to understand Mr. Morrison, there is no set procedure to follow, no scientific formula involved."

Madame Alice joined the conversation, her voice dry, mechanical. "We cannot predict what the outcome will look like. We cannot even be sure there will be an outcome. Perhaps no one from *Eldridge* will reach out to us. I don't think that will be the case. I believe there will be more contact with these unfortunate servicemen, but I cannot promise that."

"I suppose that's not a very encouraging position. Must be difficult to remain upbeat. But then you have your faith, right. Should I use that word?"

So many times, over the years she had faced this same dilemma. People wanted to believe that a mystic hand reached out from another galaxy and enlightened her soul or that cryptic revelations hidden in the night time constellations, discernible only to Madame Alice, had given her deity-like insight into the workings of the universe. No, it wasn't anything as complex as that, it was a simple unpretentious ability bestowed upon her without warning and without her consent.

"Mr. Morrison, you can call it faith," Madame Alice replied. "But you may be complicating the process. I have been given this ability, why, I simply do not know. It often tells me more than I want to know, such as this mission we find ourselves in. I am well aware of the urgency behind it. Both Simon and I have witnessed its growth. We will help you in any way we can."

The lieutenant commander scratched his head. "I'm not sure if you clarified anything for me, guess I'll just continue to believe there will be an outcome. I hope it won't be as bleak as you predict."

"Every day I wake up with my own version of astonishment," Madame Alice said, "and I suppose Simon does too." She looked at Simon and he offered a simple nod and a soft blink of his eyes. "We never know who or what mystic event will invade our lives."

Brewster Morrison looked directly at Madame Alice, his voice steady. "I am a very practical man. I am not the cynic that Captain Bains is, but I must admit this whole effort tests my values and intellect. I wake each day and wonder where this adventure will take me. I'm supposed to believe in something completely unbelievable. It's like the three of us are standing on a cliff and you tell me we suddenly all have the ability to fly, just take a step off and flap your arms. I don't think so; you go first and prove it to me."

"Mr. Morrison, let me tell you a story, it might relieve some of your concerns and shed some light on my abilities and who I am."

Madame Alice began a tale of when she stilled lived in the U.K. "I lived the first sixteen years of my life in Nottingham, England. I was a small child when my strange ability began to surface. Relatives, friends, and strangers began to seek me out for my singular insight. As it became more profound, it caused me a great deal of anguish and unnerved my parents. My father owned a lace mill there, but was committed to relocating his business to New England in the US Now with the added inconvenience of people unexpectedly showing up on our door step desperately looking for my counsel, the move to America seemed the right thing to do.

"Several months before our departure date for the US, I was approached on the street by a young couple. My older brother and I were heading to my father's business. It was not far from our home. I found out later that they had followed us from our house. They immediately launched into a story of how their father had suddenly passed away without revealing to a single soul where he had secured a great deal of the family assets. Their father had amassed a great deal of wealth from his manufacturing business, but was not trusting of the local banks, supposedly harboring large amounts gold, silver, and currency in obscure and secretive locations. The family found this out only when they went to claim their assets. They were stunned when banking officials told them there were very limited funds available once they cleared probate. They were now close to being destitute. Properties and assets were being sold off or repossessed. They had heard of my gift and begged for my intervention.

"My brother stepped in to protect his little sister. Episodes of being confronted on the streets by frantic people were occurring more and more and they began to frighten and overwhelm me; mind you I was just sixteen, probably a little younger at this time. My brother told the intruders they should leave before he called a constable. They left quite begrudgingly, but I would see them often in the next few weeks, on the streets or public squares. Sometimes they would approach me and begin their tragic narrative all over again. Lack of personal hygiene and tattered clothing only reinforced their claims of poverty. They seemed to be truly destitute. I finally gave in to their pleadings and I sat with them on a park bench near the center of town. I had my younger sister with me and she thought the scene quite entertaining.

"Remember I was just a young girl and wondered how they could be so convinced that I could help them, and I asked them exactly that.

"Surprisingly the couple admitted they were indeed not convinced my assistance would even be productive, but were anxious for any insight into where their father had squirreled away their very livelihood. My ability had developed its own traction; in fact much of what I had done had been embellished and had only added to its legend. If I could help them locate these missing funds, they were prepared to compensate me quite handsomely.

"They told me more of their background and family history. Priscilla and Horatio Cummings were their names. They had been a happy family, quite content in their existence. Their mother had passed away from consumption a number of years ago and that was when their father's behavior suddenly changed. He loved his wife and their mother quite deeply and missed her terribly. He began to turn inward and his trust in people and institutions quickly unraveled. His mood dark and disturbing, they became concerned for his physical and emotional wellbeing. He dismissed their pleadings to see a physician. Less than a month later, a servant found him hanging from a crossbeam in the basement.

"I was touched by their tale and agreed to help in whatever way I could. This was a whole new dimension to my gift, but knew I must help; what was the purpose of this insight if I could not help, especially those in need.

"They asked if I could visit with them this coming Saturday. The whole concept of gathering as a group in an effort to contact the dead frightened me. I struggled with the reality of it all. Was I becoming a charlatan, offering services that most thought were despicable? Taking advantage of people in their weakest times was not a dimension that I wanted added to my identity. Yet something inside me drew me closer to this couple. I felt compelled to visit their home on Manchester Street on the west side.

"Looking back on it now, it was a very daring move for me, a young girl just barely sixteen, to do by herself.

"I arrived at just after noon on a Saturday in early June, an unusually hot and humid day. The weather was very unstable with all the moisture. There would no doubt be thunderstorms later in the day.

"The house was impressive in its size, but detracting in its condition. Doors, windows, and trim were in desperate need of a scraping and painting. Glass portals were coated with years of industrial soot. It gave the exterior of the home a smoky, unhealthy look.

"I knocked gingerly on the front door and was quickly received by Priscilla. She was dressed in the same clothes as when I met them in the town square. I wondered if it was the only fashion she owned.

"'Please come in Miss Sheppard,' she offered, and showed me to the living room. I could tell by her awkwardness it was a responsibility rarely assigned to her. Servants did these types of things.

"'Horatio, Miss Sheppard has arrived,' she yelled towards the other end of the house. She turned back to me, her hands clasped together at her bosom. 'Will you have tea?'

"I nodded my head. 'Please.'

"'Bring some tea.' It sounded more like a command than a request, and then added, 'Please dear,' in an attempt to soften its harshness.

"We walked a long hallway that was dusty with neglect, but marked with the shoe prints of a thousand steps. The long corridor offered entry to numerous rooms, large fireplaced living rooms, parlors, library, and dining area. Most of the furniture had been removed from these rooms, with stained sheets covering the few items remaining. Our shoes echoed off the empty walls and high ceilings. Wiring from now missing chandeliers hung loosely from their ornate escutcheons. Supporting hardware was all that remained of the many paintings that must have adorned this stately home. Elegant furniture, tiffany fixtures and priceless artwork, all of it probably liquidated to sustain their accustomed lifestyle.

"We arrived at a grand entryway, its huge double doors pulled back and open. A tall, imposing south-facing window flooded the gathering room with bright sunlight. Numerous portraits of past family members in grand fashion still spotted the high walls, probably the only remaining artwork of the once stately home. Near the window, four Queen Air chairs offered their comfort while also highlighting the emptiness of the once grand ballroom.

"'Please have a seat,' Priscilla said, and extended her hand towards the chairs. 'Horatio should be here shortly with tea.'

"I was about to take a seat when I heard what sounded like muted groans. I turned towards the source of these bizarre sounds; in the shadows of a massive stone fireplace was a middle-aged man awkwardly seated in a wheelchair. His face was contorted with his mouth twisted open at one side. Several teeth were missing and those that remained were large and heavily stained. It was obvious the man was mentally compromised.

"'Oh! Of course, Howard, you want to be introduced to our guest,' Priscilla said, sarcasm and irritation in her voice. She turned to me and offered with no attempt to shield her words, 'Howard is rather simple, we're not sure if he really comprehends much,' her words painful even to me. Howard's grunts seemed to escalate.

"'This is my brother,' Priscilla said, and went directly to him. Grabbing the back of the wheelchair, she forcefully spun him around and was quickly back in the bright sunlight, its piercing rays illuminating a frail and unhealthy man. As if in pain, he recoiled, his arms against his chest and head, twisted hands and curled fingers tried to shield his eyes from the penetrating glare.

"Unable to witness this cruelty, I instinctively stood between the window and this poor soul. Howard's relief was immediate, his moans softened and I sensed the look from behind his crooked digits communicated gratefulness.

"'You should thank Miss Sheppard for her kindness,' Priscilla said. 'I should have known better.' Howard only continued his soft murmurs with his forearms still awkwardly curled around his head. I wondered how she could not have anticipated his reaction; it seemed a harsh and deliberate act.

"Priscilla turned Howard's wheelchair away from the sun. 'There, isn't that much better?' she said. Howard slowly dropped his arms and stared off vacantly.

"Pushing a teacart, Horatio entered the room. There was a mishmash of teacups, with a creamer and sugar bowl.

"'Young Miss Sheppard, so good of you to come and so brave,' Horatio said. 'For such a young lady, it seems that much is being said about you. We would be extremely grateful if you could help us through this fog that has consumed us. We know that our father would never have wanted this outcome. He was a troubled man but he loved us dearly.'

"Howard's grunts became more vocal and his hands spasmed. He was painfully thin, almost undernourished. His clothing soiled and torn in several places; his hair and beard, a rust color with specks of gray, was matted and uncombed. I wondered when the last time he might have bathed was.

"Priscilla saw her brother's restlessness. 'Even Howard loved him and my father had a special place in his heart for him.' And she faced her brother; her voice for the first time had compassion. 'My father's family had a lineage of unstable personalities and he blamed himself for the sadness brought to Howard's life.'

"The mumblings became more pronounced and Howard began to twitch in his wheelchair. 'Perhaps we should take Howard to his room for some quiet time,' Horatio said, annoyance in his voice. 'I'm afraid his uneasiness might distract us.'

"Howard's agitation quickly settled back. It was obvious he understood our conversation and was not the simpleton as described by his sister. I was once again offended with their indifferent treatment of Howard. Sensing that this poor man probably lived a life of isolation and deprivation, I insisted he should stay, that his presence might actually help.

"'If Howard was as emotionally connected to your father as you say, then he needs to be in this room with us. His presence may be critical.'

"'Of course, Miss Sheppard, if you insist,' Horatio said, and asked, 'How does this all happen? We will do whatever you say. We are so grateful for your help.'

182

"The last few days I had anguished over exactly that. My unique gift was expanding its magnitude almost daily, but there was never any order or direction with its progress. Pronounced feelings of dread or abstract visions of the future began to invade my life, at first with no warning, and then I began to notice that certain thoughts or focused conversations could trigger some of these manifestations. Sharing these communications from a universe beyond my understanding seemed to be the only reasonable thing to do.

"As a young girl, when my gift had begun to shape my identity, my father once told me that this unique ability was now my own responsibility, an obligation to help those you can. 'I have no idea where this will take you and I don't believe you do either,' he told me.

"My father was right; I had no idea where this bizarre gift would lead me. I was simply along for the ride. But I would help all those I could. It caused great concern for my parents.

"Having the ability to receive messages from beyond and the whole concept terrified me. It was a dimension that I wanted to know very little about. Understanding how the universe of the deceased moved along frightened me.

"'Perhaps if we just sit quietly in this large room. It seems a peaceful room now, and no doubt there were many happy times within it. Perhaps the fond memories you all must have of those occasions and the energy from today's bright sun will be the mixture we need to reach your father. I wish I knew, I really do.'

"'Tell me about your father, his favorite meal, what did he do with spare time, hobbies, were your parents in love. How did your mother pass away? Talking about your father and your lives together is our only hope.'

"Awkward silence suddenly consumed the large ballroom. Only a steady breeze and the sound of rustling leaves outside could be heard. I was struck with the lack of energy Priscilla and Horatio now appeared to have. They had hounded me for days to come to their home and assist them in a bizarre task and now they had little they could offer.

"'This will go nowhere if you cannot contribute, I can assure you of that,' I said. 'Your emotional connection to your father is critical.' I began to sense a disharmony in the gathering.

"'I suppose we could think of some lively times,' Horatio replied, arrogance and sarcasm defining his reply.

"'Oh, come now Horatio, don't sound so trite,' Priscilla needled her brother. 'Miss Sheppard is here to help us.'

"'Every Christmas Eve this ballroom would be filled with people that worked at my father's business, some family members on my father's side would also attend. Our mother loved the event, she was a very societal woman and treasured all the planning and interaction leading up to the Christmas gala. However, my father could scarcely tolerate the affair. He was a caring man, he loved my mother dearly, but his social skills were not obvious. His employees always enjoyed the holiday event and the small stipend he distributed at the end of the evening. After our guests left for the night, the family and close servants would gather around the big Douglas fir in this room and open presents.'

"Howard became very animated in his wheelchair, his hands curled inward and he rocked back and forth. His grunts became more pronounced, a wide and twisted smile spread across his face, exposing again some very neglected teeth. It was obvious he had fond memories of the yearly event.

"I felt very conflicted for this lonely man child. I wondered where and how his thoughts connected on this holiday memory. It was obvious that this discussion of Christmases past had stirred up some very personal recollections. I reached over and rested my hand on his gnarled and curled fingers. Cold and rough, they felt like the hands of a lifeless being, but he immediately ceased his rocking and stared directly at me. It was as if I suddenly soothed a confused and anxious soul. He in turn clutched my hands and brought them to his lips and began a soft and tender kiss of them. He murmured soft grunts, all the time casting a penetrating gaze into my eyes. I sensed that this poor man had not often been the recipient of a caring or loving gesture.

"Energy and warmth slowly returned to his hands and his piercing eyes drew me in further. I sensed a spiritual connection was occurring, to what or where I knew not, only a strange feeling that Howard in all his tortured and empty existence was struggling to share something with me. We locked eyes on each other and the sights and sounds of a very ordinary day began to fade away.

"'Howard you must stop this now, you are making our guest quite uncomfortable,' Priscilla said, and she attempted to separate his hands from mine.

"Howard shook his head and tightened the grip on my hands.

"'No, he is not bothering me at all,' I said. 'Please give us a few minutes. I believe he is trying to tell me something.'

"'You do realize he does not have the ability of speech,' Priscilla said with cruel objectivity. 'These grunts and groans are the extent of his vocabulary.'

"'Please just give us a minute,' I pleaded.

"Priscilla and Horatio apathetically nodded their heads and moved closer to the large windows and took in the warmth. They carried their cups of tea and began an intimate conversation. No doubt Howard's quirky behavior had been a trying lifetime daily event.

"Howard's anxiety melted away and he loosened his grip, offering the same fractured toothy smile as before. A calm settled in around us, Howard's grunts softened and likened to the purr of a contented cat. His eyes grew wide. Large black pupils took all surrounding color with them and they began to search within my soul. Something commanding was about to happen and I knew I had no choice but to participate.

"Suddenly his facial features softened, his smile no longer tortured, only welcoming. Hands and arms relaxed, shoulders slumped and settled back into his frame. Sitting there in his chair, with his father's large portrait in the background, I was stunned with their likeness.

"'They have killed me,' a voice spoke to me. It seemed to emanate from behind the large black pupils of Howard's eyes, his face was without expression.

"'Who has killed you?' I repeated, my response instinctive. Suddenly Horatio and Priscilla were by our side. My question had hastily demanded their presence.

"'Who has killed who?' Priscilla probed, 'Why would you say such a thing?'

"'Say nothing to these traitors,' came the voice again, an older man's speech. Howard also pleaded with his eyes and his head moved slowly back and forth ever so slightly. I knew immediately he too had heard the voice, his father's, and he begged me to heed his pater's advice.

"'Come now Miss Sheppard,' Horatio demanded. 'That's a very bizarre choice of words. What is the origin of such speculation?"

"I panicked, I offered only the truth. It was not a preconceived approach, I simply had no other method.

"'A voice, probably that of an older man, spoke to me,' I told them. 'He told me that he had been murdered.' And then I lied, 'That was all he said to me.'

"It was obvious that I had struck a nerve. Priscilla and Horatio peppered me with questions. How could such an odd statement have ever entered my consciousness? Was I sure it was older man's voice? Were there any other facts revealed? Their concerns only escalating with every unanswered question.

"Howard continued his wide-eyed gaze, never taking his suppliant eyes off of me, his head tactically telling me to ignore the questions.

"'I think I should leave now,' I told the agitated couple. 'I don't think I can help you anymore at this point.'

"They were stunned. 'You came here to help us. We told you that our very existence is a stake here,' Horatio said, panic in his voice. 'And all you can offer is some bizarre statement about someone possibly being killed.'

"'It's Howard isn't it,' Priscilla interrupted. 'It's his strange staring, all wide-eyed.'

"She turned to Howard and cuffed the back of his head. 'Howard, stop your incessant staring at our guest. You're all bugeyed. It's making Sarah very uncomfortable.' Howard never flinched; his stare only more penetrating.

"'The fools poisoned me, a potion in my evening wine. My wealth was too much of a temptation for them.' The voice again, this time sad, despondent. 'They came for me in the early hours, lying in my bed, thought I was dead. I was not. I could offer nothing; I couldn't talk nor move my extremities. My eyes frozen, I could only observe and witness their evil plan. They took me to the wine cellar and hung me from a crossbeam. It was to look as if I had taken my own life.' Now his tone grew darker. 'My death was agonizing. I spasmed violently in my noose. They knew then the poison had not done the task and ran horrified from the room. The buffoons did not have the stomach to witness the outcome they desperately wanted.'

"Stunned and troubled, I tried to process the profane message put before me. I looked at Howard, the piercing stare was gone. Back in the moment, he nodded as if to say there was only truth to what had been shared with me. I felt only pity for him. He was trapped in a body by a disease that had consumed him years ago, but also imprisoned now within a deadly secret that he could share with no one. His brother and sister would continue their abuse and neglect, only increasing his helplessness to a level I could not possibly imagine.

"'There is nothing else I can tell you,' I lied further. 'I'm not sure I can make any sense of the words I heard, they were garbled, rather indistinct. Perhaps I misunderstood. But what I do sense is that Howard knows more about your father's financial affairs than you might think. I believe he and your father had a special bond. Perhaps if you stopped your neglect of him and offer some kindness. I believe he wants to help.'

"'We have never mistreated our brother.' Priscilla's face grew red and she angrily challenged me. 'You should be careful...' She stopped, knowing that I just witnessed her striking Howard. Lowering her head, caught in a lie, she turned away from me.

"'My dear sister's anger and frustration is always to close to the surface,' Horatio offered. 'But perhaps we have unknowingly mistreated our poor older brother. We have been through some very trying times. My brother was very close to my father, but in his compromised condition I never considered how deep their bond may have been.'

"'Oh, I am convinced they had a close bond. A brief image of a dusty wine cellar, with large beams crisscrossing the ceiling came to me. Perhaps the money you seek is hidden or buried in that room. Do you have such a room in this house?'

"Priscilla turned quickly to me; her eyes focused with panic, but Horatio's intense glare checked her before she could say anything.

"Horatio replied, 'No there is no such room in this house, but there is a pickling and canning room as well as other rooms in our basement, maybe that is the image you saw. We should look into that possibility.'

"'Yes, yes we will look into that and I know Howard will become the ally that we have needed all this time. Isn't that so Howard?' Priscilla nervously offered. She walked to his side and, where minutes earlier she had struck him, now offered a gentle caress.

"Howard nodded his head, a subtle smile with it. I had secured a better future for him; at least I hoped I had. I grasped his hand, smiled, and offered a soft squeeze. His awkward smile and eyes that opened wider and repeatedly blinked told me he was grateful.

"It was time to leave, this sensitive visit had been draining and the air was filled with tension. Perhaps only Howard had gained some emotional relief, maybe his days ahead would be more tolerable. His value to his diabolical brother and sister had increased. They walked me to the front door, told me of a pressing engagement later that day, and thanked me for my visit.

"'I hope things work out for you and your brother,'" I told them. 'Maybe, the significance of the image of the wine cellar might reveal itself. I am convinced there is a mystery waiting to be solved there.'

"'As I said, Miss Sheppard, we have no wine cellar,' Horatio said, his voice steely cold and his stare piercing. Priscilla would not look at me. 'Thank you again for coming,' he said, and they stepped back into the hallway, closing the door behind them."

Her story complete, her eyes staring off into an event from long ago, Madame Alice brought herself back into the moment.

"Commander Morrison, the point of my sharing this old memory, is that I had been deceived by two evil people into helping them. They had murdered their own father for his money and had abused their brother, but in the end, I had revealed the truth. That is always the outcome, how or why I get involved is a mystery and the journey to that outcome is unpredictable and often difficult but, in the end, it always provides the truth."

Brewster rose from the mess table and paused to gather his thoughts. "What a strange tale, very compelling, and to think you were only sixteen years old. Quite precocious on your part." He paused then continued. "War always has a disturbing truth, Madame Alice. I hope you are wrong about this certainty you say we are sailing towards, but I am prepared for that. Excuse me ma'am, Mr. Bouchard, I have things to do." He placed his hat on his head, set it square, offered a casual salute with his right hand, and left the room.

USS *RENO*

s scheduled, they refueled and took on supplies north west of Hawaii. Viewing the transfer of diesel and provisions was impressive, a test of ship to ship coordination. It helped break up the string of uneventful days at sea.

Madame seemed most comfortable in the confines of her cabin, her privacy an important element of her daily routine. It took some persuasion to get her to leave her quarters. After the breakfast they would walk about the foredeck. Their strolls were slow and deliberate; Madame Alice was still unsteady on her feet. Simon was always close by with a supporting hand. The warm sun and tropical air seemed to energize Madame Alice, although her appearance remained a lifeless pastel color, puzzling to Simon.

Today the winds were steadier, out of the northwest, and had a coolness to them. Simon sought shelter on the lee side of the ship away from the chilling breeze. The plainness of the Pacific horizon before them, they leaned on the railing of the lower deck and sought each other's thoughts.

Since their hasty decision to leave Prudence Island on their patriotic mission there had been no interrupted dreams with the unexplained, no eerie visits from a desperate, cursed crew member of the USS *Eldridge*. Simon shared his concerns with his old friend.

190

"Why have the visits from members of the *Eldridge* crew suddenly stopped, each day goes by and we can offer nothing to Brewster Morrison or Captain Bains."

"It does seem strange that our nights have been free of the bizarre visits or visions that have been the driving force behind this journey." All of it was mystifying to her. "But I am certain that we have done what has been expected of us. We are on the right path; if not, there would have been visits or communications letting us know of our missteps. When time and conditions are right, the sailors of the *Eldridge* will advise us."

"I will trust your insight," Simon conceded. "It has proven itself over the years."

In an attempt to escape the gravity of their charge, Simon shared a casual observation of their time on the *Reno.* "I believe the crew of this destroyer is quite perplexed with our presence. Either they have been ordered to steer clear of us or the presence of two mystics has unnerved them. Have you noticed how little conversation is ever directed at us by junior officers and crew alike? There is the polite tip of their hats or—"

"BATTLE STATIONS, GENERAL QUARTERS." A blaring horn screamed out from the ship's speaker system. The ship was suddenly alive. Sailors scrambled all about, but always forward on the port side and aft on the starboard. Simon and Madame Alice stood frozen; panic had crippled them. Captain Bains was shouting from the bridge after deck. "Seamen Howell and Conroy please get our guests below deck now. We have three enemy aircraft about two minutes out. Move."

The two sailors guided Simon and actually carried Madame Alice, her movements too slow and cautious. The seaman grabbing her from behind, a gentle bear hug, her legs and arms hanging limply from her sides. They guided them to the nearest hatchway. Inside the narrow corridors, crewmen were dashing about. Helmets, life vests, and flak jackets were passed along and donned. Frequent inadvertent collisions with panicked sailors required Madame Alice's escorts to keep a firm grip on their charge.

The P.A. system blasted, "Jap zeros bearing 274 degrees, dead ahead 10 o'clock."

Suddenly the *Reno* was hard over to port, her bow digging in and pushing a wall of Pacific blue to starboard. At the entrance to her room, the momentum of the sudden change of heading tumbled Madame Alice to the floor, her young petty officer cushioning her fall by throwing himself between her and the steel plated decking.

"Oh my goodness," Madame Alice said, now breathless. "Have we been hit?"

"No Ma'am," Seaman Howell answered. "They have just brought her hard over to port so we can get a better look at the incoming nips."

"All weapons stations ready," the update again for all to hear on the ship's intercom.

The ship's weapons erupted. Explosions from the forward 8-inch turrets rocked the Reno. 40mm and 20mm antiaircraft mounts released their hell. Fifty and thirty caliber machine gun positions opened up. The recoil of her big guns, the jolting vibrations, and the piercing noise of heavy automatic fire all frantic efforts of a vessel fighting for its survival.

The single glass porthole in the room suddenly became the focus of the foursome. It drew them in and they witnessed the fury of war. Below them was a 20 mm gun crew. Two men desperately struggled to stay ahead of the gunner's mate's demands for ammunition. He was directing his fire straight ahead only slightly up from the level horizon, the outgoing assault lit up randomly with tracer rounds. And then they saw it, a dark olive silhouette of a plane outlined against the bright blue skyline. All around it the air was filled with the evidence of exploding shells, expanding puffs of black and white smoke formed small clouds that the plane sliced through. *Reno's* machine gun fire tore at the attacking plane's fuselage, its debris flying outward and into the sea.

"My god he's coming right for us!" Madame Alice shouted. No one said a word; no one could take their gaze from the glass portal. They stood frozen.

The plane bore in on them; its Japanese pilot flew towards his destiny. Five hundred feet, four hundred feet, measured in fractions of seconds. They could see the shattered glass canopy, the pilot's bloodied face with half-closed eyes. Flashes of light burst out from the aircraft's wings and two sailors at their weapons station below them were shredded, their flesh and their crimson blood everywhere. Machine gun bullets pierced the room they stood in.

The pilot's head slumped; he was no longer a pilot of a plane, now only a cadaver attached to a missile. The plane suddenly exploded, shattered into a thousand particles. A shell from the US warship had found its mark. Smaller pieces of the plane's fuselage fell harmlessly into the blue water, the larger pieces striking harmlessly against the sides of the *Reno*.

The two sailors in the room with Simon and Madame Alice quickly surveyed the damage to the stateroom, asked if they were ok, and fled the room. This battle was not over and they would be needed elsewhere.

Simon looked at Madame Alice, the horrors of war had suddenly found them. "We should have died," he said. His voice a whisper, empty of feeling.

"No!!" Madame Alice said plainly, "There is much to be done. Death is not our outcome right now. I am sure of that."

The *Reno* survived the assault; all three attacking planes had been shot down. Two crewmen had been killed and others injured, only superficial damage to the vessel. Lieutenant Commander Morrison had shared with them that the assaulting aircraft were probably flown by very inexperienced pilots and that the results could have been tragically different if battle tested pilots had been at the controls. Apparently, Japan had lost many of its qualified pilots in their fight to control the Pacific. These were desperate acts by young men convinced that their supreme emperor was worthy of their lives.

They sailed on, pausing only briefly to give up their dead to the sea. The entire ship's company gathered on the foredeck. The warship, its engines idle, the propellers still, sat motionless on the flat sea. Madame Alice and Simon stood among them. It was another beautiful tropical day, late in the afternoon, the air warm and the ocean shining like a big blue mirror.

Two companions wrapped tightly in bands of white cotton and covered with America's colors were about to be eased into the sea and granted eternal peace. Captain Bains offered his praise and words of comfort for the brave young men before them. He asked that the ship's company join him in the Lord's prayer.

Hats were removed and they began together, "Our father, who art in heaven," and then Simon saw him, a lonely figure up on the decking just outside the bridge. Burnt and disfigured, it was the same young officer as before. He stood there, his right hand pulled to his charred forehead, a salute to his fallen comrades.

Simon slowly turned to Madame Alice; she too was staring up at the navigation bridge. "Do you see him?" he mumbled under his breath.

Her response was instant and startled. "Oh, I see him." All about her, navy men recited their solemn prayer, no one noticed the strange visitor staring down on them. But then Madame Alice knew that she and Simon were the only ones that could view this odd visitor.

"Attention," came the directive from the second in command. All on the ship snapped to. "Gentlemen, our last respects," he continued, and every man aboard raised their right hand and offered their final salute. The board was gently raised and their comrades slid into the waiting depths. Madame Alice watched and prayed for them. She looked up to the *Reno's* superstructure and the tortured spirit of Lt. Estrella was gone.

Back in their cabin, the two sages knew that the milestone that they had been waiting for had been reached.

"I sense our journey has been validated," Simon acknowledged with relief.

"Yes, it has, the young lieutenant's visit has assured us that we are on the right path. My lord, what must have happened on that ship? I believe we will be shocked when we finally solve the mystery."

NATSUGUMO

"Captain, I have radar contact at 282 degrees, 14 miles." Ensign Tanaka stood up from his station and looked directly at his superior. "It's our ghost ship." His eyes gleamed wide with excitement and his head nodded up and down, adding to his certainty.

"Good work Ensign, please give your coordinates to our main batteries," Captain Saito asked.

"Already done."

"Fire when ready and it better be quick." His order was briskly relayed through a microphone. He watched the forward mount slowly turn to port, its muzzles elevating as it moved. A stop, a brief tick of time, and then the eruption of flame and sound, huge projectiles heading out across the horizon at 3,600 miles an hour or about one mile per second.

USS *ELDRIDGE*

0400 hours; the USS *Eldridge* was rolling through calm seas at 15 knots, her crew weary and distraught, their undertaking and captain slowly unraveling. They seemed to be a wandering warship locked into a desperate battle with a persistent Japanese destroyer. Little information was shared with ship personnel as to course and objective, only adding to the crew's mistrust of their captain. Sleep was their only escape and that had become elusive. Watches were doubled up, standby conditions had been enacted, and of course there were Van Noy's sporadic drills. Men were tired, dog tired.

In the control room, officer of the watch Lt. J.G. Robinson leaned into the corner wall of the bridge and took a mouthful of black coffee. Other men stationed there, their faces reflecting the lights of the instrumentation all around them, struggled to stay alert at their posts. Quiet, the ship gently, almost hypnotically, moving up and down as she sliced through deep Pacific blue. Lt. Robinson gazed vacantly out past the bow of their destroyer. There was no moon and the separation between ocean and the heavens was indistinct.

A flash of light in the distance and several more in rapid succession.

"Mr. Calaman, do you have any radar contact about twenty degrees off starboard?"

Second class Petty Officer Calaman, Williams Hanes's backup, had dozed off, watching the repetitive sweep of his radar screen in the early morning hours had done its trick.

"Mr. Calaman," he shouted this time. And then almost together, the sound, like that of small car being pushed through the air at a tremendous speed, and the ocean to the starboard side of the ship erupted. Huge plumes of water jumped up out of the sea, the ship shook violently and then the forward deck exploded in flame.

"General quarters!" Lt. Robinson shouted. "Helmsman bring us hard over to starboard. Engineering full speed. Get our fire crews moving!"

The blaring alarm for battle stations had the ship alive in seconds, although the forward explosion had alerted most sailors that something was wrong, quite wrong. Weary, tired men found new energy.

Captain Van Noy burst into the bridge, his jacket unbuttoned and beneath it a coffee stained T-shirt. His red rimmed eyes were wide with bewilderment.

"Mr. Robinson," he barked his voice loud and demanding.

"Sir, we have taken a hit near the forward crew's quarters and the chief's mess room. I have fire crews scrambling as we speak. We are hard over to starboard at full speed."

"Have you notified the Rainbow Room to engage?"

"No sir."

Suddenly the ocean to their aft and port exploded, four plumes of sea water erupted skyward. The *Eldridge* shuddered from the near impact. Those in the bridge gripped what was near to steady themselves.

Van Noy grabbed the mic that connected directly to the Rainbow Room. "Ensign Williams, engage our device, let's move gentlemen. I know you boys heard the explosion." He turned to his radar tech. "Mr. Calaman, do you have a bearing and distance to your contact?" Without waiting for his reply Van Noy continued. "Provide that to the helmsman and our gunnery officer."

"Helmsman, I want us dead on to that target, all head full. Let's move people."

NATSUGUMO

Sailors aboard the *Natsugumo* that could view the horizon saw the clouds in the far distance illuminate with the flash of an explosion on the American vessel. A cheer went up, the first step towards retribution for the slaughter of their shipmates on the *Myoko*.

"Captain Saito," Ensign Tanaka's voice pitched with excitement, "I believe we have scored a hit on the enemy destroyer. He has turned dead on to us and is at full speed. Right now, I have him at 27 knots. I believe we should immediately turn about and make our run."

"Quite so," the captain agreed, confident for the first time since they began their confrontation with the phantom American destroyer. "Steering, bring us hard over to port, bring us about, all ahead full speed. I believe this strategy of yours just may work Ensign Tanaka." He nodded and encouragingly winked at his young subordinate.

USS *ELDRIDGE*

"Why haven't our forward mounts fired?!" Van Noy yelled. "What the hell are they waiting for?"

The forward 8-inch rifles soon bellowed with fire, smoke, and sound. The *Eldridge* shuddered from the powerful recoil.

"Find the bastard," the captain whispered to himself as the projectiles roared out into the early morning light.

Those on the bridge suddenly sensed the dramatic reduction in the ship's speed; it was as if the *Eldridge* had suddenly encountered a vast area of water that had the viscosity of honey. Ship personnel leaned forward with their loss of momentum. Collectively they all knew their stealthy weapon had been activated and fear now consumed them as to who would suffer more from it, friend or foe?

The bridge speaker crackled with the radar technician update. "Captain, our Jap has turned tail and is making his run. Got him at about 35 knots. With our reduced speed, he'll be out of range shortly. He did this before, shoot and run, maybe this is his new strategy."

The captain shook his head ever so slightly, his front teeth barely visible through a vindictive sneer. "No, he's not that smart. He wants a piece of us, he can't help himself."

The forward mounts fired another salvo at the fleeing Japanese ship and the *Eldridge* again trembled.

199

NATSUGUMO

An explosion just aft of the control room rocked the *Natsu-gumo*. A round from the American destroyer found its mark. The communications room was hit; critical components destroyed. Two sailors were killed and three seriously injured.

All about the ship men scrambled to contain the flames and damage done to their ship. Those in the bridge focused on their course and speed.

Short minutes later they stood in the chaos, the control room still heavy with smoke. Those assigned to quickly determine the damage stood before Captain Saito, ready to report.

"Gentlemen, let's have it," he requested.

"Captain, I'm afraid the damage to our radio room is beyond repair."

"Ensign Mashito, our communications officer, and his senior technician were both killed. We have some spare components but just not enough. I'm afraid we lost all ability to communicate with naval command."

"Do what you can. Stay on it." The captain's voice was robotic, but committed. "What about our radar capabilities, Ensign Tanaka, I'm more concerned about that."

"Only minor damage, we were lucky, some wiring torn or charred. I've got a man on it right now, should be up and running within the hour," Tanaka replied.

"And our American menace, what's his position, status?" the captain asked, trepidation in his voice.

The ensign told his superior that the enemy destroyer had quickly disappeared from his radar screen.

"I can't believe he would pursue us with such a speed disadvantage." He continued that it was his belief that the enemy vessel had by now figured out their new strategy. This was the third time that they had fled the battle after only brief minutes of engagement, although this last one had been a deliberate, pre-planned tactic.

Captain Saito contemplated. "My guess is their captain is contemplating his next move very carefully. He did score a hit on us and is no doubt aware of that, as we are aware of our strike on him. Neither of us knows how much damage was done to the other and we must gauge our next action very prudently. This battle is over for now, but the chess match goes on. There will be no draw in this contest."

USS *ELDRIDGE*

Breaking off their confrontation with the Japanese destroyer, the *Eldridge's* fire teams worked to control the flames in the forecastle bunking area and goat locker to assess the ship's damage. The lone enemy shell had penetrated the forward berthing area. Fortunately, most men had been at their battle stations, only Seaman Louis Camire, who had been restricted to his bunk because of extreme nausea and vertigo, was seriously injured in the explosion. Numerous shrapnel wounds to his upper torso and head made his outlook very bleak. He was not expected to survive the next twenty-four hours.

However, their secret weapon took two more seamen to their deaths. This time the loss was devastating. Chief Petty Officer Vincent "Bruiser" Bruno and young crewman Diaz were found horribly burned near the Rainbow Room. Their bodies gruesomely singed into the steel grating in the bowels of their ship. Normally not an area of the vessel where they belonged, but ship personnel had thinned and responsibilities now needed to be shared. Chief Bruno was a solidifying personality on the *Eldridge*, his leadership and calming influence both vital elements to the ship's identity. It was determined that he died trying to save the young sailor who was imbedded in the scorching steel grating. The chief had taken the fledgling under his care. It was an act that surprised no one. A very personal loss to all, this was a devastating event that could splinter the *Eldridge*. Crew and officers knew they had breached a barrier that would offer no retreat.

Seamen retrieved steel plating from ship's stores, ship fitting and welding repairs were well underway, but the ship moved with little energy, the man that was a source of most of that energy was dead.

The attack by their Japanese nemesis and the emergency repairs needed pushed the scheduled meeting to even later in late afternoon. A 1600 hours gathering in the wardroom, Van Noy entered, wide-eyed, disheveled, ravaged by the lack of sleep, and once again his sergeant of arms accompanied him. Officers that he had requested were in attendance, as were professors Mueller, Bjurman, and Kincaid. All the men rose from the table and acknowledged his entry.

"At ease gentlemen, I'll take a fresh cup of coffee," he told the attending yeoman and placed himself at the head of the table. His hands trembled as he sipped at the coffee placed before him, some of it spilled.

"Gentlemen, I am in a foul mood," he began, his voice tired but committed.

"Earlier this morning, we had a close call with a Japanese destroyer." He went on to identify areas of the ship and the responsible officers that contributed to the near fatal confrontation. "Ensign Cabral and engineering were negligent in their responsibility to provide adequate power to their cloaking device as well as maintaining sufficient speed and maneuverability during battle conditions. The coordination between firing control and munitions was slow and unorganized." He saved most of his wrath for the officer of the watch when the attack occurred and expressed extreme displeasure with the radar technician for dozing at his post, a blatant dereliction of duty. "Seaman Calaman will pay dearly for his negligence; he could have directly contributed to the loss of this ship and all of us. Tomorrow at noon, with the ship's company assembled, he will be openly chastised for his carelessness. I wish flogging was still tolerated by our navy; some countries still permit its application. What a pity. He will remain secured to his bunk with reduced rations until I can think of a more suited castigation."

Captain Van Noy pushed back the hair on scalp with his open left hand and massaged the back of his neck as he turned his head side to side. In the last few weeks it had become his signature reflex at briefings, simple discussions on the bridge, or in his movements about his ship. It did not convey confidence or stability to his crew.

"Now to the other pressing issue," he continued.

"As you know, yesterday afternoon, I also confined our ship's corpsman to his quarters. Some of you may be opposed to that action. Frankly I don't give a damn. My authority on this ship will not be challenged. Luckily, I was warned by a loyal officer of Doc Bellows's intentions. Fortunately, there are still patriots aboard the *Eldridge.* I will not tolerate such insurrection. Is that understood?" And he searched the table for dissension.

"I don't think anything the Doc said could be considered treasonous," Lt. Commander Lapierre nervously offered, "I believe he honestly cares."

Slamming his fist on the table, he confronted his subordinate, "Mr. Lapierre, I don't remember you being present at that meeting, how the hell do you know what he said or meant. Perhaps he reviewed his intent with you; that would make you a party to his insubordination. Shall I put cuffs on you too?"

"No sir." His eyes were now only focused on the table directly below him.

Professor Klaus Bjurman sat muted during the captain's rant; he had witnessed the unraveling of their mission. In the beginning the potential for their new weapon was limitless. Defense and naval authorities were intrigued with its possibilities; perhaps a horrific war could be quickly ended. The schedule to test and develop their high-tech device had been too aggressive, driven by unrealistic optimism. Too little beta testing and even less actual sea trials had secured the outcome they all wanted. The device that he and Professor Mueller had developed had become unstable, but they never reasoned these horrific deaths and injuries would be the product of this instability.

Weeks ago, Klaus had voiced his concern to his associate in the confines of their cramped quarters. Conversing in their native German dialect had allowed them to guard their concerns from an already nervous crew. But Hans would not agree with his assessment. These were wartime conditions, testing and development would have to be accomplished at sea, it was the harsh reality of it all.

The pushback and combative disagreement from his colleague had taken Klaus off guard. The deaths and severe injuries of these American sailors should have been enough to convince Hans that their lethal weapon was falling apart. But Professor Mueller insisted that minor adjustments should be attempted, cooling pumps could be tweaked, diesel generators fine-tuned, calculations related to their own specific equipment could be rechecked. None of these efforts bore any promising results, only more deaths and disturbing injuries. To Klaus, the fact that their secret weapon was falling apart should have been as obvious as the hand in front of your face, and he told his colleague exactly that. Hans vehemently denied such was the case. Klaus was speechless.

Something else was at work here and it took little reflection to uncover the truth behind his colleague's stubborn defense. Adolph Hitler's madness had brutally taken all that was precious to Hans, his beloved Emma and their daughter Lena. He would never forget the day he and Hans had fled their country and finally found sanctuary when they crossed over the border into Switzerland. Their families were supposed to be there waiting for them. Only Klaus's wife and young Otto stood there. Hans' eyes searched frantically for his family; he turned in all directions hoping to find them. Finally an older man, part of the rescue group, confided that Hans' family would not be joining him, and their whereabouts were unknown. Klaus saw the life suddenly sucked away from his friend. His colleague's face contorted with pain and he stared off into the distance, looking but never seeing. It became the expression Hans now wore most of his days. He was living, but lifeless on the inside.

Now, their new weapon had given him purpose. A long-denied revenge was finally his. The USS *Eldridge* and their powerful armament would crush Hitler's Germany and its war machines and when they were done with them, they would do the same to the Japanese. It did not matter to him, Germans or Japanese, he would destroy them all.

Captain Van Noy had experienced the same horrific loss as Hans. A bloody, horrific Sunday in Pearl Harbor had turned his world on its head. Now, retribution had also become his only reason for living.

Unwittingly the US Navy had brought together two twisted, vengeful men, placed them on the same destroyer, and let them loose on the world. They would support each other and together conspire, manipulate, and contrive whatever was required to complete their obsession. Professor Mueller had created a unique and deadly weapon and he prayed daily that Captain Van Noy would use it without discretion or hesitation. He had, and was ruthless in those efforts. And now the crew of the *Eldridge* was about to mutiny. It was as plain as the hand in front of his face.

"Captain, I don't believe you have been fair with the men of this ship." Klaus's words had suddenly stolen the air and humidity from the wardroom. Each person in the wardroom was stunned with Klaus's assessment, a challenge to Van Noy's leadership. Those seated looked directly across the table at their colleague. Eyebrows arched and weary officers began to search the room from the corners of their eyes. The professor had expressed what most in the room had long held, but lacked the courage to say. Professor Klaus had crossed a dangerous line.

Nervous and in broken English he tentatively continued his reprimand. "I believe that they have done quite well under terrible conditions, and what of the good men lost this day, especially your Chief Bruno? You have had evil words but not once did you mention their loss. If you keep on this destructive, twisted road, you will have a rebellion on your hands."

When finished, he folded his hands on the table and looked directly at Van Noy. Whether from a subordinate or crewman, the confrontation was long overdue

Total silence had quickly taken a seat at the wardroom table. Only the hum of the ship engines and the Pacific trade winds whisking by open portals could be heard.

Van Noy studied the German scientist; he had not anticipated the challenge originating from his engineering staff. Nevertheless, he would meet it head on. He raised his hands, folded them in front of him, and rested his chin on his thumbs.

"Professor Bjurman, are you speaking on behalf of the small scientific community onboard this ship, or do you represent the officers and crew of the *Eldridge*?" he queried, his words crisp and direct. He began to rub the back of his neck, his head slowly twisting. "Before you answer, Mr. Bjurman," now a piercing stare accompanied his blunt words, "know that you do not have the capacity to represent the men of this ship, for rather obvious reasons, so then this assertion of yours I suspect must be a joint statement from you and your colleagues." He turned to look at the other professors. "Is this the case gentlemen, has this been a topic of conversation among just the three of you and you now feel it so urgent that you must challenge my authority?"

No response was forthcoming from the two scientists as they hurriedly searched each other's expressions for a collective response.

"Well, gentlemen, is it?" Van Noy's words rang loud and direct.

The researchers and others in the conference room twitched in the chairs. "Ah, no sir," responded Professor Kincaid. Professor Mueller shook his head no and a supportive nod quickly followed.

"It seems you are alone in this thinking, Mr. Bjurman. I will not tolerate insubordination from within the ranks nor from outside them. You have ventured into a very dangerous place." He turned to his sergeant at arms. "Mr. Pierce, please escort Professor Bjurman to his quarters and restrict his movements. In regards to the loss of two men today, I do not take lightly the loss of any member of my ship's company."

Those in the wardroom suddenly sensed a loss of bearing. An unknown world had unexpectedly engulfed them. Thoughts of what happens now or where do we go from here raced through the mind of every man in that room.

Confusion and panic gripped the young petty officer now charged with the scientist's incarceration. He was unsure of his next move.

"Wait just a minute," Professor Bjurman pleaded, "is there no discussion here, no effort to reason our way through this? Captain please, things have come unhinged. Our device has become unpredictable and that is mine and Dr. Mueller's responsibility. If I have to, I will take complete blame for the carnage brought on by it." He searched the captain's face for the slightest sense of compassion. "But I beg you Captain Van Noy, we can't continue like this."

The stifling silence continued, some officers awkwardly rose from their chairs and migrated slowly to the rear of the wardroom, others remained seated near the captain. Were sides being taken? It quickly became the dangerous unanswered fear.

Commander Preston stepped into the standoff. "Skipper, why don't we try this again? I'm sure Professor Bjurman can re-word his concerns."

Captain Van Noy abruptly raised his right hand in a stopping gesture. His face was red with pent up anger and restraint, spittle jumped from his lips when he spoke.

"Commander Preston, we've been through this already, but we can do it one more time. Professors Mueller and Kincaid, do you think your weapon is unbalanced, the threat to our mission that Mr. Bjurman says it is?

Professor Mueller's reply was quick and confident, "Not at all." Professor Kincaid's answer, weak and without conviction, "I don't think so."

"End of discussion." And he slammed his open right palm on the wardroom table.

"Petty Officer Pierce, bring Bjurman to his quarters and handcuff him to his bunk. Now gentlemen, somewhere out there a Japanese destroyer means to sink us. They damaged our rudder and only a few hours ago put a round into our forward deck. I'll be damned if I will let things continue along those lines. I'm going after that son of a bitch. Stand ready."

He immediately rose from the table and left the briefing. Those buying into the captain's mindset followed him out. Those remaining knew a frightening new reality had been forced upon them.

Commander Preston pulled on Lt. Estrella's sleeve. "Tonight, 0100 hours, portside engine room, the same men as before. I am including Chief Ponterreli. Without Chief Bruno, his participation is now critical."

Lt. Estrella looked directly at his superior. "My god what did we just witness."

"Just have everyone there, lieutenant." And he left the wardroom.

USS *ELDRIDGE*

Early, dark, the lonely hours of a new day. A resolved committee, they gathered in the port side engine room as Commander Preston had requested. Lt. Estrella and Lt. Junior Grade Gomez, Ensign Williams, Ensign Hughes and Lt. Commander LaPierre, Chief Morretti and Petty Officer Louis Cievetti, his tattoed forearms and the lucky strikes rolled up in his T-shirt, straight from central casting, represented the enlisted men in this act of mutiny. A role no one wanted.

"First we need to know where the rest of the crew is with this, we were a company of 207 officers and crew when we left Philadelphia," Preston began the rebellious dialogue. "We cannot move ahead with this if we are just a very vocal minority. I am convinced we are not, but what did you discover, what is the mood of the crew?"

"Captain Van Noy has been very systematic with his perverse vengeance and hatred," Ensign Hughes offered. "Our recent confrontation with the Japanese destroyer showed how reckless his tactics have become. We're about to loss Seaman Camire, he's not expected to make it through the night." He paused, his tone turning sarcastic, "and our game changing, fabulous, freakin secret weapon added to the gruesome count. That device must not be used again. The entire

210

collection of NCOs on this vessel, with the exception of three, are completely in line with our sentiments."

One by one they shared the comments gathered from the crew of the *Eldridge*. A strong and committed consensus showed they were a united front. Van Noy had been thorough on how he sowed his vile seed and now would harvest only resentment and hatred.

They talked quietly and quickly, the hum of the steam turbines guarding their conversation. Ship's weapon storage would be accessed with the keys that Ensign Hughes had custody of. When the time was right, rifles and side arms would be issued. Officers and seamen with weapons would secure vital areas of the vessel. Engineering, communications, radar and sonar, the CIC room, and fire control. The few officers and crew that still supported their captain would need to be located and apprehended. Some of the senior officers had their own side arms in their personal belongings. These would need to be recovered and secured. They would also need to be confined separately, away from their commander. Communication was critical, the ship's intercom was to be used at all times until the *Eldridge* was secure.

"When the time comes, the coded phrase 'President Roosevelt though naval command would like to issue the following statement,' or something to that effect, will be issued over the P.A. We will apprehend the captain when he is in his quarters. His sleep schedule is unpredictable now, but when he grabs some shut eye, we'll make our move. I want him rousted and brought to the bridge. He won't know it, but we'll be watching him like a hawk. Be quick and follow your directives. Also, be aware that we will all be judged very harshly when the time comes. This has to be done professionally, by the book so to speak, no one can be hurt. We cannot act like thugs; that will not help our cause."

Lieutenant Estrella felt a need to speak. "Gentlemen, we met as a group three weeks ago in the confines of turret number five. One very good man that was part of that conference is now dead. Chief Vincent Bruno, he held this ship together. This is a big loss to the *Eldridge*. It was horrific the way he and crewman Diaz died. Two weeks ago Lieutenant Wickersham died, another casualty of that freakin death machine. I know there is a festering sense of revenge now because of this, it's about to put us over the edge. We've all lost good friends."

They paused as group to reflect; some nodded their heads, others stared vacantly beyond.

Estrella continued, "I just came from sickbay, Seaman Camire did not make it, as Ensign Hughes alluded to. That's four of us in the last two weeks. It's a goddamn shame these decent men and the others had to die before we did something. We need to honor these men by ending the insanity. Now, before someone else dies. But let's be smart about it. Everybody stays cool. This is all gonna end real soon. It's how Chief Bruno and Lieutenant Diaz would have done it."

"Let's not forget about the elephant in the room," Commander Preston added. "We have one pissed off Japanese destroyer on our tail. Van Noy has put a bug up his ass, so he's not going away anytime soon. We have to pay close attention to him. Lucky for us he doesn't know how chaotic things are on this ship, otherwise he'd be all over us like a Sears & Roebuck suit." For emphasis he added, "Gentlemen remember, Tojo is the wildcard in anything we plan."

Slipping away one by one from their gathering, they sneaked along dark passageways, back to their berths or early morning stations. All of them now with a knot in their stomachs. In a short time, they would become a cast of mutineers, the thought itself chilling.

USS *RENO*

Madame Alice seemed to be regaining some of her vitality. Tropic air and ample sunshine appeared to have energized her. She seemed not as pale and was animated in her activities and conversation, or at least Simon thought so. Her appetite hadn't improved that much, actually what little she ate was done in the privacy of her stateroom; she refused to allow Simon to critique her eating habits. Simon sensed a burden lifted from his spirit. For now, his fear that this pilgrimage would be her undoing had subsided.

This morning Simon sat alone in one of the rockers that Captain Bains had provided for his two VIPs. Madame Alice had yet to join him, she had been sleeping late the last few days, often missing breakfast but later confessing to a hearty lunch.

"Good morning," she called to him.

Startled, he twisted in her direction; he hadn't seen her walk up to their "station for relaxation" as Lt. Commander Morrison would tease them about their spot, high up behind the pilot house. It provided ample sunshine and protection from the stiff winds.

"Yes, it is a good morning," he returned. She stood there in a loose-fitting off-white dress and a light blue navy fatigue shirt much too large for her. She looked lost, almost delicate in her outfit. The last few days she allowed her long gray hair to hang freely, no longer pulled back and tied with a ribbon.

"My goodness Sarah, where did you find such an ensemble?" Simon chuckled. "If I didn't know you, I might suspect you of being someone who has crossed over."

Madame Alice laughed heartily. "I haven't laughed that hard in a long time and I wonder why, I think you just insulted me." This time they both hooted. "The shirt is an old one of my Milton's, many years ago, he was in the navy," she added.

But then Madame Alice's expression quickly changed, her smile gone and her eyes intent. "Last night I had a visitor, the tortured young lieutenant that has become my companion. He told me that we are on the wrong path; we should travel west from here. He was not asking; he was demanding we do this. We need to let Captain Bains know right away." And she walked briskly towards the bridge, not waiting for Simon to accompany her. Simon had to be quick on his feet to catch up to her, a little irritated by her lack of patience, but pleased with her new-found energy.

Entering the control room, they found neither Captain Bains nor Lt. Commander Morrison there. Madame Alice quickly became anxious and was unsure of her next action. Simon stepped in.

"Please ask Captain Bains and Commander Morrison to join us on the bridge," he told the ranking officer. Madame Alice began to pace the bridge.

"This is the part that always challenges me; we'll see just how receptive they really are. You know how this works. Skepticism is always our biggest obstacle."

"Good morning people." It was Lt. Commander Morrison. "Hope you're comfortable folks," Captain Bains added. They returned the greeting.

Too anxious to restrain herself, she placed herself in front of Captain Bains. "You need to head due west from here." Her voice was almost frantic.

Bains studied Madame Alice, her face stoic, her eyes piercing. He looked at Simon and then Morrison. They could offer no advice nor would they. This was his decision. They had arrived at the point that would test his mettle, he was about to trust his command of

214

a million-dollar war machine to a woman whose abilities her seriously doubted.

"Please Captain Bains," she pleaded, "if you want to find that ship, we have to do this now."

The skipper examined her face again, searched her eyes. "Helmsman, hard over, bring us to 270 degrees, maintain current speed," he said loud and clearly, never taking his stare off Madame Alice. The helmsman repeated the order and they felt the center of gravity shift on the massive ship. Captain Bains gave Madame Alice a quick reassuring wink.

"Thank you so much captain, you will see that I am right." Madame Alice's voice was now almost mechanical, puzzling to Simon.

Captain Bains removed his hat and scratched his head, once again his sensibility tested. He wanted to pound his fists on the nearest bulkhead with frustration, walk out to the outer deck, turn his face into the strongest wind his destroyer could fashion and scream for clarity.

He would belie the turmoil within. His was voice calm. "I hope you are indeed right, Madame. What a strange journey we are on. I need to go to my quarters; I have some paperwork that needs my attention. I will assume there will be more revelations or should I say course changes as we travel. It seems we are navigating by the stars in an afternoon starless sky." He shook his head and left.

"This is all very difficult for our skipper to comprehend," Brewster Morrison shared with them. "He's got thirty years traveling the oceans of the world as a navy man, all of it practical, structured, and all of it very black and white. Orders given; orders followed."

"We understand his cynicism; we're used to it," Simon offered. "This is by far the most unique setting for anything we've ever been involved with. For an old salt such as Captain Bains, it must be extremely trying."

"You have no idea how challenging this is for him." Brewster tipped his cap and excused himself.

Madame Alice and Simon were relieved that a critical new course heading, delivered by the crew of the troubled *Eldridge,* had been shared with them. A lifetime of bizarre disclosures delivered by eccentric spirits had become their norm.

Simon walked Madame Alice back to her cabin. Before entering she reached out, softly patted her good friend's shoulder, raised her eyebrows, offered a soft smile, and closed the door behind her.

USS *ELDRIDGE*

Early evening, Ensign Hughes and Lieutenant Gomez were huddled at the after DC station. A gray overcast day, intermittent rain showers had descended on the *Eldridge* since late afternoon. The ship was active with repairs to the forward deck. Both officers wore their rain gear, they had been at the 1600 hours briefing and had witnessed Van Noy's madness.

"You saw what happened in the wardroom yesterday afternoon, he was out of control," a statement of the obvious by Ensign Hughes, a nervous frustration consuming him. "Cuffing the professor to his bunk because of a legitimate concern—it shows you the extent of Van Noy's paranoia. Although I did hear he was only in his quarters for about five hours before the captain released Bjurman to the custody of his pal Mueller. Guess he's back in the Rainbow Room."

"The captain is not stable." A blunt and simple assessment by Gomez. "But what we do about that frightens the hell out of me, and we need to do something. I know there was a meeting late last night in the engine room. I've been told Preston is about to assume command. We're about to enter a strange reality. I can't imagine he feels good about that."

"It scares the shit out of me," Ensign Hughes revealed, little hesitation in his objection. "There's no walking a fine line on this.

217

You become part of the mutiny or you align yourself with a very unstable man. When we answer for this, our futures will be debated by a bunch of admirals. I have a wife and child, they're all impacted by the decision I might make in the next few days."

"Is there any other possibility here? Our fucked-up skipper hasn't given us many options."

"The fact that mutiny has become our only option doesn't give me the warm and fuzzies, and it don't fill me with a lot of confidence either."

"Keep your hearing sharp, there will be an announcement on the P.A. regarding a communication from President Roosevelt. That's the signal that Van Noy has been removed from his command and we have become a ship of mutineers."

"What are we supposed to do, what do we say to the crew?"

"I would say as little as possible to the crew. Just continue with your normal duties, have your people go about their responsibilities in the usual manner. Commander Preston is a good officer. He will quickly update everyone, he'll keep you informed. I don't expect the transition to be difficult."

"In the meantime, we keep chasing the nip destroyer that Van Noy has become obsessed with." Ensign Hughes cast a nervous look about their ship. "Maybe Commander Preston will make his move before…that."

General Quarters rang loud and the ship's intercom was alive with bearing and distance to the threat. Again, the *Eldridge* was alive with the actions of men who were close to total apathy.

"Looks like Van Noy found his adversary, or he found us," Ensign Hughes said. "God help us." He turned to his ranking officer.

Lieutenant Gomez was already sprinting to his battle station.

NATSUGUMO

Ensign Tanaka's head snapped up, as if stabbed in his back side with a sharp pin, suddenly alert, the adrenalin surging through every fiber of his body. A foggy blip on his radar display jolted his survival instincts.

The crew of the *Natsugumo*, a 387-foot Japanese destroyer, had been at their battle stations for the last twenty-six hours, they were exhausted and their nerves unraveling. Long hours of watching the endless, mindless sweep of his radar screen had lulled the young officer into a restless, almost hypnotic sleep.

Tanaka yelled the bearing and distance to the last known location of the *funa yurei*, a mythical name for sea ghosts dedicated to sinking ships. All too fitting that the crew had dubbed the American ghost ship as such. The general quarters alarm was sounded. Officers and sailors, most of whom were already at battle stations, cleared their heads and refocused on critical responsibilities

An impressive sunset with clouds from a soft yellow to scarlet pink and reaching far into the heavens had given way to twilight.

There would be rain tomorrow. Tired eyes, at the bearing and distance given by Ensign Tanaka, searched the vanishing horizon. Tension among the crew was escalating with the knowledge that an invisible enemy lurked nearby waiting for the perfect moment to strike.

Then again, another sudden blip on Ensign Tazawa Tanaka's screen, with no previous indication, this time only 600 meters off the starboard bow, dead ahead. Tanaka hollered his new warning along with bearing and distance to the lead officer on the bridge. Those on the bridge turned to the direction given and raised their field glasses in unison. The phantom frigate should have been clearly visible even without their binoculars.

There was silence on the bridge. Lookouts saw only an empty sea spotted with whitecaps.

An irritated officer addressed him. "Ensign Tanaka you need to recheck your findings, perhaps calibrate your device, there is no American ship there." Lack of sleep had long ago depleted the senior officer's patience.

Baffled and exhausted, Tanaka rose from his radar station and viewed the empty ocean off their starboard side. He returned his gaze to his radar screen and once again saw the distinctive image on the screen. And as if his head was on a swivel he looked back at the vacant sea, back to his screen, back to the ocean. A small line appeared in a section of ocean several hundred yards out. The line quickly grew in length and depth; water began to push out from its center to either side of the expanding line. As it grew in height, each side formed its own wave with its own distinctive white crown. Between the two opposite moving waves the ocean turned flat and calm like a mill pond. Only the small funneling eddies that seemed everywhere told of the depth that lay below and hinted to a shape that might be responsible for such a phenomenon before them. A mystifying image begged for clarity, it temporarily halted all movement and thought aboard the *Natsugumo*. All they could do was stand there, unsure in what their next actions should be. They reasoned enough that before them was a wake from a very large ship. But what had caused this ocean mystery, and where was its genesis.

Officers, petty officers, and sailors on the bridge stood bewildered. Had they really witnessed such an oddity? Had their lack of sleep caused their senses to fail them? How close had they actually come to becoming a casualty of war, victims of an American ghost ship? They were not allowed to dwell on that possibility.

Captain Saito quickly took charge, shouting orders that all starboard gun crews immediately open fire on the empty patch of ocean where the image of the wake was last seen. Machine guns, 20 mm and 40 mm mounts erupted, soon followed by their forward and aft 6-inch artillery. The *Natsugumo* sprayed the area with lead and explosives, this ghost ship could be anywhere and their fire should be random and indiscriminate. An eerie but impressive display unfolded: the area before them was alive with the fury of war, shells exploding in the air or when they hit the water. Phosphorus tracer rounds lit up the sky, like swarming fireflies on a hot summer's night. The whole event much like an evening's celebration of the emperor's birthday. And yet no secondary explosions, no strikes to the phantom warship. Most of the projectiles streaking into the empty darkness of the night, disappearing forever.

Suddenly the flashes of several explosions and the upper bridge of the enemy destroyer with its foredeck aflame immediately became visible, silhouetted against the evening sky. A separate, single image with no superstructure below or around it; it floated separately thirty feet above the water line, an eerie image with the fires of hell consuming it. A brief glimpse of smoldering, shattered gray steel bulkheads and men, sailors with their uniforms and bodies aflame, some throwing themselves from the bridge observation posts to the sea below; then, just as quickly, the images vanished as if slipping into a thick fog bank.

The *Natsugumo* increased the fury and the randomness of their bombardment, but no additional hits were scored on the enemy frigate and orders to cease fire were finally issued. Star shells exploded in the area above the battle, turning the dark night and their ship into an eerie bleached white, but there would be no more sightings or unexplained radar images to torment the weary crew.

A search of the immediate area revealed a small oil slick and miscellaneous debris, along with two severely burned bodies, their uniforms too badly scorched for identification, nor were they wearing their typical dog tags. A puzzling revelation to the crew of the *Natsugumo*.

Captain Saito's second battle report to the Japanese naval command would again be difficult to prepare and he knew it would once more be received with skepticism. Reinforcing the existence of a phantom, disappearing American destroyer was a disturbing prospect. But their ability to share this new information with the admiralty was lost when return fire, a shell from the desperate American destroyer, found their communications room. The damage was extensive to both men and equipment. No critical update would be forwarded. The Natsugumo was on its own, not a comforting option when dealing with an American *funa yurei*.

USS *ELDRIDGE*

"**P**rofessor, activate our device again and quickly. We're going to make another run at that nip destroyer," Van Noy hung up the connection to the Rainbow Room. He turned to those on the bridge. He was an exhausted man and yet his eyes were alive with anticipation of battle. He no longer cared about his appearance, abandoning his broad hat when on the bridge. His hair was unwashed and appeared glued to his scalp. His shirt was notice-ably loose at the collar and was spotted with sweat stains, some fresh, others quite stale.

Officers and crew present on the bridge cringed once more when they heard the directive given to that vile room in the bowels of their ship. There would be more carnage.

Van Noy believed their device brought them invisibility and with it invincibility, perhaps at the beginning of the voyage that may have been true. However, that reality had long ago vanished. No one believed the lies anymore, now he was only deceiving himself.

"Navigation, please plot a course to intercept the Japanese destroyer. Helmsman, be ready for that course change." The captain rattled off other commands.

Two similar attacks barely a day apart were unsuccessful, an-other day and the *Eldridge* was about to engage for a third time. No one on the ship thought this outcome would be any different than the previous.

Course changes were calculated and implemented. Their secretive device was engaged and the *Eldridge* slowed her forward speed, confirming that progression. The ship shuddered as ocean waters dragged on her hull. Familiar heat and with it nausea, spread out from its center, like early symptoms of a deadly plague, each sailor fearing he might be next to be claimed by its fatal touch.

"I want it clear; no shot fired until I give that command." Van Noy stuttered, his face a portrait of instability. "I want to get as close to those wife and baby killers as we can. I want them to see my face." Those collected on the bridge all in their sea vests and steel helmets froze where they stood, baffled by their captain's bizarre comment. Their world stranger, more inexplicable by the hour.

"Engine room, bring us to two thirds," Van Noy screamed at his minions. "Where is Professor Mueller?!" He frantically searched the pilot house. "Hans needs to be here, where is he?" His voice ratcheted upwards.

"Captain, Professor Mueller is still in the Rainbow Room," Ensign Babbitt, the communications officer, revealed. "I have him on the phone right now. He says they're having trouble with our device. Very unstable he says."

The captain grabbed the phone. "Hans you should be here, this may be our most glorious moment," he said, his eyes wide, the phone shaking in his hand. "What, no, no we will not reduce speed, I finally have the prick right where I want him. Try, try Hans you must make it work. This is our chance." He passed the phone off, and with raised binoculars, he searched the ocean before them.

Ensign Hughes approached his executive officer. Leaning in, almost whispering, "Commander, I think our time is here, he's completely lost his grip," the tension in his voice obvious. "We better do something real fucking quick or we may not be around to try it again."

Grabbing his junior officer by the wrist, he guided the two of them to the recesses of the control room. "Calm the fuck down Ensign, you want me to declare mutiny as we're about to engage with an enemy warship, that'll work real swell. Ensign Hughes, let's pray we survive this attack. The minute we get through this, Van Noy will be in custody. I promise you that. For now, just do your job, make sure everybody does theirs. We need to survive this." He turned and was quickly beside the captain, his glasses searching the seascape.

Their increased speed quickly closing the distance, visuals without field glasses were now possible. The enemy no longer a profile in the distance; her shape, her characteristics more defined as the *Eldridge* drew closer.

"Captain," Babbitt said, holding the ship's phone off to the side, "Professor Mueller says his device is becoming unstable, says we need to break off this engagement."

Van Noy turned to his subordinate with a puzzled look, as if he had just been told the most obscure, irrelevant detail. "I will not do that. We're about to have him."

"Sir, shouldn't we open fire? We are well within range," the firing control office pleaded.

"NO NO NO!!!" Van Noy bellowed. "We'll open up when I say so. We'll do this just like the other ones. Real close, no quarter given, they have to feel the pain."

Close and closing, the *Eldridge* steamed towards their Japanese foe. Fear and prayer by those who no longer believed in their invincibility. Van Noy squealed with delight like a child on Christmas morning. "My god he can't even see us, I can smell the bastard."

Without warning the *Eldridge* shuddered, strong, pulsating vibrations along the length of her hull. A sensation of a dramatic increase in air pressure. Numerous seamen covered their ears, the pain excruciating.

Ensign Babbitt was once again on the phone with someone in the Rainbow Room. "Captain, our device is breaking down, they cannot guarantee our invulnerability. It sounds quite serious sir."

Suddenly the evening air around the *Eldridge* lit up with explosions. The enemy destroyer had suddenly found them, the incoming fire overwhelming. Two large explosions wracked their ship. Her forwarded 8-inch mount burst into a ball of fire and twisted steel. Soon after, another round devastated the radar room. Heavy machine gun fire ran along the deck.

Van Noy grabbed the phone to the Rainbow Room. "Hans, What the fuck are you doing to us?!" He listened intently and then machine gun fire found the bridge, windows exploded inward, controls and instrumentation shattered. Helmsman Mello's head exploded, his entrails and blood pressed against the nearby bulkhead. Ensign Babbitt, a serious wound to his left shoulder, twisted on the floor.

Captain Van Noy dropped to the control room deck, the ship's phone still at his ear. Suddenly he yelled above the fray. "Reduce our speed to 10 knots, bring us to 155 degrees, do it quickly." A panicked crewman with blood dribbling from both ears dialed backed the indicator for the engine room. Another pulled desperately on the ship's wheel, freshly covered with his shipmates' blood and skull fragments.

The *Eldridge* slowed and the crippling pressure that had squeezed at the sides of their heads and ruptured the eardrums of some abruptly eased. Those on the bridge now moved with purpose, they manned their stations, others tended to the wounded.

The twilight sky around them was still alive with explosions and screaming projectiles. Tracer rounds searching for the American destroyer lit up the evening sky. Machine gun fire still randomly found her flanks and superstructure, with more sailors wounded.

And then the fury of the attack was gone. Larger rounds from their attacker no longer found the *Eldridge*. Smaller arms and machine guns ceased their onslaught. The Pacific air was suddenly still, an unnerving silence quickly pushed aside the harsh noise and turmoil of war. Their Japanese attacker halted its fire.

The *Eldridge* had once again slipped into her own unique fog. She steamed north-northwest, disappearing into the night. The *Eldridge* had survived, but at a terrible cost.

USS *ELDRIDGE*

"**D**amage control?" Standing in the bridge of the USS *El-dridge*, a stunned Captain Van Noy wearily shouted to his hastily gathered collection of junior lieutenants and senior petty officers. They had received two, possibly more, devastating hits from the Japanese destroyer, one to the communications room, amidships, upper decks, and the forward 8-inch mount was reduced to a mass of twisted steel. Machine gun fire had also sprayed the lower decks. Casualties would be numerous. There was controlled chaos all about the ship. Orders were shouted above the sounding alarms. Smoke seemed to be everywhere, complicating the search for dead and injured crew. Fires raged in three different locations. There is a saying among navy maintenance personnel, "If it moves grease it, if it doesn't paint it." Now fire teams raced about the vessel, dragging their two inch hoses with them. They cursed the numerous layers of paint and the grease that now fed the inferno. High pressure pumps were engaged and sea water was soon attacking the crumbling and burning steel bulkheads. Drills are a way of life for the navy and happen all the time, all the practice critical, but the reality of the dead or severely wounded shipmates, no one trains you for that.

"Sir," Lieutenant Estrella, who had been on the bridge and now visibly shaken by the carnage, was the first to pipe in, his voice

227

trembling with emotion. "We took several direct hits to the radar room and CIC, two dead four injured, two very seriously, probably won't make it. A lot of equipment damage. We cannot transmit or receive at this point. Chief Rossi will need some time to determine if the damage is repairable. Sir…" he paused. "Captain, why didn't we fire when we had the chance?"

Van Noy angrily confronted his junior officer. "You are not here to question your captain's strategy." His stare was demonic and long, finally turning to face the chief gunners' mate. Sanchez stood there in his tattered and charred uniform. His left shoulder and arm injured and burned; a bandage had been hastily wrapped around his wounds. Blood was oozing from the white dressing.

"Chief, are you OK?" he asked, unsure he wanted the answer.

"I'm fine sir," he paused a bit, distraught with news he was about to share. "The forward 8-inch mount took at least two direct hits, sir. All five of the gun crew are dead. The ammunition in the room made that a certainty. Two seamen adjacent to the mount were seriously wounded. The forward mount is toast sir. There's just no way to repair it."

"Thanks Chief, you get down to sickbay as soon as you can."

"Did you hear what I said sir, eight of our shipmen dead. Don't you care about that?"

"Am I to be grilled by every underling on my ship?" Van Noy challenged. "Petty Officer Sanchez, I can't afford to care right now, I'm trying to keep this ship afloat and you are way out of line for asking that." He moved on.

"Lieutenant Cohen, you're up next, did you sound the ship?" And he forcefully massaged the back of his neck, his face a flustered red.

"Yes, I did sir. The ship is water tight. We took no hits below the waterline. Port side was raked with heavy machine gun fire, three crew members killed, two injured, lots of superficial damage."

Captain Van Noy curled his lips and slowly moved his head back and forth as he did the math in disbelief. "Lieutenant Cohen, what about our scientists in the Rainbow Room?"

"Still trying to access that sir. There are injuries to people who were near the room. Don't know the extent yet. Inside the room, can't say, no one's got in there yet."

"What!" Van Noy screeched, his agitation escalating. He began to pace about, rubbing the back of neck all the time. He stopped. "Then we need to get the fuck down there right now."

Captain Van Noy and his lieutenant worked their way below decks, the sounds and smells of destruction and chaos fading the deeper into the bowels of the ship they traveled. Reaching the restricted lower level, the stifling heat and humidity quickly engulfed them. They found the two seamen, part of a security detail continually stationed at the entry to the controlled area. One man was dead, his lower torso severely burned, still smoldering. The pants of his uniform now resembling shorts, tattered and charred. The flesh along both legs was like legs of lamb on an outdoor barbecue spit. His companion sat nearby with arms braced, propping himself up. His chin rested against his chest.

"Seaman Ross," the lieutenant called out to the sailor.

Slowly raising his head, he moved it side to side, as if unsure he heard a voice. His sluggish search finally found them and he stared emptily.

"Franklin," he used the sailor's first name, "it's me Lieutenant Cohen, and Captain Van Noy."

Seaman Ross struggled to his feet, his movements slow and deliberate, his uniform soaked with the humidity.

"Carl didn't make it," he said in a daze, and looked at his friend's charred body on the floor. "Sorry sir."

"It's alright son," Van Noy consoled. "What happened down here?" he asked, and looked around the area. Overhead piping and conduits were covered in condensation and water dripped everywhere. Bulkheads were covered in their own sweat and added to the little inlets that were forming on the floor and again the heat was oppressive.

"Don't know, sir," the bewildered senior sailor replied. "Started getting real hot down here and then we started to hear a sort of pulsating hum, and then the deck and bulkheads started vibrating,

229

nasty, like the whole ship was shaking; and it got really loud, hurt your ears. The heat just kept increasing, everything became too hot to touch, especially anything metal," and he displayed the severe burns on most of his fingertips. "I think we passed out, sir," and he looked again at his friend, "guess I only did, Carl he ..." He never finished, just stared at his shipmate.

Captain Van Noy grabbed the sailor by the shoulders. His body and uniform still unnaturally warm and sweaty. "Seaman Ross, anything from the Rainbow Room?" He jostled him, returning him to the moment. "Anything from the restricted area?" he asked again.

"Might have been, sir. But there was vibrations and noise all over the place down here. It was hard to tell. Carl said he heard something. Before..." and the sailor again never finished his thought.

Van Noy quickly reached for the intercom mic that connected directly to the bridge. He buzzed several times, finally somebody picked up. "Lieutenant, I need a detail with a corpsman sent down to the restricted area ASAP. Tell them to bring air fans with them."

The captain turned back to Lieutenant Cohen, who was now assisting the confused and injured sailor.

"Lieutenant Cohen, forget about Seaman Ross, get the keys from his belt. We need access to the Rainbow Room now!"

"Sir, I think we should wait until people get down here, Seaman Ross needs our help right now."

"That was an order Lieutenant, not a suggestion," Van Noy barked at him.

"Captain, it'll be just a few minutes," Lieutenant Cohen challenged. "Carl could go into shock. Please, just a few minutes."

Van Noy angrily stared at his young officer, agitated he rubbed the back of his neck and began to pace about. They would wait.

The team from the bridge arrived; two men tended to Seaman Ross, the rest entered the Rainbow Room with Captain Van Noy and the lieutenant.

Inside the scene was staggering. The room was stifling hot. Fans, ordered by Van Noy, were quickly set up and pushed cooler air into the room. Their innovative mechanism had somehow been shut down. Van Noy and his men discovered the bodies of both Professor

Mueller and Bjurman. They were dead, their torsos terribly scorched, barely recognizable. Professor Kincaid, showing serious symptoms of heat exhaustion, was still alive; somehow, he found a small nook where he eluded the piercing heat. A young sailor assigned to be a technical assistant was found embedded from his shoulders up in an interior bulkhead. His neck gruesomely torn apart, the gore splatter was wide and copious.

Van Noy was stunned, seeing the seared body of his friend and ally pushed him closer to the precipice. He squatted next to his comrade and studied his burned face. "We were so close, Hans," he whispered. "Oh my god, what becomes of us now?"

Standing he began to pace the room, rubbing the back of his neck, he mumbled to himself, "We were so close," over and over.

The ship's speaker screeched, "Captain Van Noy, please report to the bridge, we have a coded message directly from President Roosevelt." He was a man suddenly without purpose or bearing, his face a portrait of complete apathy, he turned to his entourage. "I suppose I should go now." Unsure if any of his actions mattered at this moment, he shuffled out of the room.

A panicked bridge, the result of deadly enemy fire was beginning to gather its senses and with that a sudden uncertainty of their survival was beginning to give way to the understanding that things were not as perilous as initially thought. Bedlam had been replaced with hurried, controlled reactions. The countless fire drills, practiced over and over, had paid dividends.

"Mr. Estrella, let the engine room know, I want us at flank speed immediately," Commander Preston told his helmsman, his voice loud, his diction clear. "Maintain current heading, let's make sure we remain beyond the range of our Japanese friend."

He turned to the gathering before him. "We do it now, or we don't it at all." There was silence among them. They nodded their heads. A long, weary road had brought them to this point; a final destination long ago anticipated was finally here.

"Van Noy has been notified with our coded phrase. He's on his way up here. I will be assuming command of the *Eldridge*. This isn't quite the way we planned it. But we can no longer wait for the perfect moment. Others have heard the warning and we have to assume they are acting as planned. There's no turning back."

USS *ELDRIDGE*

A lifeless, shattered man, Captain Van Noy floated into the CIC. He was groggy and irritated. They all feared this moment. No one was sure how it would happen. Commander Preston knew how it would evolve; he went directly to Van Noy when he entered the CIC.

"Captain Van Noy, under the authority of paragraph 1008 of *U.S. Navy Regulations*, for your reckless hazarding of your command, I am relieving you of all duties and responsibilities. I have consulted with the ship's corpsman and it is clear that you are medically incapacitated. I assume full responsibility with this and will forward a complete report to the next higher authority."

Preston continued, "I believe we have gone well beyond the parameters of our mission." Commander Preston's hands were shaking but his voice was composed. "You will stand down as the commanding officer and remain confined to quarters until such time you are notified otherwise. Seamen Davis and Newhouse, please escort Captain Van Noy to his cabin. You will alternate guarding his stateroom and will carry a sidearm at all times, if the captain tries to escape, shoot him."

Captain Van Noy leaned into his second in command and looked him directly in the eyes. The numbing confusion that had engulfed below decks was gone. He was being attacked. He would defend himself with the deep hatred festering within since that Sunday morning in Pearl Harbor. It had become been his own secret weapon.

"What the fuck do you think you're doing, Commander? I believe you have your head up your ass, as you know the navy examines mutiny very thoroughly and treats it with absolute disdain."

He twisted free of the two seamen that had placed their hands on his forearms and shoulders and continued his condemnation of Commander Preston.

"What a stupid, fucked up thing you're doing. We had a chance to end this goddamn war with our new weapon. It was always going to be a dangerous mission, not without its risks, we all knew that."

He looked around at the other officers in the bridge; their faces staring only at the floor beneath them. *Cowards, all of them*, he thought to himself.

"But you lacked the drive, the fortitude to see it through—" and then the captain's eyes widened and his face became frozen with fear the way it had many times these last two months. Drifting off to a place where paranoia and self-doubt existed, he was no longer among them.

Officers and crew had seen these hasty departures to another world more and more as their ship suffered. Hideous indescribable deaths and injuries can do that.

"Captain, I will not allow a debate on this. Gentlemen, please bring Captain Van Noy to his room." Once again they took him by his arms and then he was back in the moment. He turned again to his subordinate and sneered, "You will hang for this or spend the rest of your life in Leavenworth. You all will. You have cast your die now." He turned and strode off towards his cabin, the seamen following.

Preston spoke. "Lieutenant Estrella, make sure those officers and NCOs that are sympathetic to Captain Van Noy's cause are confined as well and are adequately guarded."

Commander Preston stared out on a vast, flat calm horizon, there was no breeze and the air was heavy with moisture. His uniform was stained with sweat, his hair unwashed, and a patchy beard was well underway. He was exhausted.

The dangerous first step taken, the enormity of it sinking in with all those on the bridge.

Commander Preston turned to his helmsman. "Bring us to 025, maintain flank speed." The order was repeated by the helmsman. The directive had brought some sanity to what had been a nerve wracking experience. An anxious gathering of men took a deep breath.

"Gentlemen let's get back to business." Commander Preston dismissed those not required in the control room. "We are still an American navy vessel; we will continue to act that way."

USS *RENO*

"What's the latest from our mystics, Mr. Morrison?" Captain Bains asked, trying to curtail his skepticism.

The two officers met daily, shortly after their evening meal. One the leader of the search, the other the captain of the search vessel. They discovered they both enjoyed the semi-dry bouquet of a cabernet wine and looked forward to their end of the day libations. The captain had stocked his cabin with an ample supply.

Most Fletcher class destroyers were being assigned to the Pacific theater. The navy discovered that their new class of wide beam vessel fared much better in the relatively storm free waters of the Pacific.

Tonight, they enjoyed the comforts of a smooth flowing sea, their wine glasses stable on the skippers' small, square end table.

"Most of my information comes from Simon; Madame Alice has become more selective with what she shares with me. Simon says that he has never seen her more consumed, more committed to any of her undertakings. I know she was quite relieved when we made that turn west. All I can offer is that both of our sages sense that we are on the correct course, for now. How they know this is beyond me and it frustrates me as much as it does you."

"You know the navy has been my life." The skipper paused, staring at his goblet as he swirled the wine in it, "and I mean my whole life, my father was a chief petty officer and I was a navy brat. My mother, sister, and I traveled up and down the east coast from one of my father's assignment to the next. He was always away for long extended times. It was hard on my mother. For me and my sister it just became a way of life."

He paused again, finished his wine, and returned it to the table. "But nothing could have prepared me for this bizarre assignment. I was suddenly pulled from my command, directed to San Diego where I am to skipper a new vessel that hasn't even had the benefit of a shakedown cruise. I take aboard two people, an old woman with science fiction credentials and her middle age understudy. I'm directed to treat them like royalty and I move qualified senior officers out of their quarters to assure that."

"Captain, I know you're aware that my journey to this ship is almost as inexplicable as yours."

"Hear me out Brewster." They had ventured into referring to themselves by their first names.

"So now we are to wander the very risky waters trying to locate a ship that has no idea that we're looking for them, but how do we look for this missing, highly secretive ship, not by any proven maritime search method, no we're at the whim of two mediums that communicate with the stars in the heavens. Is this freaking nuts or what?"

Brewster Morrison chuckled at the captain's very personal take on his twisted assignment. The thousand-foot view of the whole operation was incredulous.

"It's hard to grasp," he admitted.

"Admiral Carlson was very specific in his communications with me about this search and rescue or recovery effort. He could not stress enough the importance of our mission."

Now they were dangerously close to Japan, no ship had gotten this near to the island nation since Doolittle's raid almost two years ago. They had been attacked by suicide pilots and suffered causalities. There would be more confrontations. More injuries, more deaths. War always guarantees that outcome. They were deep into the Sea of Japan.

"I've got to keep this ship afloat and wandering around Japanese infested waters makes it goddamn difficult. It's my intent to travel through these seas at max speed. This ship is intended for 40 knots. I plan to challenge that design." The captain's frustration was growing.

"We are well north of the last reported location of the *Eldridge* when she last checked in on July 16th. Actually about 300 miles northwest of that position," Brew Morrison corrected himself. "It seems an odd course for them to take. I am constantly talking with Madame Alice and Mr. Bouchard regarding that concern and as I said, they are united as to the course we are traveling. I simply do not ask how they know that, I'm afraid their explanation would only create more doubt."

There was a soft knock on the captain's cabin door, both men paused, unsure if they heard it. It probed again. Captain Bains shouted, "Enter." The handle turned gently, slowly, and then the soft rap once more. Brewster Morrison moved to the door and opened it.

Madame Alice stood there, the same off-white dress and oversized navy shirt as before, her hair frizzled and moving about with the wind that often funneled down the passageways. "I'm sorry to bother you gentlemen, but it's urgent we turn due north, I think I said that right." She began to twist her hands in a nervous motion and rocked back and forth on her feet.

Captain Bains stood and waved her into his quarters. "Please come in, Madame Alice."

"No! I think we need to make our course change first, due north," she repeated, "this will be our last change. The *Eldridge* will now lie straight before us."

Lieutenant Commander Morrison looked directly at the captain, again this alone was the skipper's decision and he was grateful it was not his. In two slow steps, Captain Bains was at his desk. He picked up the phone that led directly to the control room.

"Lieutenant Billings, change in course, bring us due north, zero degrees, maintain current speed. I will be on the bridge shortly."

He turned to Madame Alice. "Would you join us, maybe a glass of wine?"

"Thank you, Captain, I do not drink and I need to share this with Simon, excuse me." She left to find Simon.

"A very committed woman," Captain Bains shared with his cabin mate. "Maybe when this trip is over, I will gain a new understanding of her and with that some respect. I gotta get to the bridge."

USS *ELDRIDGE*

Things had quickly settled down on the *Eldridge*. Captain Van Noy, banished to his cabin, was accepting of his confinement, his demands few and his words even fewer. Officers were convinced he was plotting something. Guards were alerted to be extremely cautious in their interactions with him.

Sailors that had aligned themselves with Van Noy soon expressed their regrets and pleaded for a second chance. Most were released from their confinement and returned to their normal activities.

Officers and crew took deep relaxed breaths now, the suffocating atmosphere that was their daily existence was gone. There was widespread relief, the hate they carried for Van Noy no longer there. Hate can be an unbearable burden. Perhaps brighter days lay ahead.

"Hansey, where is our Japanese tour guide?" Commander Preston stuck his head into Seaman Hanes's little alcove. "Still keeping his distance?"

"Yes sir, been like this for a while, even after our turn north."

"Alright, good, keep an eye on him. I'm headed down to the mess for a cup of joe, can I get you one?"

"No thanks sir, had my fill. Hey Commander, I've been thinking about our Jap friend, been wondering why he's not called for reinforcements. We're right in their backyard, you'd think it would

240

be pretty easy to do. But he don't, and I think he can't. We know we put a round or two into him, I think we took out his communications room."

"Good thinking, Hansey. Real good." Commander Preston reflected for a bit. "I guess that will keep the odds even for a bit." And he headed for the galley.

When he got there, Professor Kincaid and Lieutenant Commander LaPierre were seated, mugs of coffee in their hands. A chart of the area was spread out on the table. LaPierre was smoking his usual Lucky Strike. The new skipper poured himself a coffee and joined them.

"Gentlemen," he offered and tipped his hat.

Professor Kincaid was first to reply, he seemed a little edgy.

"Commander, I've been tracking the ocean temperature, it's been getting steadily cooler the further north we go. I was just telling Lieutenant Commander LaPierre about a strategy we might try."

Commander Preston laid his mug on the table, looking directly at Kincaid. "I'm all ears, Professor."

"I know we have a meeting in the wardroom in about an hour. We have to re-evaluate our situation pretty fast. Just keep this in mind: with these cooler waters I might be able to squeeze one more operation from the Rainbow Room, maybe. Scavenge up one more sneak attack. I'd be willing to talk about that in the wardroom and further explain if needed."

"How confident are you, Professor?" Preston inquired.

"Somewhat, and that's the best I can offer. My guess, the water temp will be even cooler and that will help. I know enough about our mechanism to operate it."

Preston pondered their conversation. "OK, let's talk more about this in the wardroom," he looked at his watch, "in about forty-five minutes. Gotta run." He stepped quickly away from them.

USS *ELDRIDGE*

Its hull slicing through enemy waters, the *Eldridge* traveled due north at 25 knots. Ship radar continually showed their Japanese pursuer always on the outer fringe, neither ship within range of the other's artillery. Matching each other's speed seemed to be their current strategy. Their enemy seemed committed to the chase, obviously content for the moment in the way it had evolved.

They gathered in the wardroom, their first since yesterday's mutinous act, although no single man even considered it a treasonous act, to them it was collectively an act of survival. Commander Preston, Lieutenant Commander Lapierre, Lieutenant Billings the communications officer, Lt. J.G. Robinson of engineering, Chief Bergeron the ship's quartermaster, two seamen representing the crew, and Professor Kincaid, although still weak from his ordeal in the Rainbow Room.

Commander Preston opened the meeting for discussion. "Mr. Lapierre, you have some updates."

"Commander, or should I address you as captain?" Lieutenant Commander Lapierre inquired of their new leader. "We're heading for a fuel problem."

"Do not call me captain, this was never how I envisioned achieving that rank," he said. "Commander will do just fine. I'm not

242

surprised with our fuel status. We missed the last hook up with our tanker. I got a list, about a country mile long, as to why that happened. So, tell me, when do we start running on fumes?"

"Commander we have 80,000 gallons. Maintaining our current speed, which cuts into it rather aggressively, we burn 25,000 gallons a day, Math is pretty easy, three days and we'll be pulled over onto the side of the road and then our options become rather bleak."

"I can imagine," Preston conceded. "Our communications room can't receive or transmit. Any update on that?"

"No change on that, Hansey sees no fix until we can get some parts, a lot of them. The damage was pretty extensive."

"Yes, our options are rather limited." Commander Preston perused the assembly at the table, good men all of them, unwilling participants in someone else's twisted scheme. He was proud to serve with them, now even prouder to lead them. He had no strategy to offer them. Their damaged captain, now locked and guarded in his cabin, had sealed their fate.

"Gentlemen, I have some very revealing information that Professor Kincaid recently shared with me, actually about an hour ago. It appears we find ourselves in the Sea of Japan not by accident, although nothing was ever by pure chance with Van Noy, he just chose to share very little with us. Van Noy directed this ship to the cooler waters of this area ocean for very specific reasons. I will let Professor Kincaid explain it from here." All those at the wardroom table shifted in their chairs, each head pivoted to the American professor. They waited; no cue was needed.

Continually intimidated by his German colleagues and overwhelmed by their innovative technology, Professor Kincaid had played a passive role for too long on this journey. His colleagues' sudden deaths had broken the chains that checked his actions and silenced his tongue. The futuristic device was just that, its time had not yet come. Kincaid had sensed this from his first exposure to it.

Kincaid was initially recruited by the Defense Department because of his work in the area of weapons development at Blackburn Machinery, a division of General Electric. He relished his new status and devoted himself to the defense of his country.

But then, numerous German scientists were brought in to aid the war effort. They were being secreted out of Germany and their participation to the war effort was deemed critical. Because of his firm grasp of the German dialect, a product of his mother's heritage, he was asked to be the liaison for a select group of German researchers. Newly arrived in the US, they brought with them a proposal of a weapon of innovative design with game changing potential. To him it was a step down, a babysitting responsibility. His own hard work was pushed to the side, suddenly irrelevant.

His German colleagues soon began to control the project's direction. Professor Mueller seemed consumed with its development, continually working long days on end. Professor Bjurman, the other critical team member, his passion not as robust, appeared more concerned with the pace of their project and would often confront his foreign counterpart, sometimes forgetting that the American liaison understood their language. Their arguments, heated at times, always centered around the issue of insufficient testing supporting critical assertions, stability and safety, two topics always debated.

When he confronted them on these issues, Professor Mueller's stronger personality would dominate the discussion and the concerns that they had vocally debated would quickly vanish. Professor Mueller deemed it just productive banter and they would part company with little resolved.

Professor Bjurman's feeble participation and passive acceptance in these discussions always left him feeling he had been denied the whole truth.

Professor Kincaid addressed those in the wardroom.

"The last several days before my German colleagues died, there were desperate discussions between the two; they were trying to rein in the machine's instability. It seems the ocean waters we were traveling through are warmer than the eastern US currents we did our beta testing in. Those few degrees in temperature difference were just enough to create the machine's instability that contributed to our demise."

Lieutenant Billings could not control himself. "I have been hearing all this bullshit about cooling pumps and poor design for a while now. You mean all these good men died because of a few degrees difference in the sea water. How can you sit there and tell us that, like you're reading a weather forecast? What kind of prick are you—" and he leaped at the professor, grabbing him by his shirt and wrestling him to the deck, his fists flying wildly through the air, trying to find any piece of Kincaid.

Those in the room quickly separated the two men, the professor grateful for their intervention, the lieutenant still senseless in his attempts to punish the professor. Several men strained to control him; his face flushed red with rage. Commander Preston shouted directives for the chaos to end. Billings heard not a word. He continued to struggle with those trying to restrain him. Slowly the fight left him, he stood there, his shirt torn and pulled free from his pants.

Not knowing what he searched for, Billings's eyes moved about the room. Those standing there knew he sought their understanding and forgiveness even if he did not. An empty, bewildered man, he turned and left the wardroom. No one tried to stop him.

They straightened the conference table, picked up the chair from the floor and offered it to Kincaid. Wearing a face fresh with bruises and scratches, he wearily took a seat. He stared off and beyond the men in the room. Tears gathered at the edges of his eyes.

"Gentlemen, this journey has been a very demanding one, a god damn awful one," Commander Preston said, his voice heavy with empathy, "and yesterday took its toll. That could have been any one of us," and he pointed to where Lieutenant Billings once stood. "We're all shadows of what we used to be." He turned to the professor. "I'm sorry that happened to you, the lieutenant was really venting against Van Noy, but you know that." He was about to have the professor continue his proposal, but now seeing him there, his left eye beginning to swell and his lower lip split and bleeding, he thought better of it.

"Perhaps we should try this later. Why don't we—"

Professor Kincaid interrupted him. "We do this now. There isn't time to reschedule. Some very important decisions have to be made and you need to be informed, but just in case somebody else wants to use me as a punching bag, understand this was not my invention, never was. I saw no practical good coming from this evil tool. I spoke German, so they made me a babysitter." And he looked at every man in the room. Most nodded their heads in acceptance.

Commander Preston extended his arm and open hand towards the table, inviting Kincaid to continue his dialogue.

The professor rolled out a navigation chart onto the conference table. Ashtrays and coffee cups secured the four corners.

"This is our location." He pointed to a spot on the map. "We're about 400 miles due east of Hamhung, Korea. Probably a place where no American warship has ever been before. East of mainland Japan there are some very warm ocean currents," and he ran his hand parallel to the large island nation, "like the Gulf Stream just off the coast of the eastern US." He brought his index finger back to their current position on the chart. "Here we're looking at ocean temps 15 to 20 degrees cooler. I believe my German counterparts, more specifically Professor Mueller, directed your captain to head towards this body of water. I believe they knew the device was failing and maybe the cooler ocean might extend its usefulness. That opportunity never presented itself."

Commander Preston entered the discussion again. "Navigations officer Ensign Tisdale and I've been looking at this inlet up here," again he pointed to their chart. "It's called Amurskiy Bay, it's about 900 miles due north of us. It shows some shallow depths and very strong tidal currents, maybe we can get those narrow depths to work to our benefit. Japanese destroyers draw a lot more water than this Fletcher class. I say we run as far as our fuel takes us; this is Russian territory, maybe it's enough to scare the Japanese off. We take a stand, the hell with the outcome. Professor Kincaid believes with the chilly waters we're in, we might get one more use out of the

Rainbow Room. Maybe we can set a trap for Tokyo Joe and end this for good."

He paused to let it sink in. LaPierre was the first to speak. "They died with their boots on, so to speak, our last stand." His tone was solemn with the acceptance of the finality of it all. "Trying to use a shallow draft to our advantage sounds like something out of a nineteenth century ship's sailing manual. We have reached a desperate place if that is our single defense, only an observation sir, not a condemnation," he added.

"It does seem desperate," Preston replied, "but I think it's our only option. I say we steam towards Amurskiy Bay. See what develops, we'll meet again tomorrow. If anybody's got a better approach, I'm all ears. Professor, you should have a visit with Doc Bellows."

It seemed the appropriate thing to do. They rose from their chairs, offered Kincaid condolences and soft pats on his shoulders. Later they would offer the same gestures to Billings. Both men sought understanding and hoped not to be judged.

A consensus had been reached; the *Eldridge* would push on to the Amurskiy inlet. That decision was quite easily made. Fuel, distance, and time had simply placed them there and they would turn and fight.

In the meantime, their Japanese shadow had decided to up the stakes. They began another cat and mouse scenario. The two warships kept their distance for several hours, then a sudden rush by the *Natsugumo,* firing a salvo when within range. The *Eldridge* would immediately go to flank speed and general quarters would be sounded. There was pandemonium on the *Eldridge*. Return fire was brought to bear on the Japanese destroyer and the *Natsugumo* would quickly disengage. Another few hours and the identical setup would be repeated with neither ship inflicting any damage.

For Van Noy the activities were agonizing. The repeated call of battle stations, the sound of rushing sailors on the other side of his cabin door, the roar of the heavy guns, all of it painfully distracting for him. He tortured himself about the ineptness that was surely occurring and would no doubt bring about the destruction of his ship. The fools were not even clever enough to understand that he was the only one that could deliver their salvation. He had to do something, there was no other choice.

Hidden beneath a loose decking plate, he retrieved his prized .45 caliber Smith & Wesson. It had been a gift from his father when he achieved the rank of lieutenant commander and given his first command. A bittersweet memory for him now.

General quarters had just been broadcasted. Again, there was controlled chaos on the *Eldridge*. Van Noy lay down on his stomach and fired his pistol three times into the exterior bulkhead. The sound was deafening and the armed seaman stationed outside his stateroom began pounding on his door and shouting his name. He heard the loud cursing and the fumbling of keys. Van Noy held his breath and kept completely still. The armed sentry unlocked the door, rushed into the room and to his skipper's side. The guard gently rolled him over. In one swift motion Van Noy pulled the gun from beneath his shirt and pinned it on the sailor's forehead. The young recruit froze, he knew his life would end abruptly, and he hoped the pain would be brief. Captain Van Noy smiled sarcastically and pulled the trigger. The back of the young sailor's skull exploded and splattered the nearby wall. This time no one heard a thing. The screeching alarms and panicked commotion had guaranteed that. Closing his stateroom door, he quickly removed his own uniform and donned the sailor's outfit. He was soon racing along the hallways, just another seaman sprinting to his battle station.

He was soon below decks and near the entrance to the Rainbow Room, he made a mad dash for the heavy steel hatchway. Seaman Wilson was suddenly blocking his way, grabbing his forearm. "Sir you can't go in there." Van Noy's revolver suddenly appeared from nowhere and Seaman Second Class Bernard Wilson, his eyes suddenly wide with disbelief, knew there would be no further discussion. The powerful blast pounded Wilson's chest cavity and tore a massive hole in his heart. Van Noy closed the Rainbow Room portal behind him and began to engage a weapon that had done little to soothe the hatred he harbored so deep in his soul. He had just murdered two young men for no good cause and he was entirely indifferent to its consequences.

USS *ELDRIDGE*

A sudden decrease in their forward speed signaled something was wrong, very wrong. Commander Preston was in the CIC. "Engineering, please tell me this is not what I think it is," Commander Preston shouted.

Lieutenant Cabral the engineering officer faced his superior, dread freezing his expression. "Sir, power has been diverted from our drive."

At the same time, the intercom from below decks begged for Commander Preston's immediate response. "Sir, Captain Van Noy has gotten into the Rainbow Room. He's locked himself in there. Seaman Wilson is dead."

"I want a full security team down there on the double. Get Professor Kincaid as well. Also, get six of our best machinists down there with their cutting torches. Pronto!!! We need to get in that room immediately. I'm on my way. I want constant updates on that Jap destroyer. How the fuck did Van Noy get loose?"

They scrambled below decks, sometimes leaping to the floor below; some ran ahead of their commander, others close on his heels. They gathered just outside the Rainbow Room, men were already putting their shoulders against the entrance to the secret room, its thick steel frame moving not at all. Machinists were setting up their torches.

"Spark those torches. Fire teams be ready. Gentlemen, we need to get into that room as quickly as we fucking can. Our lives depend on it." The commander's words and tone were disturbing.

Stepping back, Preston grabbed the connecting phone to the bridge. "Lieutenant what's that Jap destroyer doing?" He listened then cursed …. "Fuck!! Get a firing solution to number three and open up. Stay on him. Don't wait for him to be first." Seconds later they felt the shake and the blast of an outgoing eight-inch projectile.

Professor Kincaid arrived. He had been told that Van Noy escaped and had taken refuge in the Rainbow Room. "Commander Preston, the captain has not engaged the cloaking," he shouted above the noises of the cutting torches. "We would have felt the side effects. He really knows very little about its operation."

"Great, the one time I wish it was activated, we've got our Japanese stalker making a run on us again." Another boom from the after mount.

Van Noy opened the exterior hull valves and activated the cooling pumps. There was an immediate drain of the ship's power. Now, if he could activate their cloaking mechanism, he might save his ship. A mutinous, misguided crew had lost faith in their extraordinary weapon. He had not.

He stood before the control panel, his frustration and anger escalating. Dials and controls, relays and switches, green and red instrumentation. Some marked in German and all of it confusing.

"Goddamn their souls," he cursed the German researchers; they had been so secretive with how to operate their device. They ignored his pleas for more understanding on how it functioned, choosing only to spoon feed him information and withholding the critical data, knowing he could never differentiate between the two.

A heavy pounding on the hatchway told him his desperate escape would be all for naught. Capt. Milton Van Noy's world was rapidly collapsing in on him. Everything he ever cherished was stolen from him, and after those evil thefts, time had offered little comfort and no healing. His isolation would never be any sadder. His family was near, only a simple motion away. They would cure his loneliness.

Sparks and hot metal jumped out from the door. They were cutting through the door. It was time to go home.

Over the noise of the gas torches, the sound of a single gunshot halted everyone for the briefest moment; they looked at each other and then quickly returned to their desperate actions. Nothing was said. Collectively they knew that Captain Milton Van Noy was dead.

The torches were suddenly extinguished and Seaman Geanetti violently pushed his large frame into the smoking entryway. It swung wildly inward. On the floor, with a pool of blood gathered around his head, was Captain Van Noy. His eyes wide as if shocked by his own death. Complete pathos, no one cared, no one felt a thing.

A large explosion rocked the *Eldridge*, the enemy destroyer had found its range. On deck and probably a level below that, the damage would be severe.

Then again, the boom of the rear turret, the *Eldridge* still had her stinger.

"Get that carcass the fuck out of our way." Preston pointed to Van Noy and they immediately dragged his body as if it were a dead animal on the side of a country road, his head banging the raised rounded threshold. Commander Preston continued to shout his orders. "Here's how we're going to do this, Professor, engage this goddamn mechanism, now. I want everyone out of here." He grabbed the ship's phone and signaled the control room. "Pick up...pick up," he muttered, "Lieutenant Estrella, all engines stop, cease firing, hard to starboard, let her coast. I'm on my way up."

"Commander Preston, I'll have the system up by the time you get to the bridge, don't know how long I can give you," Professor Kincaid offered, his forehead beaded with sweat. The dizziness and heat that was the signature of their secret weapon would soon begin its lethal migration outward.

"Just long enough, I hope. Professor get in the auxiliary room just above and stay near the ship's phone. Be ready to do whatever I say," he hesitated, "good luck and thanks." He dashed for the stairs, climbing them two at a time.

NATSUGUMO

"Captain, the American destroyer has decreased his speed by quite a bit." Ensign Tanaka's voice was tired but alert. "I will provide firing solutions to our turrets, but we're not quite in range."

"Do so," Captain Saito replied. He turned to the officer of the bridge. "Bring us to flank speed immediately, sound battle stations. Helmsman, be ready for a course change. Gunnery officer ready on my command."

They waited. Minutes dragged by. "Captain Saito, something is different this time, usually he disappears from my screen after he decreases his speed, takes a minute or so but he's usually gone long before this point. Now he's still there, bright as light bulb on New Year's. We're well within range, his and ours—" and then an explosion wracked the after deck of the *Natsugumo*.

"Open fire," the order quick, instinctive, the forward six-inch rifles bellowing flame and smoke. Those on the bridge turned to see huge flames shoot out from the decks below, just aft of the rear battery. The explosion was excessive, indicative of more than one hit; an inferno was instantly raging in the levels beneath. There would be multiple deaths and injuries with more to come. Fire teams were scrambling.

"Maintain flank speed, continue firing, Ensign Tanaka you will continue to provide updates."

The shelling continued. A flash on the horizon indicated a hit on the American, quickly another explosion lit up the sky. Confidence on the *Natsugumo's* bridge was beginning to grow.

"Captain, I just lost him, no indication at all where he is," Tanaka reported, frustration choking his words.

"Why don't we see any smoke, we know we hit them!" Captain Saito screamed.

Tanaka shrugged his shoulders. "Sir, we should cease firing and reverse our course immediately."

Saito stared at his radar officer, the American once again gaining the upper hand, his frustration overwhelming.

"Helmsman, let's go hard to starboard, bring us about. Maintain flank speed."

USS *ELDRIDGE*

"Commander, he is dis-engaging, turned 180 and is making good speed," Hanesy pronounced elated, as were the men in the CIC.

"Okay, we got lucky again, wondered if he knows what a damaged ship we are right now. Suppose not. Let's go 180 ourselves, 8 knots as she goes. Hansey as soon as were out of radar range, I want us at full speed. You know where we're headed, get us there." He picked up the ship's phone, "Professor, Hansey will call you as soon as we're beyond range, shut Rainbow the fuck down immediately after that confirmation. Thanks Professor, you just saved our ass. He hung up the receiver and turned to his staff. "Gentlemen, anyone not critical to the bridge right now I want amidships. I'm sure we have some seriously injured shipmates."

They moved quickly to the mid-ship area where the medical storage room, laundry, and the forward engine room had taken hits. Two-inch fire hoses crisscrossed the decking. Sailors struggled to maintain control of the canvas serpents. Water was everywhere, often bouncing off bulkheads and back on those trying to control the inferno. One crewman, his size and weight simply not enough to direct the sea water where it was needed, screamed for help. Commander Preston grabbed the fire line and with the young sailor began attacking the flames. Others began helping the wounded and burned. Doc Bellows treated and consoled all that he could and was overwhelmed. Men were being stretchered to sickbay. Some, he knew, in vain.

When he saw Commander Preston among them, he shouted, "When can we turn off that fucking death machine below? Too many of us nauseous and dizzy, all fucked up. Me included."

"Soon Doc, soon," he yelled back, and they worked their way inside, closer to the source of the firestorm.

Professor Kincaid was suddenly standing next to the commander, grabbed his arm and yelled, "I'll take it from here, the machine has been turned off."

Preston stood among the chaos, his face, neck, and arms red from the fires they fought. They had gained the upper hand, only small flare-ups remained. The *Eldridge* was again attacking the waters at flank speed, another sign that the death machine had been checked. The wind along her sides felt good. Now they would count their dead and sail towards a place never heard of, but which would define their legacy.

USS *ELDRIDGE*

"What's this place called again?" Lieutenant Commander La Pierre inquired.

Another gathering in the wardroom, their mood darker, more somber. Tomorrow would bring their final battle and by then, they would be a ship without fuel, adrift, their ability to defend themselves now very limited. Looking for the silver lining would be challenging for this assembly of officers.

Captain Van Noy had escaped from his quarters, how, it didn't really matter. No one cared. His breakdown, long ago started, had finally completed its destructive mission. Putting his pearl handled .45 to his head and blowing his brains all over a control panel in the Rainbow Room was the easiest decision he had ever made. It was as simple as taking a few extra aspirin for a very bad headache, it's what you did when the pain became too much. Besides, his wife insisted it was time to come home. It was a travesty that he had to take two young men in their prime with him.

"It's called Amurskiy Bay, nothing really special about it, it's just a place to be when we run out of fuel," Lieutenant Cabral answered.

"Actually, I've done a little research on it, not that much to go on, just the global charts we have with their footnotes, but it shows some extremely shallow depths and that's because it has one of the strongest tidal surges of anywhere in the world," radar tech Bill Hanes revealed. "The delta in tide height, low to high, is about 26 feet. Pretty remarkable, actually. Don't have the slightest idea if that means a damn thing for us," he concluded.

Those in the wardroom didn't the see the significance either.

"Gentlemen, in about twenty-four hours we'll be steaming into the inlet at Amurskiy Bay. Things will probably get quite ugly. How do we prepare for that? I've got some ideas but I want to hear yours first."

Gunnery officer Lieutenant Commander LaPierre jumped in. "When we arrive in this Cape Amurskiy, Tokyo Joe will be right on our ass, he hasn't come this far just to sail off into the sunset. How much time will we have to prepare for the apocalypse?"

"One hour maybe," Hansey answered.

"That's not long," LaPierre replied. "OK this is how I see it from my perspective. We're in a precarious situation, both of our forward mounts are toast, we have only two of the after turrets functional. The only real threat we have is our torpedoes, they remain completely operational." And then he hesitated.

"Why the pause, Lieutenant?" Commander Preston pushed.

"Because now it becomes a strategy planning session, I can only provide opinion. In the end—"

Commander Preston cut him off. "Come on Jim, I asked for opinions, Christ, just get it out!"

"Okay, it's a long bay, I say we find a narrow inlet, steer up as far as we can, moor ourselves parallel to the opening, hope he comes in after us. Put a spread of fish in the water, we can do five at a time, and we have twenty torpedoes. If we're lucky, we put one into him. Actually, think the odds aren't too bad. If he takes the bait."

Ideas were exchanged, proposals offered and then measured. There were no egos complicating the process, all the adversity had brought them together, they cared very much for each other. No one wanted this to end badly. In the end, a clear consensus, they prepare their ship for its last engagement, as laid out by Lieutenant Commander LaPierre.

Commander Preston took in a deep breath and looked upon the men seated before him; he felt only pride and deep respect for all of them. "Tomorrow will be our toughest challenge, put on a brave face for your men, they deserve it. They have sacrificed a lot. We will put up a good defense and get through this, our strategy will guarantee it. That's what we will tell them and you will be convincing." Exhausted, unshaven, his hair greased back, he rose from his chair.

"You all should know how proud I am of you and it has been an honor to serve with you."

The mood turned even darker. Heads nodded, they were just as proud and grateful. They slowly shuffled out of the wardroom, each man alone with his own thoughts of loved ones, unfinished business, and words left unsaid.

Reaching out he grabbed the arm of Professor Kincaid. "Professor," Commander Preston raised his index finger to his lips and cocked his head back towards the conference room.

He closed the door to the wardroom. "Professor, our situation is rather delicate, although you didn't need me to tell you that. However, the plan we just formulated will not be enough, possibly something you did not know. But that is the awful reality of it."

"What do you want from me, I'll do whatever I can."

"I can't believe I'm going to ask this, but can we get one more use out of that horrible device we have? It may be our only way out of this."

Their secret weapon was unstable, one more use could prove deadly, not that it was an issue; death was always part of its horrific identity. Now the possibility of the thermal runaway they had always feared was very real.

"Commander, I have no idea what's going to happen if we activate that device. My guess, it might work for a while, how long, no idea. Its core is so fragile, all those times running close or over its design limits has done severe harm. Right now, I think it's a god damn ticking time bomb."

Preston ran his open palm through his thick black hair. "I understand the gravity of what you're telling me. There's a freaking Jap destroyer out there that's got one huge hard-on for us and he's going to be all over us like white on rice. The deck is stacked against us;

we're going to need a small miracle to come out of this alive. And again, I can't believe I'm going to say this, but that miracle might be sitting in the bottom of the ship. Please, hear me out."

BOOK III

THE FINAL BATTLE

THE FINAL BATTLE

To the east, a rather ordinary sunrise pried open a new day, perhaps their last. Sleep had been fleeting, last night they had checked and rechecked their mid-ships torpedo racks. They practiced loading and dry firing the fish. An uneasiness kept them sharp. They were as ready as they would ever be.

Before them the entrance to Amurskiy Bay. They reduced speed and eased their way into the inlet, testing the waters as they went. The bridge and the CIC were crowded with officers and petty officers, theirs was a single purpose; they would make their stand together. Normal procedures during battle were relaxed; there was an urgency to be as close to each other as tolerable. A sense that a day of reckoning was upon them had instinctively brought them together.

"What's our fuel status? Ensign Cabral?" Preston shouted out.

"I have us at 14,000 gallons. Once we drop anchors and get positioned, I can shut down the screws. I will keep the steam turbines on standby, per your request."

"Good, let's get up this channel, I like this spot here," he pointed to the map where a small peninsula jutted out into the bay. "Let's maneuver behind it and tie off. It'll be just enough to hide from his radar. Hope we can suck him in. I believe it's our most defensible position. But we gotta do it quickly! Gentlemen let's start communicating and coordinating."

Orders and directives were given. Men scurried about the deck; subtle course changes were ordered. Engines were engaged and then disengaged, sometimes reversed. Finally, the loud rattling noise of their anchor dropping into the water, and then a peaceful stillness on the *Eldridge* as she found her spot within the currents and depths of Amurskiy Bay. A soft breeze moved along her lines, teasing youthful locks and grizzled chins. All eyes turned southward, on the distant seascape an insignificant dark gray column of smoke trailed upward. The horsemen of the apocalypse were soon to be upon them.

Commander Preston grabbed the ship's mic, his voice booming and echoing across the ship and the waters around them. "Ok listen up. It's going to get pretty hairy in a short while. Do what you've been trained to do. Stay focused, stay cool, and we'll get through this." He wanted to tell them how proud he was of them, but there was no reason to make their situation any more unsettling. Perhaps, if they did survive this, he could tell them. He switched off the ship's P.A. and picked up the phone for the Rainbow Room.

"Professor Kincaid, you there?

"Yes sir."

"We're inside Amurskiy Bay, we'll be tied off shortly, steam turbines will still on line; you should have all the power you'll need. Be ready for my orders."

"Yes, but I have no concept how stable our machine will be or for how long. I know I sound like a broken record—"

"Yeah, you do Professor, relax, I understand what you're telling me."

"Commander, I have radar contact," Hansey announced from the CIC. "It's our nip and he's coming on fast."

"Stand by," he yelled to the professor and hung up the phone.

Two sudden explosions 200 yards south of them sent plumes of water high into the morning sky. The Japanese warship announced its arrival. They were ranging in on the *Eldridge*, now a stationary target; it would not be a difficult thing to do. Maybe one more separate round to complete the targeting process, after that the next salvo would be their full arsenal and it would be lethal.

With only two of her five turrets operational and the command given, the *Eldridge* returned fire. The coordination between radar and fire control was precise. Two missiles, each packed with 58 pounds of high explosives, rocked the enemy frigate. Flames erupted skyward, thick black smoke rose to swallow those red and orange swirls. Those on the bridge felt a reprieve, a sense of hope. Lieutenant Estrella muttered to himself, "Bet that hurt."

The combatants exchanged another salvo. Commander Preston could wait no longer. He grabbed the phone for the Rainbow Room. "Engage now," he hollered, not waiting for Kincaid's reply. He felt the turbines load down, the strain on them obvious. He hoped against hope that his ploy might work.

NATSUGUMO

They stalked the American destroyer to the mouth of the Amur- skiy inlet and then their unpredictable move into and up the fjord. The whole course taken by the American since their first battle had baffled them, it had challenged all naval tactical logic. The enemy had traveled west of their island nation, deeper into Japanese controlled waters and further away from the protection of the ever- increasing US fleet. The Americans had steadily increased their dom- ination of the southern and central Pacific. Several theories had been postulated as to why this single destroyer charted such a strange course; in the end no one really knew. Japanese naval command's orders were explicit, "Destroy the American destroyer at all costs, kill or be killed." The message was crystal clear.

"Captain, the American has entered Amurskiy Bay and is moving deeper into the inlet. There are lots of twists and turns; he's probably looking at the same charts as we are, maybe he wants to find a place to hide, a place where our radar can't see him. Do you want to pursue?"

"Our enemy has befuddled us." Captain Saito paced about the pilot house. "I believe we should force his hand. We shall pursue this filthy rodent. Have the ship go to battle stations, all engines ahead full, as soon as you have a fix on him, you will open fire. We are at a crossroads now, it's time for our indecisive actions to end."

Once again organized chaos, sailors scrambling, the *Natsugumo's* engines were dialed all the way up and she surged through the Amurskiy Bay waters.

"Captain, if the charts are right, we'll be in some shallow waters in about 4 miles, very strong tidal currents too."

"Noted. Steady as she goes."

This time the gunnery officer chipped in. "Captain, we should begin our ranging."

"Then do so." Their two forward batteries erupted and the ship shuddered.

Short moments later, two huge explosions shook the *Natsugumo*. The American beat them to the punch, their first salvo deadly accurate. Her number three turret, with the explosives located within, blew itself apart. The rear depth charge rack was hit; several drums exploded and the ship's stern was ablaze. There was potential for more lethal explosions.

Captain Saito turned to his gunnery officer, his face red, eyes wide with impatience. "Open fire!" he screamed. The full arsenal of the *Natsugumo* expelled its wrath.

USS *ELDRIDGE*

This time the *Eldridge* felt the sting of their Japanese foe, the CIC and sickbay took direct hits. Petty Officer William Hanes was killed instantly, a solitary blip, the last vision he would take in before he and his radar screen were obliterated. Ensign Pullhause, the junior communications officer; Lieutenant Commander LaPierre, the CIC senior officer; and Second Class Petty Officer Dunbar also died in the instant inferno; others were critically injured with severe burns and missing limbs.

Doc Bellows was killed tending to his flock in sickbay. They found his body collapsed over a young enlistee still on the examination table, the youth's eyes wide with fear. He too was dead. A section of gray bulkhead grossly imbedded in Doc's abdomen had nearly bisected the two of them.

The Doc felt some redemption when the man he absolutely detested put a bullet through his own skull. Doc was always a man of infinite compassion and the depth of his hatred for Captain Van Noy troubled him. That kind of odium eventually destroys from within. But the evil prick was dead and Doc wanted to heal the wounds inflicted by Van Noy on his lambs. But those acts of compassion had been savagely stripped from him, now they would be someone else's responsibility.

268

Four other men were killed, three of them patients. Critical medications were lost in the resulting inferno. Severe burns and gruesome injuries no longer had the indulgence of being treated with morphine.

Fire crews were attacking the flames throughout the ship; others sought to fathom the loss of life and the damage done. The CIC would no longer provide critical information to bridge personnel. Men and machine now gone. Those that had survived the explosions in the CIC, some of them wounded, made their way to the pilot house. Their bloody and battered entrance only confirmed to those in the bridge that the explosions had been close and deadly.

"Are we capable of any communication with the CIC, I've been trying to reach Hansey for some time, I need his eyes and ears. Something tells me you've got some bad news." Commander Preston waited for the gloomy update he knew was coming.

The senior petty officer answered, "Commander, Hansey is dead, the CIC is severely damaged. We're on our own. Sir."

The news took their breath away, losing the CIC and the man that made it hum only increased their panic.

"Mr. Moretti, we've been on our own for a long time." Hansey's loss hurt; that could not be denied. But Commander Preston would not amplify his death. "Let's get back on task. I want look outs aloft, get eyes on our Jap destroyer. I want every possible seaman manning a fire hose or a demo axe." He barked his commands. "Let's get our dead and wounded taken care of." He turned to his gunnery officer. "We need our torpedo tubes ready. I want the spread just as we discussed."

NATSUGUMO

The reflection on Ensign Tanaka's screen faded in and out continually. The *Natsugumo* had scored direct hits. The American destroyer's deck and superstructure were on fire, thick black smoke curled upward from behind the inlet where the American had sought shelter. Suddenly the smoke and the tips of the red flames vanished as did the image on his screen. How was that possible, a reflection on his screen and the physical reality of that image disappearing together?

He notified his captain. Although, something was different this time, he sensed the American had moved to a more defensible position. Captain Saito felt the situation dictated an aggressive response.

"Bring us perpendicular to that cove, gun crews be ready. We may finally have him."

USS *ELDRIDGE*

The phone connection to the Rainbow Room crackled with static and a slight echo chased the professor's words.

"Things are very unstable here, Commander." The professor's voice was shaky with fear and nausea. He sounded quite ill.

"Is the mechanism working?" The commander's question was direct, pointed.

"All the indicators are there; I am quite sure we have disappeared from our enemy's radar screen and any visual evidence of our smoke and fire along with it. I left the Rainbow Room just a few minutes ago, the heat is too intense. I'm above, in the auxiliary room, same as before. Two crewmen have collapsed from the heat. They may be dead."

"Just a few more minutes, Professor, that's all. We just fired our torpedoes."

"Not sure I can do that, I'll try, but metal fatigue is evident all over, like things are melting. There was a lot of steam coming from the floor below, almost like ocean water up against red hot steel plating. Loud banging noises, like flashing in a steam pipe." He stopped to get his breath, the wheezing exhausting him. "Oh my God!! We have a breech. There's water everywhere. It's already too late—" The phone went dead.

271

NATSUGUMO

The *Natsugumo* steamed beyond the peninsula, there in the inlet the American destroyer should have been clearly visible, but nothing was there, just the flat waters of a sheltered cove. Those on the bridge were shocked by the emptiness before them.

"Reduce speed to 8 knots," Captain Saito ordered.

Engines were dialed back and the mass of the *Natsugumo* pushed her lower in the bay waters. They searched the inlet waters, found nothing, even the radar screen could offer nothing. An uneasy calm settled into the pilot house.

"Captain, I have contact," the sonar man's voice screamed. "Torpedoes, inbound starboard side, two or three, maybe more."

Heads turned, binoculars raised, the unmistakable trails of torpedoes blistering through the ocean were there, heading for them.

"Flank speed, hard over to port!" Saito shouted.

The pilot house jumped with purpose; stanchions were dialed into the engine room. The helmsman pulled on the ship's wheel and she was responding. Others on the bridge froze in panic and braced themselves for the explosions they knew would come, their desperate actions would serve no purpose. The torpedoes were too near and too fast.

The first one struck just forward of the boiler room, the force of the blast pushing the warship further to port. Flames shot skyward, the inferno devastating as headwinds pushed the flames aft. A second torpedo struck the ammunition locker, the explosion was massive; the death and destruction below were extensive. The third hit pierced the number two engine room. Exterior bulkheads gave way and steam boilers exploded; cold seawater rushed in and collided with hot pressurized steam, creating a lethal killing zone. Flooding below decks was massive and immediate. In less than a minute the *Natsugumo* was listing heavily to starboard. Captain Saito gave the order to abandon ship, the sudden turn of events stunning his crew. How had the American so quickly turned the tables? There would be no report to offer the Japanese admiralty, and then a fourth hit breached another large section of hull.

In a brief amount of time the *Natsugumo* would roll over, her keel high and dry before she made her rapid plunge for the bottom of Amurskiy Bay. The loss of life would be widespread.

USS *ELDRIDGE*

The heat, the nausea suddenly ten times more intense than before, along with a force that pulled them all towards the bottom center of their ship. Sailors throughout the *Eldridge* fell where they stood, their bodies instantly gelled with the bulkheads and decking now suddenly porous. Others tried to grab nearby safety handles or lean into walls where they stood, the same fate awaited them, their limbs and torso penetrated steel barriers as if they were now made of thick jelly. All of them as before, severely burned in the process, the pain torturous and always deadly. Many of them dead instantly, others twisted and spasmed where they fell, their screams becoming a chorus of death.

Her steel hull melted away from beneath their secret weapon, opening the floodgates. Thousands of gallons every second attacked the *Eldridge*'s buoyancy. Her waterline quickly moved upward. There would be no stopping her surge to the ocean floor. A tidal flow suddenly grabbed hold of her hull, so strong her anchor chains snapped. The *Eldridge* was pulled from the sheltering inlet and pushed further up the bay.

Commander Preston and those in the pilot house would face the same outcome as their shipmates. The piercing hotness and instability that had become the reality of their secret weapon now

274

overwhelmed their room. They froze where they stood and melted into the decking below and the walls near them. The smell of burning flesh sickening and the pain immeasurable. Many of them, their last act an unselfish gesture of a helping hand, reached out to one another. No command given to abandon ship, that opportunity never arrived.

USS *ELDRIDGE*

Young seaman Kevin Connors, high aloft, next to *Eldridge*'s radar dome would be the only one to witness the *Eldridge's* final moments. Perhaps his distance out from the ship's center was his lucky break. The heat, although intense, was not as crippling. It would eventually take his life, but not before he saw the undeserved path that had been laid out for them. An undeserving legacy, one that in life the crew of the *Eldridge* would never accept as their identity but would forever become the tale always told when history reflected on them.

The fires below had been contained before the deadly plague moved across the vessel, now she was a lifeless, smoky, smoldering ship. Wanting to understand what had happened to the Japanese destroyer and to view the last moments of the vanquished enemy, Seaman Connors struggled to his feet. High in his perch, he saw the stern of the Japanese destroyer slip beneath the waves, her twin propellers still turning. A flaming oil slick now marked where she had disappeared; survivors in the water struggled to escape the flames.

He felt the sudden, powerful tidal surge as it pushed the *Eldridge* further up the bay. Their anchor no longer an obstacle to that commanding current. He had heard the recent talk that they had purposely sought out a spot that was home to one of the most dramatic

276

tidal flows of any place on this planet. Was this that tidal phenomenon?

The water rushed by, and it steadily climbed up the sides of the *Eldridge*. They were sinking and yet there was no panic anywhere. No orders shouted, no seamen rushing about trying to save their ship. They were all dead and Seaman Connors would only witness. Seawater was already above the gunnels; passageways were now flooding and still she was being pushed further up the inlet.

A sudden grinding halt told Seaman Connors that the *Eldridge*'s keel had found the bottom of Amurskiy Bay. The tidal current now pushed up and over the bow like a submarine diving for the sheltering depths of deep water. Sea water moved steadily upward, swallowing deck after deck. Debris and bodies not imbedded were dragged away. Soon the bridge was flooded; no bodies emerged from that deluge. The deadly heat was gone, but no relief, no answered prayer for Seaman Connors, his shipmates, close friends all gone. He was there to witness the last few moments of the *Eldridge*'s existence, alone and in great discomfort. It made no sense.

The rising tide still sought him out, his feet, his shins now sensing the cold central Pacific Ocean that flowed all about him. Giving his soul and what remained physically of himself to his God, he lowered himself onto the floor plating of the perch where he sat. The frigid water, now chest high, sucked the air from his lungs. The rising ocean slowly filled in his world. Soon his tiny universe would be seen through a blue green prism. The overhead sun now not as piercing swirled above him and then Buck, his faithful coon hound, his tail alive with joy, was suddenly on his lap, licking at his face. His mother stood in the distance on their South Carolina porch and waved him in for lunch. He would go to her.

USS *RENO*

The USS *Reno,* her profile dark, purposely void of lighting, was a lethal shadow quietly slicing through enemy waters. In the early morning hours, Madame Alice stood at Simon's cabin; her fragile, persistent rapping at his door finally pulled him from his slumber. He opened his door anticipating his old friend. The last few days Madame Alice had begun to seek him out at all hours of the day with unusual updates. The delicate knocking and the unusual hour only supported that reasoning.

"I sense we are close, very close to the end of our journey." Her greeting was intense with conviction. She still wore the same loose dress and worn, oversized shirt. Her hair dry, almost lifeless, hung all about. It was obvious Madame Alice was neglecting her hygiene. Simon struggled on how to approach the delicate issue, for now he would leave it alone. It troubled him. She had always been an attractive woman taking pride in her appearance. She looked tired, their trip no doubt taking its collective toll. Simon tortured himself for his decision to bring her along.

However, Simon now also sensed a culmination was about to reveal itself, but he would defer to Madame Alice, her gift much more reflective.

Sleep still had its grip on Simon, his thoughts sluggish.

278

"Why don't we go to the galley, I could use some coffee," he offered.

"You know I'm not much of a coffee drinker, never have been. It turns me into a bundle of nerves. But I will walk there with you."

They shuffled their way to the ship's galley. In the early hour, the passageways were empty of crew. They had the galley to themselves. In the back room they could hear the cooks preparing for the morning rush. Grumpy dialogue and clanging pots and pans. A seaman, his cigarette hanging onto his lower lip, the smoke making him squint, nodded towards the dispenser. "Coffee's fresh, just made it."

They sat at one of the tables. Simon gingerly sipped his coffee; fresh coffee often meant hot coffee.

"What happened this morning?" Simon asked. "You were persistent in your knocking, I'm sorry if it took me a while to answer."

"My young lieutenant visited only a few hours ago. He was quite edgy, there was no mistaking that. We're getting very close to where their spirits separated from their bodies, all of them together. A collection of fear and anguish hangs over these poor sailors like an invincible cloud. So many men terrified of losing their lives, never seeing their loved ones again, and possibly their souls wandering for eternity in some obscure location, their families dealing with a Defense Department letter stating 'Missing in Action' the only closure they would have. Simon, they desperately want us to find them. They are so worried we will miss them, especially now that we are so close. Lieutenant Estrella pleaded with me to be patient, not to give up, they were close by."

Simon had anticipated this; Madame Alice would be the communicator, the translator.

"What happens next?" he asked.

"When we are close, we will both know; I am convinced we will be overwhelmed with their presence. Two hundred and five damaged spirits will not be ignored. Simon, I have never felt such a calling in all my life. This speaks to me."

USS *RENO*

They stood on the bridge, before them an empty passage to a narrow inlet that stretch for miles inward. At the far end, one or two small fishing villages dotted the coastline.

Captain Bains was the first to speak. "We have to make a collective decision here, those are my orders, but first let me give you my perspective on where things stand, I'll keep my sarcasm in check. I just received a coded message from fleet command."

He told them that a recent Japanese message had been decoded, it told of a naval engagement about a week ago, between a Japanese and an American destroyer. Both ships were sunk; local fishermen recovered only a few Japanese survivors and no Americans. He acknowledged they had probably found the location where the USS *Eldridge* had gone down.

"It seems Japanese naval authorities have been notified and they are sending a vessel to investigate, that could mean a destroyer or a patrol boat; whatever it is I don't want to be here when they arrive. That could be in two days or two hours."

Lieutenant Commander Morrison was next. "My orders were to help you locate the *Eldridge* by whatever means possible and it appears we have done that. The other part of my order, probably your orders as well Captain Bains, even more critical, is to destroy the highly secretive mechanism in the bowels of that ship. We have to make that attempt."

"I just laid it out, how precarious things are. Mr. Morrison, any idea where we should search, I'm all ears." The frustration of a taxing assignment clearly was plainly catching up with him.

"You will not need to search for them, they will find you." Madame Alice's response was quiet, mechanical, as if she read from a holy scripture.

Perplexed, they searched her face for clarity. "We haven't come all this way for nothing, don't disrespect these brave men. We can't leave them here. You must be patient." She moved to leave the pilot house, and then turned back to them, said, "I'm tired," and then again, "Be patient," and she drifted from the room, her long dress skimming the floor, her hair moving stiffly in the breeze.

"Gentlemen," Simon now offered, "if Madame Alice believes these men and their ship are here, you can take that to the bank. I have too many experiences that reinforce such a statement and if she says they will show themselves, then they will."

"It better happen pretty goddamn soon," Captain Bains offered. He spoke to his helmsman, "Begin a search pattern of this inlet, I want men aloft as well as along the rails."

Simon left the bridge, stopping at Madame Alice's room for more talk, but there was no response to his knocking. Convinced she was already asleep, he would leave her alone. Standing there in the pilot house she looked quite fatigued. He continued to blame himself for her condition.

Eight hours of crisscrossing Amurskiy Bay turned up nothing, The *Reno's* two launches were lowered to aid in the search efforts.

Anxious for an update, Simon left his cabin and headed for the bridge. He stopped at Madame Alice's cabin on the way; despite his persistent knocking he was unable to rouse her. He rejoined Lieutenant Commander Morrison and Captain Bains still on the bridge.

Taking turns raising their binoculars and searching the waters around them, they waited together, impatient for any news. Captain Bains nervously paced about the bridge.

"Captain, we're experiencing some extreme outgoing currents or tidal flow. We're getting pushed around pretty good," Lieutenant Palmer, his watch officer, informed him. "Our motor launches are having a tough go at it. Suggest we recall them."

"Then do so," the captain replied. "Also, notify our boatswain mates to drop our anchor ASAP. I want to ride this out where we are. No sense trying to conduct a search if we're getting muscled around, only end up covering the same area over and over.

They retrieved their launches, secured their anchor, and were stabilized against the aggressive currents. Her movements silent and secretive, no one noticed Madame Alice entering the pilot house. She moved deliberately towards the large forward windows, staring up the bay and to the near starboard side. She raised her right arm and extended her bony, pale index finger, pointing to an empty area of sea.

Simon moved to her side; he raised his field glasses to where she pointed. After a while, he leaned in and whispered to his friend, "There is nothing there, Sarah."

She turned to him. "Patience, Simon, you of all people. Patience." She returned to her vigilance off their starboard side and Simon returned his glasses to his eyes.

Only through his glasses was he able to see it, a small, quivering ripple along the surface. Then a small object, perhaps the top of a rock began to push back against a forceful current and then a short staff below the rock, the ripple now a small torrent. Simon no longer needed the aid of his binoculars; he turned to the others on the bridge to see if they shared the same observation. They stood there stunned, unsure of what they were about to witness.

A small strip of red cloth was suddenly being pulled out from the staff, then a blue and a white mixed in with it. Their country's colors were soon hanging limply from its staff, the tide surging outward and now below it. Soon *Eldridge's* radar dome was revealed.

Stunned silence was the shared response on the bridge of the *Reno.* Captain Bains jolted them back to reality. "I want our launches in the water now. Let's get over to the *Eldridge* ASAP. I want all bodies that can be recovered returned to this ship. Lieutenant Commander Howard, prepare your detonation crew for their assignment.

The rushing tide receded steadily, revealing more and more of the *Eldridge's* superstructure and then her lower levels. The water raced along her flanks. Seaweed hung from her gunnels, early barnacles and new marine growth appeared all about the vessel.

The launches pulled alongside the *Eldridge* and tied off. The vessels, despite the huge difference in size, were at the same level. Stepping from one to other was easily accomplished.

Handheld radios soon sent disturbing information back to the *Reno*. Numerous bodies throughout the *Eldridge,* burned and horribly embedded in bulkheads and decking. They would require more men and more tools. A launch returned to the *Reno*, tools and twelve crewmen were taken on, but there were two added, unexpected passengers. Simon and Madame Alice.

Simon strongly protested her decision to travel to the *Eldridge*. He could see no sense in testing her already compromised stability.

"Please do not do this, what good can possibly come of this. Do you really want to see these men in such a horrible state?"

"I promised these men I would find them and give them closure. That has been my life. Do you think I would come this far, commit so much of myself to this cause and then drop the ball when we're at the finish line? Simon, you know me better than that."

"You are not well! This entire trip has taken a toll on you. How you've struggled through it is testament to your resolve. But why must you continually push yourself? You have nothing to prove to me."

Simon pleaded to Captain Bains and Lieutenant Commander Morrison for their support, but neither had issues with her decision to go; her insight had resulted in a successful mission. A tremendous load had been lifted from their shoulders, they owed her this much.

The *Reno* had already notified fleet command that a certain vessel had been located and secured. More details would be forthcoming. But navy brass could relax. Simon did not have sufficient backing to prevent Madame Alice from going to the *Eldridge*. They did however assign a sailor to stay by her side at all times.

The launch struggled against the rushing tide but was soon tied off. They stepped gingerly from their craft to a ghastly reality, for the lifeless sailors of the USS *Eldridge* a horrifying and unjust eternity.

Salt water algae had begun its process of reclaiming the *Eldridge*, movement would require some caution. They began their trek to the bridge. Skeletal remains still cloaked in their uniforms hampered their travel. Some hung from passageway bulkheads, their arms or legs disappearing into the steel walls. The edges of their uniforms burned where they touched the hallways, their bony faces, now void of any flesh, showed the pain they had endured. Jaws still frozen wide screamed their pain in another world. Others were found in the same condition but stood before them like midgets, only their bodies from the waist up remained. Some with their hats hanging low, shielding their eyes from their new terrifying reality. The same scream as the others, framed by their outstretched mandibles.

"Oh, my savior," Madame Alice said, her voice low and woefully sad. "How could we ever leave them like this?"

"Not to worry, ma'am," the young ensign in charge of the detail offered. "I have strict orders to bring every man back to our ship."

They made their way to the bridge, the trip challenging and gruesome. Numerous personnel slipped in the slimy walkways. Madame Alice continually required a helping hand.

The scene in the pilot house was just as depressing. Lifeless skeletons, still wrapped in navy attire, all in gruesome positions. The air stale, foul with the smell of death.

Madame Alice confronted Simon and the ever present lieutenant commander. "He's not here, Lieutenant Estrella is not here." Her voice escalated, objective and demanding.

"We'll find him," Brewster replied, resolve in his voice.

"He's in the room behind us." A statement not a suggestion, she pointed to the CIC directly aft and below the bridge. "I need some air." Her complexion grew even more ashen.

They walked her to the area just outside the bridge, sun and a soft breeze greeted them. They leaned against the waist high railing and Madame Alice, removed from the foul air in the bridge, gathered her legs beneath her.

A single seaman joined them. "Sir, I think you better take a look in the CIC, not good."

"Oh my," she whispered. "Please find Lieutenant Estrella for me," she pleaded. "I'm feeling better, but I will wait here."

They nodded their consent and moved towards the dark news that waited for them in the CIC. "Keep an eye on her," Simon reminded her escort.

Light now filtering through algae covered portals, they stepped into the dungeon-like Combat and Information Center. It was obvious the room had taken multiple hits; the damage was extensive. Two charred bodies, unrecognizable, barely human in form lay near the broad chart table in the center of the room. Their tattered uniforms indicated they were not officers. Stunned, Brewster and Simon searched the room. Back in the corner, nestled among the debris they found him, his face and hands severely burned, his right leg inserted up to his knee in flooring below. They stood speechless, all the gore they'd seen since boarding collectively attacking their composure.

"My God," Brew Morrison said, his tone empty. "What must have happened here."

There was commotion on the bridge deck. "OSCAR, OSCAR," the navy term for man overboard, was shouted over and over. Suddenly a young midshipman stood in the silhouetted hatchway, he called to them. "We've lost her, you need to come now."

Simon raced to the outside bridge station. People frantically searching the rushing waters below. The youthful sailor who had been charged with the care of Madame Alice stood dumbfounded. He shook his head back and forth, his arms raised in astonishment.

Simon grabbed the sailor by the collar. "What happened? What happened?" he screamed. His hands finding the man's throat.

"I don't know," his voice gurgled from the chokehold on his neck. "She was there against the retainer; I turned my back for just an instant and she was gone. Maybe she slipped, I don't know. I think I saw part of her dress as she dropped below. By the time I got to the rail she was gone, the water is flying by down there if you haven't noticed."

Brew Morrison stepped in with other crewmen and separated the seaman from Simon's death grip. "You goddamn fool," Simon shrieked at him.

Lieutenant Commander Morrison took control. "I want a crew along the port side rail searching, let's get our launches over there, quickly," he reinforced.

Simon was immediately lifeless on the inside, this sudden unexpected loss more numbing than the death of his first wife. Panic consumed him and he began to make unrealistic demands of the sailors surrounding him, pacing all about as he did.

Morrison instantly sensed the reality of the incident. The long drop, the strong, speedy current below, the frailty of Madame Alice offered only one outcome. Even if they found her, she would not survive the ordeal.

They searched for the next hour, both crafts moving up and down the adjacent waters, all the time others worked to remove the bodies of *Eldridge* seamen and placed them along the gunnels, ready to be moved to the USS *Reno*. Both launches broke away from their search efforts and rushed along the *Eldridge*. The ensign in charge shouted to Lieutenant Commander Morrison on the bridge.

"Sir, radar on the *Reno* reports two ships heading this way. Could be Japanese patrol boats. We got about thirty minutes. Captain wants everyone, including the bodies, back on the *Reno* in twenty-five."

One of the launches had already tied off and was moving the bagged bodies on board.

Simon reached a new level of panic. "You can't be serious, you're going to leave her here, after all she's done for you," he screamed. Spittle jumping from his lips.

"Mr. Bouchard, I am truly sorry for this, but that is exactly what we're going to do. This is not open for debate." He called two sailors over. "Gentlemen, make sure Mr. Bouchard gets on the first launch leaving this ship, bind his wrists if he protests." He turned to Simon. "Why don't you help with getting the bodies off this ship, they deserve that courtesy. It's what Madame Alice would have wanted you to do. I can't spend any more time on this. Decide quickly Mr. Bouchard." He turned and left, there was much to do and not a lot of time.

The words sobering and on point, Simon knew Brewster Morrison was right, alive she would have demanded that effort of him. His heart crippled with pain, he pushed himself to where they were loading the bodies and offered a helping hand.

On board the *Reno* they had gone to battle stations. The first launch had returned with some of the bodies, Simon, and the demo unit. They had not gotten around to placing their demolition charges on the *Reno*. In the meantime, the fire control officer had offered a different solution to Captain Bains.

"Think we should put three fish into her, we can set the depths down, put them right on her lower deck. We can use the high explosive compound, that's four hundred fifty pounds of high-end TNT. They won't find anything after that. I can guarantee it."

"Then get it done, we'll do it as we pull away. Do not say one freaking word to Bouchard about this. We need to be crystal clear on this."

Others officers on the *Reno's* bridge entered the discussion and conversed about the approaching patrol boats and what their course of action should be.

USS *RENO*

he last launch returned from the *Eldridge*, the remaining bodies offloaded to the *Reno*. They had already retrieved their anchor, their drive engaged and engines torqued so they held their place next to the *Eldridge*. The bridge speaker crackled to life. "Captain, we've got fish in the water, sonar reports two separate high frequencies."

The captain picked up the mic for the CIC. "How far out Ensign?"

"A good ways out, sonar says they're on the very outer fringe. Hoping for a lucky shot. Sonar doesn't give it much of a chance, not in these currents."

"We're not going give them that chance. Lieutenant Howard, fire your torpedoes NOW! All head full, bring us hard over to port, bearing 175 degrees." He barked his orders and those required to repeat those orders did so, some trying to be heard above the others. It had the bridge alive with energy and charged with adrenaline. The excitement was real. "Have our rear mounts target those incoming patrol boats and open fire."

The torpedo team was standing by, depth settings had been adjusted and fuses set. "Fire" the command given. The torpedoes

288

leaped from their starboard side housings, at this range there would be no miss.

The *Reno* was charging forcefully to port, her engines pushing her hard against the angry tide. They looked back at the *Eldridge* and watched the trails of the torpedoes as they closed in on her. Three quick thunderous explosions broke the *Eldridge* at midships, her middle rose twenty feet into the afternoon sky, smaller parts of her even higher. Intense flames shot upward as if chasing the destruction. Her center fell back into the sea, pushing huge waves outward. Her bow and stern would soon follow her to the bottom. The USS *Eldridge*, DD-628 was gone, a casualty of war.

Horror stricken, Simon watched as the *Eldridge* exploded into a thousand pieces, and then a numbness consumed him, he could only witness. He was not capable of words or actions. An outcome never imagined and its impact never contemplated.

He heard the *Reno's* rear guns fire on the pursuing Japanese patrol boats but they were quick to break off their chase when it became clear they lacked the speed or fire power to continue that pursuit.

Now there would be a mad dash for home, and if they survived, he would have to break the terrible news of his dear friend's passing to her unsuspecting, loving husband. The burden tore at his soul.

USS *RENO*

The long journey home to the *Reno's* home port in San Diego, day after day of torturous self-reflection. Angry at times, over and over, Simon challenged the sailor that was to watch over his friend. Harsh words, attacking his character, his intellect. It was such a simple task, one that only required the most basic common sense and the ability to stay focused. Every time their paths crossed, Simon would lose all self-control and would begin his verbal assault.

The young sailor apologized a thousand times; he tried desperately to avoid their being in the same room. He began to push back, often people felt the need to intervene, separating the two men, steering them away from each other.

"You know what I think," the sailor finally shouted after the tirades began to wear him down. "I think she jumped overboard, yeah that's right, she friggin' killed herself." He locked eyes with Simon and he stood his ground. His fists clenched, eyes wide with rage, Simon wanted to attack the source of the bitter words, but something inside quietly resonated with that message. Perhaps a thought he too had harbored but would not allow. Returning to his cabin, he let the confrontation fade. There would be no more angry words directed at the faultless seamen, only at himself. A smothering sadness became his constant companion.

When they docked in San Diego, he instantly called his wife. They hadn't talked in months; the classified mission had restricted that type of communication. Deborah cried tears of joy. Simon told her his flight home from southern California would begin tomorrow; however, there would be one very sad addition to his itinerary. Madame Alice, his good friend from so long ago had died on the mission; he needed to tell her husband himself. Simon would not allow that to be someone else's dirty task. It was his burden alone. This time both he and his wife cried.

The bouncy, sometimes jarring plane rides, the lonely stops for fuel and overnight resting made the journey only more torturous. He searched for the right words to say to Milton, their conversation would be difficult. In his dreams, she stood there on the open deck of the *Reno*, the warm sun and tropical breezes teasing her long gray hair, her lengthy skirt quivering in the wind. She would always turn to him, pull her hair away from her eyes with her right hand, and offer a tender smile.

Now in the distance he could see the seaside inn, the same PT boat as before skipping along and up the waters of Narragansett Bay. A late morning ride, the sun already high, flooded the bay with the sparkle of a million crystals. Knowing the gloomy purpose for Simon's second visit to Prudence Island, the skipper and crew provided all the privacy he might want; few words were exchanged. PT-231 tied off at the rugged shoreline piling and with their small skiff, put Simon on the sandy shorefront. The ensign and his petty officer companion would wait by their dory. Simon began his lonely walk.

Between the hotel and the beach, he stopped at Milton's work shed. Sarah was always chasing him from there for lunch or when his hours there had been too long, it was where he "tinkered" she would say. He was not there.

Simon moved his way up and around to the front entrance. Some of the lower windows were boarded up; he wondered if they had been that way at his last visit. There on the front door, a puzzling sign, "For Sale by Owner." He knocked several times with no answer, he tried the door; it opened effortlessly. His voice bouncing along the wall papered room, he shouted his greeting, "Hello." Inside most of the furniture facing the panoramic view of the east passage was covered in graying sheets. For Sale signs, boarded windows, covered furniture, Simon suddenly realized the depressing news he carried with him had somehow already found its way back to Milton Post. The burden now heavier than ever. He immediately envisioned the day the Western Union telegram arrived; the news must have been devastating. How absolutely insensitive and callous of the navy. Simon twitched with bitter annoyance.

A noise from the rooms below, and then the noise of heavy feet slowly climbing the stairs to where he stood.

Milton entered the room, his shoulders slumped; he wore the same long billed fisherman's cap as he often did. Bright sunshine silhouetted Simon against the broad windows. Milton pulled his cap lower, his expression tired, his face more wrinkled.

"Who's there?" he called.

Simon stepped away from the blinding sunlight and closer to Milton. He thought about the last time they spoke on the phone. Milton's brother in Connecticut was about to die from serious heart complications and Sarah had confirmed he had passed away only days before they began their Pacific journey. Milton was away, helping his brother's family with their loss.

"Hello Milton, it's me Simon. I am so sorry for your loss." He embraced the lonely old man before him. "She was a remarkable woman."

"Yes, she was," he murmured, his eyes welling up, "she was my rock. She thought very highly of you. I thought I would see you sooner than this, but I'm glad you came."

"I got here as soon as I could. I haven't been home to my wife yet. Looks like you're getting ready to sell. And I'm so sorry for the loss of your brother. My God, Milton you have been given a heavy burden, if there is anything I can do."

A puzzled expression crept across Milton's face, "Yes, I will sell the inn, it's just too empty without my Sarah."

He paused. "Mr. Bouchard, what do you mean about my brother's death? He had a serious health scare, but he is doing just fine. Spoke with him this morning."

"Milton something is wrong here." An eerie feeling from a long time ago began to revisit Simon. "The day I arrived to talk about our potential journey Sarah told me about the loss of your brother, that was why you weren't here, you left to be with family. We left the next morning, telling me she had your blessing. I traveled to the other side of the world with her." He searched Milton's face for clarification.

"Simon, this gift that you and my Sarah shared always mystified me. I think it has always bewildered the two of you. I believe it finally turned itself on the two of you, it was something Sarah continually feared." Milton's expression softened, his words filled with compassion.

"That day you visited this inn, I had no idea you were here. That's because I was in Newport burying the love of life next to her father in the Newport Cemetery. Sarah passed away in her sleep two nights before. Her heart finally gave out. Who you traveled with to the other side of the world, I have no idea."

"

ABOUT
THE AUTHOR

orn in Providence, Rhode Island, and a lifelong summer resident of Prudence Island, K. W. Garlick is the beneficiary of a rich and varied professional background, from marine tradesman to educator to commercial contractor.

Ken finally realized his enduring passion for writing and recently published his third novel, *The* Eldridge *Incident,* a sequel to his first book, *Call Me Madame Alice.* His second book, *George's Hurricanes,* is a murder mystery which takes place on Prudence Island.

He and his wife currently live on Prudence Island, Rhode Island.

Member: Association of Rhode Island Authors

Chapter 18

The Quinton Mansion is on Fire!

Everybody jumped up to see where the commotion was coming from. Somebody came running up the road and hollering, "The Quinton Mansion is on fire!"

Elsie let out a shriek. "Oh no!"

John struck out as Mr. Bill and a few other men followed. By the time the group arrived, the mansion was engulfed in flames. Elsie dropped to her knees at the sight; she had planned to retrieve her bedroom suit from the house on the next morning. She cried and moaned, but it was too late for them to save the mansion.

Some of the Klan came to view the fire. They couldn't blame this tragedy on a black man. The blacks were now leaving to go up north.

John held Elsie in his arms. Susie and Hilda stayed outside of her house, looking in the direction of the inferno. Susie had such look on her face that it made Hilda suspicious. Could her sister have had something to do with it?

Susie saw her sister's expression and said to her, "Don't look at me!" Susie walked back inside the house, and couldn't resist smiling to herself. John, Elsie, and Mr. Bill returned to Susie's house without saying a word.

One of Elton's men came up to the porch and took his hat off. "John, it appears that your daddy got drunk and sat the house on fire. His body was found in there."

Elsie fainted. John picked up his sister and laid her on the sofa. Hilda went to get some cold compresses to put on Elsie's head. John was devastated. He didn't have any money except what Elton left them in the bank, which was $10,000. He knew what he had to do now. Go get Jenny and get out of Tallahassee.

The next morning Mr. Bill went to help John get the remains of the land. The gazebo was the only thing still intact. While some men came to help, while sifting through the rubble, Mr. Bill found a music box. He brought it to John, and as John takes it into his hands, he realizes what it is. It was Mother Quinton's music box. When he was a little boy, his mom would play it for him. The melody it played was "Swan Lake." Mr. Bill eventually left to return to his own house. John stayed there at the remains of his childhood home for three hours.

Susie saw Mr. Bill return to his house and yelled for him. "Come here Bill." When he neared Susie's porch, she said, "You get yourself together and get out of here, too."

Mr. Bill was shocked at the suggestion. "Where am I going to go with five children and a wife? How would I get anywhere? I don't have any money to catch a train like you and John!"

Susie left the porch and grabbed him by the arm. "Now you listen to me. What is wrong with you folk? You got to take a chance for once in your life, or you will die in poverty the way the white man wants you to. Haven't I been telling you what's going on around this damned country? They're lynching black men like crazy, and I'm not going to stand here and let you stay here so you can be killed, Bill!"

Bill was astounded at her earnestness, and he sat down on the porch and started to cry. After a short time, Bill wiped his face and got back up to walk home. He paused to look around at the area where he lived one long time. He thought about his friend that was hung in the town's square and how his children couldn't go to school with white children. He turned and yelled back at Susie, "I'm going home to tell my family that we're leaving, too."

"There you go, Bill." Susie whooped and laughed.

John came home and told Susie, "Baby, take the children and go to Louisville, Kentucky. I'll stay here and make sure everything is sold. I'll be up there with you in a couple of months. Don't be afraid; I know that you are a strong woman. I love you. Where are my children?" Susie looked at her husband with much concern. John hugged his wife and kissed her. The children came in from playing outside. "Come here, children." John took his children into his arms to hug them. "You all know that Daddy loves you, don't you?" The children nodded their head in agreement.

"We're moving away from here." The children jumped up and down with joy. "I want you to behave yourselves, because Daddy needs to stay back, but I'll be coming to be with you all soon."

Louise asked her Daddy, "Is Aunt Elsie coming?"

John answered his daughter, "No, I'm afraid not."

"I'm going to miss her, Daddy," Louise said.

Elsie finally went to visit her sister Jenny, who was staying about ten miles from the mansion. "Ten miles," Elsie thought. All these years, her sister was only ten miles from her. She didn't even know what she was going to do once she saw her sister. She hadn't laid eyes on for over twenty years. The house that she was approaching was a cottage where people like Jenny live for the rest of their lives. Patty was the overseer of the house.

Patty had received word that Elsie was coming. She was standing on the porch waiting for Elsie to come and get her sister. Elsie walked up toward the house after getting out of an old wagon. Patty opened the door to let Elsie in. Elsie looked around for the house; it appeared somewhat comfortable but had a strange atmosphere. An atmosphere that made you feel uneasy, like something wrong had happened there.

Patty led Elsie to Jenny's room. Jenny's mental state was very childlike. Jenny didn't even recognize Elsie. "Hi Jenny! It's your sister, Elsie." Jenny continued playing with her dolls and swinging them around, singing very low to herself. Patty looked at Elsie to say. "It's going to take a long time for her to get to know you."

Elsie said, "I don't care how long it takes." Patty left them in the bedroom.

Elsie continued to live in Florida to be near her recently found sister. William also made the decision to remain in Tallahassee.

Everybody was ready to go. John purchased their train tickets. Susie, John and their children all looked at the house one last time. Mr. Bill was next to leave. His family didn't look back at all.

After nearly sixty years of leadership of oppression and bigotry, Tallahassee would go through a big change. Through sixty years of pure hell, that the so-called Quintons and many others inflicted upon the Indians and blacks spanned from the Trail of Tears to the Civil War and the Battle of Chickamauga through economic slavery.

Susie Poohtawn Quinton made her way through this life with the strong spirit of her father to fight for her freedom as a Cherokee Indian by helping her people to gain their pride and dignity necessary to live their lives as they saw fit. She helped the blacks too, in spite of racism. Susie made a way for them to stand strong and to have the courage to fight for their rights.

Even though the struggle continues, the natives of this country died fighting for their rights from Tallahassee, Florida all the way up to Kentucky, all across Virginia down to South Carolina. While at the train station, Susie thought about all that had been accomplished and looked back one last time to never to see the Quintons again.

About the Author

Terry D. Bible is a resident of Louisville, KY and a retired SFC U. S. Army Veteran rendering 21 years of service as well as a retired U. S. Postal Worker rendering 29 years to the U. S. Postal Service.

Terry Bible is a 1971 graduate of Central High School. Terry furthered her education by obtaining an Associate degree in Mental Health from the Jefferson Community College and an Associate's Degree in Christian Education from Simmons College of Kentucky. Ms. Bible is an ordained minister at Oak Grove Missionary Baptist Church, single and the mother of one daughter, Toya Boyd and the grandmother of four, BeShaunha Moore, Jr., Lamont Montez Shavers, Jr., Briya Burton and Nicholas Brown, Jr. and one great-grandchild, Shaun Anthony Moore.

Ms. Bible is currently enjoying retirement while continually her journey as a writer. For more information regarding Ms. Bible, visit www.bkroystonpublishing.com/terrybible and look her up on Facebook.